Patches through Time

By Sian Turner

Copyright Sian Turner 2022

Published in the UK in 2022 by Sian Turner

ISBN: 978-1-7392441-0-1

Cover design: by Julia Horobets

Thanks and Excuses

Thanks

Huge thanks to **Barry Segal** at Kent Glassblowing for all the technical info about how to hand blow glass and for sending me photos of his workshop. Barry makes stunning oil lamps and obviously loves what he does. Thanks for your patience with my lack of knowledge, Barry.

My gratitude also to **Nathan Dylan Goodwin**, whose book 'Hastings at War 1939-1945' provided useful info and insights. Nathan also helped me with some of the other local historical info from WW2 and did some fact-checking on parts of my manuscript for me. I'm so grateful for your time, knowledge and patience, Nathan.

Thanks also to the members of FB group **'Hastings & St Leonards History Group'** for their help, comments and obvious enthusiasm.

Big thanks to **Deb** and to my band of lovely **Beta Readers** for their time and brilliance, my small but so important band of **writer friends** for encouraging me when I needed moral support, to **Martin and Abi** for too many things to mention here, to my fantastic editor, **Alison Jack**, who helped me turn a draft into a finished manuscript and my talented cover designer **Julia Horobets**.

Excuses

If I got any of the historical bits factually wrong, it's definitely on me for not asking the right questions (or not realising a question even needed asking) not the fault of anyone who advised me. Also, I sometimes needed a level of detail that has not survived the passage of time (or I failed to find it, despite my best efforts) in which case I made my best guess/used artistic licence.

Regarding the (much) older historical descriptions of Hastings in this novel, I researched to the best of my ability but opinions differ substantially. I filled in any gaps with whatever worked best. If you imagine it differently, that's fine!

Oh, and some locations are completely fictitious (see also copyright info) because overall it's a work of fiction, not a historical recount (think Downton Abbey, which also has both factual and fictional elements interlaced).

More Thanks (and Meaningful Musings)

Finally, thanks to Hastings Crazy Golf for helping me with a small but significant detail that took me on a wander down memory lane to the many childhood outings with my brother when we would walk over the West Hill and then descend the long, steep steps to Hastings seafront to play Crazy Golf on Sunday mornings in the 1970s. These memories make me feel simultaneously ancient and youthful, for such is the true nature of time.

Dedication

This book is dedicated to those who lost their lives at the Battle of Hastings in 1066, and to all who perished in Hastings, East Sussex due to enemy action during WW2. Your lives, struggles and heroism should not be forgotten, despite the ever-marching passage of linear time.

PART 1: THE BARGAIN HUNTER

Chapter 1

A Unique Find (21 October 2019)

Jake Patch knelt on the dusty wooden floor of the shop, his dark eyes bulging in terror. A bead of sweat trickled into the hollow of his pallid cheek and his right arm hung stiff and useless at his side like a length of lead pipe.

Concentrating hard, he tried again and again to make his right hand release what it was holding. His fingers curled around the grimy object on his palm, clenching it as rigidly as an eagle's talons grasping a hapless rabbit. The artefact was roughly spherical, greyish in colour and about the size of a shot-put ball, although nowhere near as heavy. He ought to be able to let go of it easily enough. Hell, a simple twist and flick of his wrist ought to make it drop right out. But he'd tried that – with the help of his other unaffected hand. He'd tried everything.

Patch growled with frustration. *Let go. Drop the damned thing!* Focussing intently on his incapacitated limb, he glared at it as one would at an arch-enemy. It made no difference at all. His fingers continued to disobey him.

Stop panicking, idiot! Be logical.

Steadying himself, he tore his eyes off his beleaguered arm and stared up towards one of the overhead strip lights, the only means of illumination in the shop basement. Patch took one slow deep breath, then another, blowing out between puckered lips. His speeding pulse rate abated slightly.

There, that's better. Now then, numbness on one side, what could cause that? A stroke or a heart attack, perhaps.

Was that what was happening to him? Certainly he was on the young side for it, but it wasn't unheard of at his age by any means. If it was one of those conditions, he could be on the brink of death, and if this were only about him, he knew it wouldn't matter. But what about Cass – what would she do without him?

No!

The thought of leaving her alone made blind panic surge through him once again, filling every fibre of his being in a single rapid heartbeat. He couldn't die now; not without putting up a damned good fight. He parted his lips and filled his lungs with dusty air, ready to cry out for help.

'Hello,' said a feminine voice. It was calm, deep and mellow, with an odd hint of a following echo.

Patch released the breath he'd taken and scanned hurriedly around to locate the speaker. He shook his head and checked again. Apart from him, the basement of the shop was deserted.

Must be a trick of my imagination. Stress can do things like that, right?

He lifted the dead weight of his right arm into his lap and swallowed hard, preparing once more to call for assistance.

'Greetings, Jacob,' said the disembodied voice, interrupting him before he'd even drawn a breath this time. 'I am Drusilla, the sprite of The Infinity Glass.'

* * *

Jacob – or 'Jake' – Patch liked to think of himself as a semi-professional bargain hunter. He'd have it printed on business cards – less the "semi", of course – if he were not too tight-fisted to buy any. His daughter Cass kept telling him they'd be a good investment and wouldn't cost much, but he didn't see the point. Those who traded with him already knew his name and how to get hold of him.

He'd taken up this part-time occupation five years earlier. Initially, it had just been an engaging hobby, but, as his knowledge and enthusiasm increased, it had expanded into an actual business venture. Over the last year or so, he'd been using more and more of his free time hunting for one profitable purchase after another – whenever he wasn't working his "boring day job" as a supermarket delivery driver, or at home with Cass. His side-line career kept him busy, and he liked that it kept his mind off both his past and his future. He would turn forty-six tomorrow, and anything that could distract him from that had to be a good thing.

One of his regular bargain-hunting haunts was *Unique Antiques* in Hastings Old Town. That Monday, he arrived at around 2pm and elected to make his way straight to the basement, which he hadn't visited for at least a month. Descending the open wooden staircase that funnelled customers down from the centre of the expansive ground floor, he ducked slightly to avoid a beam bearing a sign that read "More Downstairs. (Mind your head!)".

Patch rubbed his palms together, then interlaced his fingers and cracked the knuckles loudly. He grinned with satisfaction at the popping sound that used to irritate his mother; a fact which, during his youth, had fed his desire to crack them at every possible opportunity. He could almost hear her voice saying, 'Jacob, do stop making that godforsaken noise. You know how it affects my nerves.' How she could claim to *have* nerves was beyond him when she rarely showed signs of feelings at all, except for animosity aimed cruelly and relentlessly at her only child.

Patch shook off the memory of his deceased mother and returned his focus to the bottom shelf of the corner cabinet. He never looked at the goods displayed at eye height, because he knew the real bargains and treasures were not to be found there. This was how he wore holes in the knees of his black jeans: kneeling on antique shop floors, rifling through stock. The very back of the lowest shelves was where half-forgotten trinkets tended to lurk: items less expected to make a hefty profit for the seller. He had learned that dealers would often accept a cheeky rock-bottom offer on such an item. Occasionally, he was fortunate enough to buy something relatively valuable for a real steal of a price, although he had considerably better luck on that score at boot fairs – your average Joe was way less savvy than a dealer. Sadly, boot fair season was a long way off, and Patch was itching to make money straight away.

Anyone able to delve deeper into his motivations – not that any ever tried – would discover that Patch was more than a casual trader in antiques and collectables. He had an all-encompassing mission: to make enough money from his dealings to see Cass through university. It was an expensive business, higher education, even if she lived in halls for her first year and got the full grant. Patch's incentive was his love for his daughter, even though he didn't want to deal with the idea of her growing up and moving away. Everything he did, he did for her. For her, and in memory of her mother.

The furthest corner of the basement was poorly lit and uninviting to shoppers. The nasty strip light which hung nearby had been on its last legs for a while and cast significantly less light than the others on this floor. Patch glanced up at it, and it gave a brief, ominous flicker.

Turning his eagle eyes back to the shelf, he spotted a tarnished and battered-looking chatelaine. *Could be silver if I'm lucky,* he thought, deciding it worthy of closer inspection. If it bore a hallmark or was stamped with the number 925, it meant it was solid silver, whereas EPNS meant plate. Solid silver would be a good result, but a Chester mark would be a bonus – nice and clear and unrubbed. Even if it had a barely visible hallmark, it might still be worth his while making an offer on it: the scrap price of silver was pleasingly high at the moment, and the bargain hunter never felt the slightest twinge of guilt when selling an antique to be melted down.

As he pulled the item towards him, another object became hooked on it and was dragged to the edge of the shelf. He estimated this second piece to be ten to twelve centimetres across and roughly spherical, although it was caked in a thick layer of unsavoury-looking greyish grime that made it difficult to assess. The object fell to the floor with a dull, hollow clunk. Patch grabbed it to stop it rolling away and tried to put it back on the shelf.

It was at this moment that his previously ordinary day became decidedly extraordinary. Instantly his arm stiffened, like it had turned to solid stone, and his rigidly clamped fingers refused the desperate instruction from his brain to let go.

'Aghhh!' he exclaimed. He leaned back, staring in horror as his arm dropped like a dead weight to the dusty floor.

* * *

'Greetings, Jacob. I am Drusilla, the sprite of The Infinity Glass.' The unseen voice spoke deliberately and slowly, as if its owner had decided Patch was stupid or dull-witted.

Still unable to locate the person who had thwarted his cry for help – and more than a little surprised to recognise the voice – Patch chose not to respond. Instead, he tossed the chatelaine back onto the shelf using his left hand and began clawing at the fingers of his right, which was still wrapped around the object. It had only been a few minutes, but he'd had more than enough of this nonsense.

To his increasing annoyance, his efforts were in vain. On the positive side, he felt fine apart from his stiff arm, so he probably wasn't dying after all. Admittedly, the disembodied voice gave him some concerns, but he was sure it would go away if he simply ignored it.

'Jacob?' said the voice, an irritated edge to it. 'I *said* I'm the—'

'Yes, yes,' he muttered, angry at both the voice's persistence and himself for giving in to it. 'I heard you, "sprite of The Infinity Glass".' He made one-handed air speech marks around the words. 'What utter drivel. You're nothing but the voice of my old dead mother, and I'm not listening now any more than I did when she was alive, so piss off and leave me alone!'

'I extracted the voice of your mother from your memories so you wouldn't be afraid of me,' explained the speaker, returning to a softer tone. 'It is an excellent example. I found an exceptionally diverse range of words in your memory spoken by it.'

'Pfah. I'll bet you did. But you chose very poorly, if you ask me, especially considering what a pompous fake she was. Why can't I let go of this thing?'

'The Infinity Glass is bound to you by *strong* forces.'

Patch swore under his breath. 'What, magic, you mean? There's no such thing. You've been reading too much *Harry Potter*.'

'Harry who?'

'Potter. Children's story. Full of magical nonsense. Ring any bells?'

'B-bells?' asked the voice. 'I can't hear any bells.'

'Look, Druella, if you're going to just yab away and not contribute anything helpful to the situation, I'd rather you left me alone. I've got more important things to do than converse with the dead.'

'My name is Drusilla, not Druella, and I am not dead, I'm using your mother's voice. I. Am. A. *Sprite*,' she rolled the "r" in precisely the manner Patch's mother would have done.

'Pah,' he spat. 'Voice in my head. Load of nonsense. Lah-lah-lah. Go away!' He flapped the air around his head as if trying to swat a fly.

Redoubling his efforts to let go of the object, he tried to lever a single finger off its lumpy surface, but couldn't manage even that. He wished he had longer nails, but he was prone to biting them.

His new companion gave a deep sigh followed by a tut – both sounds Patch remembered his mother making with annoying frequency.

'Honestly,' said Drusilla. 'I've never come across a man as disagreeable as you in my entire existence, and let me tell you that's been several centuries. I shall have to persuade you of my credentials. This ought to do it.'

Patch's fingers spasmed and every hair on his arm stood simultaneously on end. His skin buzzed with static electricity. The grimy object dropped into his lap.

'Bwah!' He stared at his now unstuck fingers, which glowed red and raw like he had dipped them into boiling water. 'What did you do to me?'

'I freed you,' said the sprite, nonchalantly. 'I expect you'll want to thank me.'

He blew on his throbbing fingers. 'Thank you?' he growled.

'You're welcome,' replied Drusilla.

'You burnt my fingers,' he said reproachfully, adding a string of swear words for good measure.

'Ah, but you believe I am what I claimed to be now, don't you? Not before time.'

The sprite sounded amused and self-satisfied, which served to rile Patch more. His lip curled into a snarl, exposing a crowded row of teeth.

'Maybe I do and maybe I don't,' he said. 'I need more information to make that judgement.'

'I am a sprite.'

'Yeah, you said that already. Tell me something I don't know,' he demanded, crossing his arms defiantly across his puffed-up chest.

'Very well, then, I shall. The Infinity Glass – or, more accurately, it together with its contents – enables its custodian to travel through time.'

Chapter 2

Cass

'What a pile of utter bullshit!' exclaimed Patch, shaking his head.

'Jacob, I'd appreciate it if you would curb your use of profanities.'

'Oh, would you now? Well tough. If you don't like it, you can go and jump in a lake.'

'I have to inform you that I am bound to The Infinity Glass resting in your lap, and it, in turn, is now bound to you, Jacob – although no longer physically so. I cannot jump in the aforementioned lake, although now I think about it, I'm guessing you didn't mean that literally.'

Although hearing a disembodied voice was odd to say the least, Patch was enjoying winding up this thing that sounded like his mother. It was like getting revenge for years of being on the receiving end of the old lady's nastiness.

'You can't be bound to it if you haven't got a body, can you?' he said. 'I think you're having a giraffe. Pulling my leg.'

The sprite hesitated for a good five seconds before responding. 'Making my best guess at interpreting your meaning, I assure you I am not pulling your leg.'

'What if I break the – what did you call it? – Infinity Glass? Would you go up in a puff of smoke?'

'Oh, dear me, don't do that. That would not be wise. Not at all.' The sprite's tone reminded Patch of the day he'd defied his mother's instruction not to climb the ancient oak tree in the park. In truth, he'd fallen out and badly sprained his ankle, then spent an uncomfortable few hours in A&E, but it was worth it, despite all the '*I told you so*'s he'd endured for weeks afterwards.

'There would be no chance of time travelling without The Infinity Glass. None whatsoever,' she said. 'It would be an utter disaster; and such a missed opportunity for you, too.'

Patch scratched his head. He'd been revelling in aggravating the so-called sprite so much that he'd temporarily forgotten her far-fetched claims.

'Tell me more about the time travelling,' he said, 'although it'll take some major persuasion for me to believe such a crazy idea.'

'Aah.' He could hear a smile in her voice and imagined his mother smirking down her nose at him, her arms folded across her chest in the certain knowledge she had won. 'It will be easy to convince you. The device is simple to use.'

He licked his lips slowly. Time travel was impossible, but then sprites didn't exist either, and yet here they were.

'So, Druella. How exactly do I make it work?'

'Well, Jacob—'

Patch interrupted with a string of angry profanities. 'Don't call me Jacob. Only Mother ever called me that and I hated it. You can call me...' he hesitated, chewing over the options. 'You can call me *Mr* Patch.'

After a long pause, there was a slight tightness to the sprite's voice when she finally responded.

'Very well, *Mr* Patch it is. You may call me Drusilla. *Dru-sill-a.*'

If he wanted Drusilla on his side, he realised he'd have to make an effort to play nicely, regardless of the voice she was using. Giving a deep sigh, he reluctantly conceded.

'OK, OK, I get it. Drusilla, not Druella.'

The child inside him wanted to test the sprite's warning that breaking "The Infinity Glass" was unwise. However, he was apparently conversing with a supernatural being. A being who had informed him that his odd find would enable him to time travel. He would give Drusilla a chance to prove it. Just in case her claims weren't impossible after all.

'You keep calling it a glass,' said Patch. 'But it isn't made of glass at all. I don't know what it is made of; is it clay or plaster, maybe?'

'Ah, on the outside, yes. That is because its previous owner wanted to disguise it. Hidden beneath the outer layer is an infinite knot fashioned from tubular glass, mounted inside a hinged metal framework. It is a wonder to behold, *Mr* Patch, truly an outstanding and unique piece.'

'If you're going to say *Mr* like that every time, call me Patch,' he said irritably, his eyes scanning the object in his lap with interest. 'It will do just as well, I suppose.' Intrigued by Drusilla's reverent tone when she was speaking about the artefact, he touched its knobbly surface gently with his fingertip, but then whipped it away in case it glued itself to him like before. He was still sore from being released earlier.

'It won't fuse to you again,' the sprite assured him. 'The binding function works but once with each custodian of The Infinity Glass. I broke the part of the erm… charm, if you like, that binds it physically to you, but it is still bound in a manner the eye cannot see.'

'You're sure I can touch it safely?' asked Patch, momentarily imagining how difficult life would be with the object stuck to his hand forevermore.

'Absolutely,' replied Drusilla, with conviction. 'Try it for yourself.'

Grumbling quietly, he acknowledged he'd have to trust the sprite if he was going to benefit from the powers of this object – assuming it had any, of course. He dabbed at it warily with his fingertip. After three dabs, he dared to place the whole length of his forefinger on it. When that didn't stick, he picked up The Infinity Glass, grabbed a fruit knife with a mother-of-pearl handle from a nearby shelf and gouged eagerly at the grimy clay with which it was coated. A chunk cracked and fell away almost immediately.

'Do be careful,' Drusilla advised, sternly.

Now he could see inside, the sprite's description was borne out – enclosed within the heavy layer of clay was indeed an object made from tubular glass. He couldn't see much of it through the meagre opening he had made, but Patch caught a glimpse of something green – maybe oil of some kind – contained within a node-like swelling. The glass artefact was held in a white metal framework with elongated 8-shaped decorations on each bar, a bit like a miniature bird cage. He gazed at the object, mesmerised – he had a good eye for spotting quality and he couldn't wait to take his find home and give it a proper, thorough clean-up.

'You said that it's both the glass and its contents which possess the power. It looks like regular glass, with some kind of green oil and a metal frame, though. It's fancy-looking, I'll give you that, but not supernatural.'

'You aren't qualified to pass judgement, though, are you?' asked Drusilla. 'How many time travel devices have you seen before today?'

Patch shrugged. She had him there.

'It is not an everyday object at all, and does not contain common or garden oil which one might use to fry eggs. It contains...' she paused like a reality TV-show host about to announce the winner. '*Essence*. And the proper name for the device is The Infinity Glass.'

Patch was about to laugh – Essence sounded like something from the latest fancy perfume ad to him – but a deep male voice barked, 'Oy, mate!' making him jump with surprise. 'Put the fruit knife back where you found it. You can't use the goods if you 'aven't paid for 'em.'

Patch shoved the artefact roughly into his carrier bag and folded the knife. 'This piece of junk?' he said, examining it swiftly, his heart thumping. 'It isn't worth a fiver and you've got twenty on it. There's no hallmark and the mother-of-pearl handle is badly chipped and cracked. How about you keep it?'

Scrambling to his feet, he thrust the folded knife into the outstretched hand of the shop owner's slow-witted nephew, Cody, and strode past him towards the stairs that led to the ground floor. Patch had done many a deal with this gangly, useless boy – Cody could be persuaded an item was worth half its true value if you caught him on a day when his far more astute uncle was off at a fair or auction and unavailable to give an opinion – but today, Patch just wanted to escape with his interesting new find.

'Oh. Sorry, Mr Patch, I didn't realise that was you. I 'spect I can do a fiver on the knife if you want it.'

Patch called back over his shoulder. 'Nah, fruit knives aren't worth my bother: a dime a dozen, those things, especially in that condition. It isn't even sharp.'

Before Cody could answer, Patch disappeared up the stairs. The boy's voice echoed after him.

'See you again soon, will we, sir?'

Patch noted a hint of desperation in the lad's voice. 'Maybe you will, or maybe I'll take my business elsewhere,' he called back. Continuing on his way, he grinned, pleased to have shaken the foolish boy up a bit. Patch had no respect for stupid people, and Cody fitted that description to a T.

'He's trying to be helpful, you know,' said the sprite.

Patch cussed loudly, pressing his palm against his chest. 'I forgot you were there. Can't you wait until you're called, like when Aladdin rubs the lamp to call the genie?'

'It doesn't work like that. I don't live inside the object.'

He gave a derisive snort. 'Of course not, I should have realised. Is there a sprite manual I can get my hands on, then, so I know what to expect?'

'Hardly,' snapped Drusilla. 'You'll simply have to work it out as we go along.'

He responded with a sarcastic, 'Oh, marvellous. Lucky me.'

'Actually, you are enormously lucky. I am one of the last of my kind. Finding me – and The Infinity Glass – is a rare privilege indeed.'

'Sure, if you say so.'

'I do. And a sprite never lies.'

'I didn't know that. No manual, remember? I'll bear it in mind, although I only have your word for it that you'd never tell a lie. Honestly, the ridiculous yarn you spun me sounds like a fairy story, but then, that's what you are, isn't it – a fairy?'

'Gracious, no, I'm no fairy. Sprites are far more refined, controlled and distinguished.'

Patch grinned, enjoying the sport of riling the sprite again.

Man and invisible sprite exited into the narrow street, the brass bell on the shop's front door jangling noisily in their wake. From the corner of his eye, Patch saw Mr Parsons, the shop owner, dashing from his tiny office towards the top of the stairs, presumably to find out how his idiot nephew had offended a regular customer.

After zipping up his worn leather jacket and turning the collar up against the biting wind whistling straight off the rolling grey sea and along the deserted High Street, Patch shoved his bony fingers into the pockets of his black jeans. A wavy strand of mousey shoulder-length hair whipped across his face and he tucked it quickly back inside his collar before starting up the long hill towards home. He'd talk to Drusilla again once he got indoors. A rush of pleasure gave him a brief 'high' when he realised he hadn't paid a penny for the artefact now in his possession. Parsons would be none the wiser; Patch doubted the shop owner was aware the object had been languishing on his bottom shelf with no price ticket.

Letting himself in through the tatty wooden front door that he kept promising he'd update to what Cass would call 'Something modern – and *way* more secure', he was surprised when the girl flew into his arms, her shoulder-length buttercream-blonde hair flopping across her face.

'Hey, Dad,' she said brightly, giving him a peck on his icy cheek.

'What are you doing here at this time of day?' he asked, tossing his key onto the chest of drawers, as he always did. He'd assumed he'd have at least an hour before his seventeen-year-old daughter arrived home from college. Time during which he could clean up the item and interrogate the sprite further about her time travel claims.

Cass's shoulders slumped. 'Gee, it's great to feel so wanted,' she said, sarcastically. 'Teacher off sick so double Psych cancelled. Yay!' She pressed her wrists together and clapped her hands like a fluttering clam shell.

'Homework?'

'Nope. Lucky me, hey? I thought I could maybe bake a cake.'

'A cake?' Patch asked, blankly.

Her expectant smile faded and she sighed deeply, shaking her head. 'I know you don't like a fuss, but it *is* your birthday tomorrow, Dad,' she reminded him.

Jake Patch shrugged. When he frowned, a wrinkle line appeared between his eyebrows.

'You know I don't do all that birthday nonsense, Cass. Haven't done since I turned twen—'

'—Since you turned twenty-one and your best friend hijacked your party by planning his own separate party on the same day. I remember. It's time you let that go, Dad. You're...' she paused, counting on her fingers. 'Forty-six now?' She waited for confirmation, looking apprehensive as if hoping she hadn't offended him by getting it wrong.

He held a finger in the air. 'Not until tomorrow, I'm not. Besides, it doesn't matter how old a person is, does it? Time is all in your head – a human construct, or to be more accurate, one of many nonsensical human constructs.' His own words made him wonder: maybe sprites and weirdly shaped artefacts were not tethered to a particular point in time in the same way that a world full of closed-minded humans were.

'Yes, yes,' said Cass, her head tilted to the side. 'Time is a human construct, I know. But then, why do we celebrate my birthday every year? By which I mean *properly* celebrate with gifts and cakes and trips to the cinema and stuff.'

'That's different,' he insisted. 'Your mother would have killed me if we didn't make a big deal for your birthday. Mine isn't important.'

Patch knew Cass didn't remember her mother. Jennifer had died after being hit by a car when her daughter was twenty months old, leaving a hole in their family that Patch had no intention of filling. He had tried dating after Jen had been gone a couple of years, but very soon concluded she was so utterly unique that he could never replace her. Besides, what if he chose a partner Cass didn't like? That wouldn't do, would it? The mention of her mother never appeared to upset Cass unduly, but it always made Patch's soul twist briefly into a tight, uncomfortable lump.

Cass raised a hand, its flat palm facing her father. 'Stop right there. I know exactly what comes next. The lecture about birthdays being different for kids. I'm not a kid any more, Dad. I'll be off to uni before long. There's less than a year to go now.'

Patch gave a twitch of a grimace, then forced his lips into as genuine a smile as he could muster.

'I'm well aware,' he replied, trying to ignore the gaping emptiness that opened up inside him whenever he had to face the prospect of her leaving. Cass was the light of his life. He understood she must start her own journey, but part of him wanted her to stay seventeen forever and never leave him alone within the four demoralising walls of his house. 'Aware and proud, Cass.'

His daughter lifted her chin, her steel-grey eyes staring into the distance. 'I'm so looking forward to London,' she said quietly, chewing on her bottom lip.

And I'll worry about you every single damned day you're there, he thought, forlornly. 'Yeah, you keep telling me. London won't know what's hit it when Cass Patch arrives,' he responded, his smile coming naturally now.

His daughter nodded her agreement. 'Too right it won't.' She had a mischievous gleam in her eye. 'Well, what flavour?' she asked.

Patch was momentarily puzzled and it must have shown on his face.

'The cake,' she said. 'What flavour of cake would you like me to bake for you?'

His grin melted into a twisted sneer. 'No birthdays, Cass. I've told you a million times.'

'You aren't *that* old,' she said, giggling. 'Anyway, I've decided I'm going to bake whether you like it or not. You're allowed to eat cake regardless of whether you deign to celebrate. I'll make it chocolate flavoured.'

'We don't have any eggs,' he told her. 'I threw the last of them in the bin yesterday because they were a week out of date.'

Cass lifted her chin again. 'No worries. I'll pop to the shop and buy some. It won't take me more than ten minutes there and back.'

She held out her palm, beckoning with her fingers. Her father reluctantly slipped his battered wallet from his back pocket and gave her a five pound note.

'Go on, then,' he said, 'since there seems to be no stopping you.'

'Thanks.' She rose onto her toes to kiss his cheek again.

'You'll need a coat, though, there's a chilly wind off the sea,' he called to her retreating figure.

'Da-a-ad! I'm not a toddler,' she whined. But she grabbed her red coat from the row of brass hooks behind the door anyway and hurried outside, still pulling it on.

The door slammed, accompanied by the metallic rattle of the letterbox, and Cass's father was alone in a suddenly silent house.

'She seems lovely,' said Drusilla, prompting a string of swear words from Patch, who had again forgotten about the sprite.

Regaining his composure, he replied, 'I suppose you find it surprising that someone like me could have a daughter like her, do you?'

'Maybe a tad. Perhaps girls take more after their mothers.'

'Yeah, maybe.'

'She brings out the best in you, I think.'

Patch grumbled an inaudible response and shuffled his feet. Drusilla's intrusion into his family life made him uncomfortable.

'Does she live here, too – Cass's mother?' asked the sprite.

'No. She died. There was an accident. Cass wasn't even two,' explained Patch. Usually, he told people to mind their own business if they asked about his love life – not that he'd had one worth talking about in a long time now. Opening up to the sprite was unexpected, especially when she was using a voice with which he couldn't remember ever holding a rational conversation.

'I see,' said Drusilla.

Patch bristled. 'I see? I *see*? You could at least say you're sorry to hear it, couldn't you?'

'Very well. I'm sorry to hear it,' parroted the sprite, blandly.

'Sure you are. What would you know about death or love?' he asked, bitterly. There was no point entering into a discussion about human emotions with this creature, especially when he wanted something from her. Instead, he changed the subject.

'Anyway, now you've come out of the woodwork again, let's talk about time travel, shall we?' He drew The Infinity Glass from his carrier bag and turned it over and over. 'How do I get this thing to work? Do I rub it or twist it a particular way or what? And how far can it take me through time? Could I go back to...' his mind picked a familiar historical date, the anniversary of which had only recently passed, 'to 14 October 1066, for example? Or—'

He was interrupted by a sound like a thousand people simultaneously snapping their fingers.

Chapter 3

Historical Tragedy

Patch flinched. He was about to ask 'What the hell was that noise?' but lost his train of thought in an instant when he realised he was now in a wood. A carpet of brown leaves surrounded his feet and a tiny bird was chirping urgently from the limb of a nearby tree, presumably as shocked by Patch's sudden appearance as he was himself.

For a moment, he stood frozen to the spot – not just figuratively either. His whole body was deep frozen, like a living experiment in cryogenics. Then, as swiftly as the cold had overtaken him, warmth flushed back through him from head to toe.

'Bloody hell! Where am I?' he asked, raking trembling fingers through his hair. All around him in every direction were trees and more trees, standing like hundreds upon hundreds of darkly clad prison guards. Although he was outside, being unable to see a way out of the woods made him feel anxious – claustrophobic even.

'Where?' asked the sprite, incredulously. 'We are exactly where we were a moment ago.'

Realising the flaw in his question, Patch reframed it. 'OK then. *When* are we?'

'Precisely when you asked to be.'

For a moment, he didn't understand. He hadn't asked to be taken anywhere. Then realisation struck.

'In 1066?' he asked, swivelling through a full circle, but still seeing nothing but trees. 'This is 1066?'

'Yes, 14 October.'

'The date of the Battle of Hastings?' The shock of having time travelled disolved away in an instant. As he'd been born and brought up in Hastings, an opportunity to be here on an historic day such as this excited and enthralled him. 'Let's go, then!' he said. 'I want to see it. I want to know if the history books are accurate about what happened. Take me to Senlac Hill – at a safe distance, of course.'

'I'm afraid I can't do that,' admitted Drusilla. 'And The Infinity Glass can't do it either. If you ask for a date, it will take you there, but you'll always arrive at the same spot from which you left. I mean, relatively. Clearly, the Earth isn't located in the same place in the universe that it was on 14 October 1066, but you are in the same position on the Earth that you inhabited before the time slip—'

The sprite was babbling, so Patch interrupted. 'What time of day is it?' he asked, unable to tell how high the sun was in the sky because of the heavy cloud cover.

'The same time it was when we left. You didn't specify a precise moment. The Infinity Glass has given you the time we departed. It is 2.38pm and seventeen seconds. Eighteen. Nineteen. Twenty.'

'Damn it, stop the counting. The battle must be raging right now, seven or eight miles away to the northwest of here. I can't possibly get there on foot through terrain like this before the fighting is over and King Harold is dead. Take me back where we came from, Drusilla. There's no point staying here now.'

'Ermmm.'

Patch's shoulders drooped and he swallowed hard, making his Adam's apple bob energetically.

'You can't take me back?' he asked, apprehensively.

'No. I don't control The Infinity Glass, you do, and it only works one way.'

Every muscle in his body tensed. 'What?' he shrieked. 'You mean I'm stuck here forever?'

'No, no, no, don't fret,' replied the sprite, reassuringly. 'Your stay here will last for precisely an hour, then you'll be returned to your point of origin.'

Patch took a deep breath and exhaled it slowly through pursed lips. Stroking his rough chin, he said, 'So even if I tried to make it to Senlac Hill in time for the end of the battle, there'd be no point because an hour from now, I'll zip off back home again anyway. Will I be returned to the moment I left or will I lose an hour?' His mind spun with a million questions. 'Hey, can't I wish myself back the same way I got here?'

'Return travel is by time, not by request. In answer to the other question, you will lose the hour.'

'What about Cass? She won't know where I've gone. She'll worry and try to call me. I'm guessing this won't work in 1066.' Drawing his shiny black mobile phone from his pocket, he was surprised when the screen lit up. 'It's working!' he exclaimed.

'Your telephone functions on its battery power, but cannot connect to any services because they don't exist here. Besides, any message she sends you won't happen for well over nine hundred years.'

He slipped the phone back into his pocket. 'Why didn't you sodding warn me?' he growled. 'I'd never have come here if I'd had all the facts – the rules, you know?'

'There simply wasn't an opportunity to discuss it before you decided to randomly select a date to travel back to,' said the sprite, irritably. 'It isn't my fault.'

'Isn't it? Well then, what is your specific function with regard to the artefact?'

'To act as intermediary between The Infinity Glass and the custodian,' she replied, as if reading the line from a script.

'There you are, then. Yet you say this mess up isn't your fault?'

'Well, no, Patch. It isn't my fault. I cannot be held responsible for your impetuosity. You called a date before giving me a chance to explain the device's powers and limitations. You hadn't even asked me about them.'

Patch was ready with a retort, but became distracted by a prickling sensation speeding along the length of his spine. It was the sixth sense feeling of being watched. His eyes darted around and something fast-moving ducked out of sight behind a tree about ten metres away.

'Hey you!' shouted Patch. 'Come out, I know you're there.'

When no reply came, he strode towards the tree where he'd seen what he now realised was a hand. He crept closer and a short, slight figure shot out into the open and ran, nimbly weaving between the trees with arms and legs pumping hard. They were clad in a calf-length brown tunic, tied at the waist and worn over a long-sleeved green top.

'You there, wait!' yelled Patch. 'I want to talk to you. I won't hurt you.' He shoved the artefact roughly into his pocket.

The figure – a girl of no more than six or seven – chanced a glance back over her shoulder and cried a word that sounded like 'Ney!' before continuing into the undergrowth at full pelt.

Patch considered pursuing her, but thought better of it. She was a young child and being chased by a man dressed in clothing from another century would frighten the life out of her. He'd have punched any bloke who had chased his Cass when she was that age – or any age, come to that.

Another thought occurred to him. 'If this really is 1066, the girl must speak Old English. She won't have understood a word of what I shouted at her. What's the point of visiting the past if I can't even communicate with the people here?' he asked, directing his question into mid-air and assuming Drusilla would understand it was aimed at her.

'The *point* is up to you, and the language barrier is not my fault,' Drusilla replied, dryly.

'Not my fault, not my fault,' repeated Patch childishly. 'Well, how totally bleedin' marvellous. Nothing is your fault, is it? Are you sure you aren't my mother?'

'I am Drusilla, a sprite. I am using your mother's voice—'

He was getting sick of it already. 'Yes, yes, so I won't be afraid. Choose another, can't you?'

Drusilla remained silent.

'Don't tell me: you can't do that either.'

'You are correct. I am bound to a single voice and that voice has already been chosen.'

'Perhaps you should shut up, then,' snapped Patch, sitting on the trunk of a fallen tree. 'Hey, what if I'm not standing in the same place an hour from now, when I get pulled back through time? Might I reappear inside a wall or something? Could I have arrived here embedded in a boulder or a tree?'

'No, no, certainly not. The Infinity Glass will place you in a location where there's sufficient space for you to arrive unhindered by obstacles when travelling in both directions. You needn't worry about that.'

'Hmph! It's one of those questions I should have asked before leaping in and suggesting a date to travel to, I suppose.'

'Perhaps so, but you aren't the first to fall foul of over-eager destination setting.'

'No?'

'No. One person asked if The Infinity Glass could take him a million years into the past. He came close to getting himself killed by an immense – and ravenous – wolf. It was lucky the man was a good climber. The wolf had to make do with an inch from the bottom of his intended prey's trouser leg.'

'What would have happened if he'd been killed?'

'His body would have returned to his own time and the exact location from which he'd departed an hour after he left.'

'But mauled by a wolf and with chunks of flesh missing?'

'Sadly so. It would have been extremely unfortunate indeed.'

'I'll say. I'd better be careful, then. Hey, are there wolves in 1066 England?' He leapt to his feet, ready to scramble up the nearest tree.

'I'm not sure. I haven't been here before. Perhaps caution is the best policy.'

'Marvellous,' said Patch. He scanned around on the ground trying to find a weapon, in case he should need to defend himself. Spotting a chunk of rock with rough edges lying nearby, he snatched it up. The stone wasn't big enough to be an intimidating weapon, but it would have to do for the time being. He shoved it into his deepest pocket, but kept his fingers wrapped around it. 'I won't be travelling again without doing serious internet research beforehand,' he grumbled.

'That,' said Drusilla, 'sounds like a wise plan.'

'If I'm travelling to a potentially dangerous time, I should seriously consider carrying a proper weapon. Something portable and easily concealed, like a knife.' The idea of being armed made his heart speed. He knew he'd have no clue how to wield one effectively. After a brief silence while Patch listened intently for the sound of approaching predators, he stood and brushed down the back of his trousers with his palms.

'Or perhaps try to avoid potentially hazardous time periods,' suggested Drusilla.

'True, but who knows when those might be? I'm no historian. Any date I pick could be risky in theory.' He sighed, still deeply troubled by both the prospect of carrying a knife. He cleared his throat, hoping it would clear his mind a little, too. 'Well, I might as well explore while I'm here, rather than standing about waiting for an hour to pass. The girl must have come from a settlement. I assume that would most likely be where the centre of the Old Town is located in the twenty-first century. It will be weird to see the place not packed with shoulder-to-shoulder Victorian houses. Even the medieval buildings erected in the 1400s won't be there for centuries yet.

'Hey, perhaps I could pick up a souvenir while I'm here – something I can carry easily that will be worth a pretty penny back in my own time. A coin, perhaps – were there coins?' He'd definitely never seen money from as far back as 1066. If it existed, it would be rare, and rare meant valuable.

'Are you asking me a question, Patch?' asked the sprite, uncertainly.

'Honestly, no. Just thinking aloud,' he replied, sauntering in the direction the girl had run. The idea of finding something valuable to take back home with him had banished all thoughts of fighting of predators. 'You said you hadn't been here before, didn't you?'

'I did, yes. Do you think you might use my name if you're speaking to me? You have a tendency to think aloud and it's going to be extremely confusing if you continue doing it.'

'Whatever,' he replied, flapping a hand dismissively.

The sprite made a noise that sounded like one of his mother's best tuts. 'Well, this is going to be a challenging affiliation, for sure,' she said.

Patch elected not to respond.

Although he was by no means a tree connoisseur, the acorns crunching beneath his feet and the distinctive shape of the browned leaves carpeting the ground – and still falling from the twisted branches – told him the trees around here were predominantly oaks. After a few minutes' walk, he reached the edge of the woodland which covered where his house would later stand and emerged onto undulating grassland punctuated with both small clumps of trees and larger areas, like that into which he had appeared. He couldn't believe he'd felt trapped in such a small area of woodland. In the distance, shards of glistening sunlight were now penetrating the deep grey clouds and reflecting off an unseasonably calm English Channel. He could not yet see the shoreline, though.

He swung around, hoping to spot the girl, but there was no sign of her. How had she got so far ahead of him? She had the advantage of being more familiar with the terrain, he realised, which was ironic given he'd been born and raised in Hastings himself.

Smoke rose in a drifting plume over to the southwest – further along the coast than he'd expected. Patch altered his route accordingly. Briefly wondering how much of his hour he had left, he checked his phone, but found it still showed the time as 2.38pm.

'What's going on with my phone?' he asked. When no reply came, he tried again. 'Drusilla, why is the time on my phone wrong?'

'Your telephone cannot connect to external services. I would suggest the time function is one of those. It will most likely return to normal when you go back home.'

'Then tell me what time it is, will you, since you managed to do that earlier.'

'It is now 2.52 and three seconds. Four. Five.'

'Enough. If I ask the time, to the closest minute is accurate enough, and I don't need continuous updates.'

'I see. Understood.'

Patch knew roughly where he must be, but still found orientation a challenge. This was home, yet not home. It was a world separated from his own by well over nine hundred years and, taking in the beautiful, unspoilt countryside, he couldn't help but think that human expansion had done nothing positive to the planet. It didn't surprise him. People were hateful; all except Jen and Cass, anyway.

His mind whirled as he tried to access any knowledge he had of this period. He, like all local children, had learned all about the Battle of Hastings in school, but nothing about the reality of everyday life for the currently being-invaded inhabitants. Had Duke William passed through Hastings on his way to the battle? Should Patch be worried about bumping into armed Norman invaders?

No, they'd surely all be at the battle, not hanging around on the coast. He ought to be safe enough from the conqueror's men.

Nonetheless, when the seashore came into sight, Patch heaved a sigh of relief that there was no sign of William's ships. The shape of the shoreline, which had been constant throughout Patch's life, was surprisingly different. The coastal erosion and large-scale human interference with the natural lie of the land that would mould the area into a shape Patch would recognise had not happened. The Norman castle, of course, had yet to be built. Patch paused for several moments taking in the view and struggling internally to ground himself in a new present.

Of course it would be different. Nigh on a thousand years of passing time will change an awful lot, he told himself.

When he moved on again, the main human settlement soon came into sight. It wasn't located where the Old Town of Hastings stood in his own time at all. Instead, the settlement lay on a spur of land a fair distance to the west, nearer where the newly refurbished pier would stand in the twenty-first century, although the vastly different topography of the seafront area in 1066 made it all but impossible for him to mentally overlay what he could see with his own recollections.

The settlement was surprisingly substantial and consisted of closely packed wooden houses with straw-thatched roofs, several of which appeared to be smouldering. As the houses had no chimneys, Patch guessed that any smoke from inside must simply make its way out through the thatch. People in Hastings were going about their daily lives and several sat in groups outside their dwellings, but Patch couldn't tell from this distance whether they were men or women, let alone see what they were doing. The tower of a church loomed like a lonely sentinel on the hillside above the settlement. Religion had most likely been an important element of medieval life. He hadn't expected any buildings as substantial as the church, though.

'Agh!' he grunted, coming to an abrupt stop. His foot had found an unseen dip in the grass and he'd turned his ankle. 'Damn it. What's the time, Drusilla?' he asked, sitting on the damp grass to evaluate the injury.

'It's 3.14, Patch,' she reported, efficiently.

His ankle would bear his weight, but he imagined the pain would slow his progress significantly.

'Already? There's only twenty-four minutes left,' he observed. This was a frustrating setback. 'I could probably reach the town in that time, but if I made it, what would I realistically do? Don't answer that, Drusilla. I'm thinking aloud.' He scratched his eyebrow with his index finger. 'I should have thought about this when I first set out. What could I possibly have done once I entered the settlement? I could hardly saunter up to an unsuspecting Anglo-Saxon and say, "Hi, I've come to visit from the twenty-first century. Your king is about to die, by the way, and the Normans will take over the country and change it forever", could I? Even if they understood a word of my modern English – which they wouldn't – it wouldn't help anybody. If they decided I was an invader, that dumb rock I picked up would offer scant protection. What's the point? This whole bloody trip has been wasted.'

'I thought you were interested in historical events.'

'Interested, yes, of course. But there's no purpose to carrying on with this foolishness; 1066 is way too long ago for me to do anything useful here. It makes more sense to plan in advance and concentrate on travelling to times closer to my own, where I can source quality items to bring back to the present and sell. My daughter's uni fund would swell in no time and she wouldn't have to worry about money like I've had to do my whole life.'

'But wouldn't you like to see more of this era?' asked Drusilla.

'Who wouldn't? Cass would absolutely love it here; she's always had a thing about social history. This is Hastings, of course, but it isn't *my* Hastings, is it? These people – and their great, great, great grandchildren, come to that – are all long dead. Although I'm here, I feel detached from what I'm seeing.'

Turning back the way he'd come, Patch walked more slowly, babying his ankle. Before he re-entered the woodland, though, curiosity made him steal a final glance back towards the rising smoke from the town.

'They think between six and ten thousand men died at the Battle of Hastings,' he said. 'Did you know that, Drusilla?'

'I did not, Patch,' she replied.

'An utter tragedy,' he said, shaking his head. Being here – even this far away from the actual bloody battleground – had made the number more real. Empathy was an emotion he usually reserved exclusively for Cass these days, yet tears threatened and he had to bite them back.

'Let's get home,' he mumbled. For a split-second, he wondered whether the girl he had seen earlier had a father or an uncle lying with a sword or an arrow through his chest on Senlac Hill, having fought in vain to save his country from the Norman invasion.

He cursed and shook his head. 'Come on, Patch, it's not your concern. History, that's all it is. Done and dusted.'

He instructed Drusilla to give him a countdown, 'Since you're so good with precise timings', and when she told him he had a few seconds left, he stood stock still like a *Star Trek* crew member waiting for transport back to the ship from an alien planet. At the last moment, he wondered whether it mattered that The Infinity Glass remained inside his pocket and shoved his hand in after it.

There was a sound like a thousand people simultaneously snapping their fingers and, in a blink, Patch was home.

Chapter 4

Warming Up

'Dad! What the hell?' Cass ran forward and flung her arms around her father, but the moment she touched him, she recoiled. 'Oh my god, you're like a block of ice. You literally just appeared out of thin air. What the hell's going on?'

Patch rubbed his frozen fingers up and down his equally frozen arms and tried to stop the shaking which racked his whole body. Cass took a half step towards him, but he raised a hand to stop her.

'C-Cass, d-d-didn't you go to buy eggs?' he asked, although he was certain a casual conversation about food shopping wouldn't distract her from wanting to know how and why her father had materialised before her eyes.

She shook her head. 'What? Oh, the eggs. Yes, I got them, they're in the kitchen. Are you OK, Dad? Please tell me what's happening. I came back and you weren't here. Then you materialised right in front of me, like someone flipped a switch to make you appear.'

Asking about the eggs had given him the extra moment he needed to come up with a rudimentary plan about what to say. What he really wanted was to give himself time to think. 'I d-don't know what happened. It was s-seriously weird, I must say. I... I have to warm myself up, love, I'm f-f-f-freezing. I'm going upstairs to have a sh-shower. We'll t-talk afterwards.' He sidestepped his daughter and made a dash for the stairs.

The shower temperature was set to cold, but felt scalding hot against his flesh. Every joint in his body ached insistently. On the positive side, his twisted ankle had completely recovered. After a few minutes, Patch turned the temperature up a notch, then another and another until at last he was warmed through again and the aching in his bones faded away.

He needed to talk to Drusilla and ask if this was normal for a time traveller, but didn't want to start a conversation here and now in case Cass was lurking outside the bathroom door waiting for him to emerge. He'd seen her unsubtly following him upstairs after his traumatic return from 1066. What could he say to her about what she'd seen happen? Honesty would be best, but the truth was so implausible that he wouldn't believe it himself, had he not lived through the experience.

Reluctantly, he considered the other option – lying to her. He could deny all knowledge and say he didn't remember, insisting that, as far as he was concerned, all that happened was he'd suddenly turned into a human ice block. She didn't have to be told he'd visited Hastings in the year 1066.

The trouble was that Cass could read his expressions as accurately as her mother used to. Right from when she was a toddler, she won any game that involved bluffing every time. She'd look him in the eye and Jen's smile would light up her face.

'Not true!' she would say, pointing a finger and laughing. He would shrug, roll his eyes and confess she was right.

Back to the idea of telling her the truth, then. Could it matter if he told her? She'd know he wasn't lying.

Patch turned off the shower.

'You OK, Dad?' Cass's voice wafted into the bathroom and interrupted his thoughts. By the sound of it, her mouth was right next to the crack between the door and its frame.

'I'm fine,' he assured her. Reaching for his towel, he noticed the rock he'd put in his pocket now lying on the bathroom floor next to the grime-encrusted Glass and his pile of rapidly discarded clothing.

'You sure?' She sounded scared. He must have frightened her half to death.

'Honestly, I'm fine now. I'll be out in a couple of minutes. You don't need to sit there waiting for me. Didn't you say you were going to bake?'

'Yeah, but that was before.'

'I said I'm fine, Cass.' His words were more of a bark than he'd intended and he silently cursed his lack of self-control. He pictured her standing on the landing right now, with her arms wrapped around her middle, shuffling from foot to foot like she always did when worried.

He wrapped the towel around his middle and opened the door a crack. She was standing just as he'd imagined and her frown didn't lift even a little when she saw his face appear.

'I'm fine,' he told her, more gently this time. 'Sorry for taking that grumpy tone just now. Go and bake, Cass. A chocolate sponge cake would be lovely.'

She closed her eyes briefly and let out a sigh. Then she shrugged a single shoulder and shot him a dubious glance before edging reluctantly towards the top of the stairs.

Patch's eyes followed her until she descended out of sight.

'Damn,' he grumbled, quietly, pushing open a window to clear away the steam from his shower. He watched it billow outside and it reminded him of the smoking roofs of old Hastings. Lost in thought, he picked up the pile of clothes, The Infinity Glass and the chunk of rock, and padded through into his bedroom, shutting the door behind him. He needed to speak with the sprite and didn't want Cass to overhear the conversation.

'So what was all that about, Drusilla?'

'All what?' she asked.

'The cold when I arrived back. I was frozen to the bone. When I made the outward journey, I was cold then, too, but it wore off straight away. Coming back was a whole lot worse. Is that normal for travellers?'

'Yes, Patch. After your return, the chill does indeed linger. I believe it is worse for older travellers than for younger ones.'

'Brilliant. Lucky me. But you didn't think I needed to know about it before it happened – to have some warning, maybe?' he asked, making a conscious effort not to raise his voice in case Cass came racing up to find out what was wrong.

'It didn't occur to me, no.'

'Marvellous. Getting useful information out of you is like drawing blood out of a stone.'

The sprite declined to comment.

'I'm going to have to be properly prepared for future time travel trips. So, firstly I must research the era I'm travelling to, and secondly, I need to make sure I'm in the exact location I want, or at least very close by.' He paused, then added, 'Thirdly, I'll think about taking a weapon in case I need to defend myself.' He hesitated again, giving that idea time to sink in before continuing. He was often a brusque man, but was not inclined to violence. 'Last but not least, I must make sure there's a way to warm myself up again when I return to my own time. Is there anything else I need to know, Drusilla? Any titbits of information you can divulge that will stop me getting myself into strife?'

'I don't think so, but I can't be certain.'

'Of course you can't.'

'Are you going to take your daughter into your confidence and tell her what happened?' asked the sprite.

Patch scratched behind his ear. 'I don't want to worry her.'

'Correct me if I'm wrong, but she seems quite worried already.'

'I know that, I'm her father.'

'And you said she loves social history. Mightn't her knowledge be a useful resource when you're deciding what time to visit next?'

'Hmmm, I suppose it might, but I'm still not sure telling her is a smart plan. Besides, my next visit will take me back to visit Cass's mother and I don't need any expert knowledge for that.'

'One of the limitations of The Infinity Glass is that you can only travel to past times outside your own lifetime. Unless your wife was older than you, I'm afraid that's out of the question.'

Patch unleashed a string of colourful swear words, then gave a huff of frustration. 'As a matter of fact, she was older than me, but by barely a couple of months. There'd be no point me visiting her as a baby, would there? She wouldn't know me. Hell, she wouldn't be able to focus on me.'

'I am sorry. I don't set the rules, I simply explain them.'

He raked his fingers through his wet hair. The sprite sounded genuinely apologetic, employing an almost sympathetic tone he'd rarely heard in *that* voice.

'Yeah, yeah, I get it,' he said. 'Not your fault again. Well then, if I can't visit Jen, I guess it's back to the idea of collecting antiques and selling them to bolster Cass's uni fund. I know I can bring things back because I have this to prove it.' He picked up the rock and examined it briefly in his palm before placing it on his bedside table. It was neither useful nor attractive – just a black and yellow lump. 'Not much of a souvenir of a time travelling trip,' he commented, dryly.

'I suppose not,' responded the sprite. 'You'll choose better next time, I expect.'

'Indeed I will.' He was already thinking about times and places he could visit on subsequent adventures. Drusilla had told him the artefact could transport him through time, but not space, meaning any travelling to other locations would have to be done by means of conventional buses or trains. A destination close to home would be ideal, but also limiting. Cass would be able to help him choose his next location wisely, but he'd already discounted the idea of telling his daughter about The Infinity Glass, the Essence within it, and his newfound ability to time travel, at least for the time being.

Cass was downstairs. He could hear her whisking eggs while humming a tune from a musical. He vaguely remembered the song – something about whistling when you were afraid.

Patch unwrapped his towel and began drying his back. He couldn't face embarking upon another journey through time today, and the prospect of a slice of moist chocolate sponge was making his mouth water. After donning clean jeans and a black T-shirt emblazoned with the logo of an eighties heavy metal band, he left the time travel device in his bedroom and went to talk to Cass.

'Couldn't I just come clean and tell her?' he mumbled to himself. 'This is crazy.'

Chapter 5

Patch's Conscience

He slipped silently into the kitchen, having still not decided whether to confess everything to Cass or keep his secret to himself. He found his daughter pouring a bag of chocolate chips into a bowlful of sweet-smelling cake batter. She must have spotted him out of the corner of her eye because she stopped what she was doing, the bag of chocolate pieces poised over the bowl. Cass tilted her head towards him, her brow furrowed and her lips pressed tightly together.

He wanted to give a confident, reassuring smile, but only one side of his mouth co-operated – and half-heartedly at that.

'You OK?' she asked.

He cleared his throat. 'Fine. Perfectly fine. Can I turn the oven on for you?'

Cass sighed and returned her attention to her cake mix. 'Sure. Whatever. A hundred and sixty degrees should do it.'

While he did as she'd told him, Cass stirred in the chocolate chips, then lifted the bowl and poured batter into a pair of cake tins, levelling the mixture with a spatula.

Patch tried to think fast – to make a decision about whether to tell her all about Drusilla and The Infinity

41

Glass. His brain was like treacle, perhaps still afflicted by the extreme chill that had enveloped him when he'd arrived home from 1066.

His stomach growled with an urgent hunger, and he reached past Cass towards the mixing bowl, ran a finger through the sparse scrapings of sponge batter and stuck it eagerly into his mouth.

'Dad, there's raw egg in that,' cried Cass.

'Mmm. Delicious. How long till the cake's cooked?' he asked, ignoring her exasperated expression.

'Once the oven's up it will be twenty to twenty-five minutes, if you can wait that long,' she told him, giving his hand a playful slap when he tried to repeat his misdemeanour. 'Plus cooling time on top. Maybe an hour.'

'Really? That long? I'm starving now, though.'

'It'll be worth the wait,' she said, confidently. 'How about I make you a coffee? You look like you could use one.'

'OK,' replied Patch, dragging a heavy wooden chair from beneath the table and sitting with his arms crossed and legs splayed.

Cass filled the kettle in silence while her father tried to straighten out his train of thought. It wouldn't be long before she started asking difficult questions again. As he expected, once she'd placed a steaming mug of coffee in front of him and sat down facing him across the table, she asked, 'So, what happened earlier?'

'Nothing,' he said with a shrug. 'I mean I, erm, don't know.'

Her eyes bored into his and she arched an eyebrow. 'You're lying.'

Turning towards the window so he wouldn't have to meet her gaze, he said, 'If you're going to grill me like I'm

a bloody enemy spy, I'll take my coffee elsewhere.'
Despite the threat, he remained seated, his jaw
stubbornly set.

Cass gave an exasperated grimace. 'Jeez, Dad, this is
crazy. Something happened earlier. You weren't here
when I arrived home from the shop, then you suddenly
appeared right in front of me, freezing cold and shaking
like a leaf. Now you refuse to explain, but expect me to
accept having my questions and concerns brushed away.
It's like I don't mean anything to you at all.'

He lifted his chin and met her stare. 'Don't be daft.'

'Daft?' She threw her hands up in frustration, then
crossed her arms and wrapped them tightly around her
waist.

Her father shook his head. 'I didn't mean that; your
concerns aren't daft. I meant it's daft to say you don't
mean anything to me. You mean the whole world, Cass,
you know you do.'

She sniffed and gave a perfunctory shrug.

Patch cleared his throat. A compromise came to him
and he grabbed it with both hands. He knew what to tell
her – or, more accurately, what not to tell her.

'Yes, something happened, but for now I can't tell
you what. In truth, I'm not sure you'd believe me if I did.'

'You could try me. I might surprise you.'

He shuffled his feet, wanting more than anything to
share his experience with her. First he would make a few
more trips, though – then he'd have a souvenir to show
her to corroborate his fantastic story and he'd be able to
reassure her that time travelling was a hundred per cent
safe.

Assuming it is, his brain interjected, unhelpfully.

'Cass, I can't do what you're asking. Not yet. I need time to think,' he said. 'All I can say now is I'm fine and I'm going to stay that way.'

'When will you tell me, then? I won't stop worrying until I know what happened.'

He tapped on the edge of the table with his forefinger. 'I can't answer that yet either.'

Cass shook her head slowly and he wanted to give her something more concrete.

'Soon, love. I promise,' he said.

'Not good enough. "Soon" is too open to interpretation. Honestly, what am I supposed to think? It's utterly surreal – I'd go as far as to say paranormal – and it's seriously freaking me out.'

'Sorry. I'm doing my best. I don't properly understand it either.'

'And I can't persuade you?'

'No.'

She heaved a sigh of resignation. 'Alright. I mean, it isn't alright at all, but I have no choice, do I?'

'Trust me, Cass,' he said, quietly.

She stared at him for a moment, then Jen's grin spread across her heart-shaped face. It was a smile which, to her father, was like watching the sun rise.

'Trust Jake Patch? You've got to be kidding.'

'Hey, you're supposed to support your father, not insult him.'

'Just being realistic,' she said, waggling her eyebrows. 'I know you better than anyone.'

'That's true. But you do trust me, don't you?' he asked.

'Sure, of course, but I'm still going to hold you to that promise.'

'I wouldn't expect any less, Cass.'

Silence fell between them. It was a comfortable silence now, although her shoulders remained hunched.

Patch yawned. 'I'm feeling a bit tired. I'm going to go upstairs for a while.' He stood, sensing her gaze following him as he left the kitchen.

Once in his room, Patch lay on the bed and curled into a foetal ball. He fell asleep instantly and dreamt of swords and arrows, a bloody battle and a long-dead king of England.

* * *

He slept for an hour and a half before Cass woke him. She was carrying plate with a wedge of buttercream-filled chocolate sponge.

'It's not my birthday until tomorrow,' he grumbled, but still took the cake before she could change her mind.

'I thought you needed it today,' she said, biting her bottom lip.

'Cass, I'm fine, honestly. You've no need to worry,' he said. Lifting the cake to his mouth, he took a generous bite. 'Sh'good,' he added, appreciatively.

She was still staring at him as if he was about to pop out of existence at any moment.

'Look, I'm not going anywhere, I promise.'

'How can you be sure?'

'That's part of the stuff I can't tell you yet. I honestly am a hundred per cent certain.'

'Yeah?'

'Yeah.'

'Well, I have a bunch of homework. I'd better go and make a start.'

'I thought you didn't have homework,' he said, feigning a shocked expression.

'I lied,' she replied, grinning.

* * *

Awakened by a tentative knocking on his door the following morning, Patch sat up.

'Come in,' he said through a cavernous yawn.

Cass's anxious face appeared. 'I was worried you would have disappeared again,' she admitted, approaching the bed, her arms snaking loosely around her middle.

'I told you I wouldn't.'

'Still,' she said, her mouth twisting into a grimace. 'Anyway, how can you know it won't happen again?'

Patch patted his chest experimentally, then extended his hands, turning them firstly palms upward, and then back the other way.

'I'm definitely here now,' he said.

Cass rolled her eyes. 'That's not funny, Dad.'

'Sorry.'

'I'm relieved you're here. I listened at your door, but couldn't hear anything – not even snoring. Let me touch your arms.'

'What for?' he asked, offering them up to her anyway and choosing to ignore the comment about his snoring.

'They're warm. That's good.' She found a half smile, which he returned.

She shifted her weight from one foot to the other. 'I know you don't want any fuss, but today *is* your birthday. I thought perhaps you'd let me make you breakfast,' she said.

'No need,' he replied, gruffly. When her lips tightened, he added hastily, 'If there's still cake, I wouldn't say no, though.'

'For breakfast?' she asked incredulously.

Patch shrugged. 'Why not?'

'Ew! Gross.'

'Well, it won't keep, will it? Best eaten, if you ask me.'

'You want me to cut you a slice and bring it up here?' she asked, dubiously.

'I need to get up anyway. I'll cut my own piece – I'll get a bigger slice that way. I'll be sure to eat it out of your sight, since the concept of cake for breakfast is so disgusting to you. When do you need to leave for college this morning?'

'In around twenty minutes,' she said, peering at his clock, which read 7.58am. 'My bus is at twenty past. Unless you don't want me to go?'

'Why wouldn't I want you to go to college?'

'In case, you know. In case something happens.'

Patch climbed out of bed and pulled his daughter into his arms. He could feel the tension knotting her shoulder muscles.

'I'll be fine. Nothing's going to happen, trust me,' he assured her, although his statement was a lie. He wanted to test the powers of the artefact again, and had already set half of his mind working on deciding which year to visit next. It was a good job Cass couldn't look into his face right now, or she'd see right through his subterfuge.

'Can I trust you?' she asked, taking a step away from him.

'Probably not,' he admitted, covering his earlier lie with a joke. 'Whoever trusts Jake Patch is a fool indeed.'

'Damn it, Dad, what am I supposed to do?' she asked, stamping a foot in frustration.

'Go to college. I'll be fine. I'll be here when you arrive back this afternoon, I promise.'

This time he'd made a promise he thought he could keep. An hour was all he needed for another trip into the past.

Chapter 6

When Next?

Patch sat at the kitchen table with a particularly generous wedge of cake on a plate in front of him and The Infinity Glass, still encrusted in grime, nearby. His right index finger scrolled through an internet search on his phone and his eyes skimmed the text. He discarded idea after idea.

'Why is this so difficult?' he grumbled, his scrolling finger flicking at the screen as if trying to remove an insect from it.

Luckily, he didn't have to go to work until this afternoon – a fact he'd forgotten about when making his promise to Cass about being home when she returned from college.

What Patch referred to as his "day job" – the one that consistently paid his bills – was doing home deliveries for a major supermarket chain. He didn't mind the job, except when he got a whinger like Mr McDonald who would moan about his delivery being late every week without fail, even when his food arrived right at the start of the allocated time slot.

Patch's first plan to profit from the unique powers of the artefact involved going back in time and acquiring a high-value autograph – maybe Churchill's or Shakespeare's or John Lennon's. But gaining access to his target celebrity and talking them into signing their autograph for him with only an hour in which to do it was a tall order. No. Besides, how would he look John Lennon in the eye and not warn him of his fate?

Patch had been seven years old when Lennon was shot and, although he hadn't heard of either Lennon or his famous band back then, the singer's murder at the hands of a man named Chapman was Patch's first taste of what the big, ugly world was really like. It was one of those infamous events that could stick in a child's mind and rumble around in there for years. Patch cleared his throat as if doing so would dislodge the mental image of the BBC news report headlining Lennon's death playing over and over in his mind's eye.

Forcing his focus back to the job at hand, he next considered acquiring England World Cup memorabilia from 1966. He typed the words into the search bar, but very soon abandoned this idea, too. Not being a football fan, he had no idea where such an item could be bought, nor what might be suitably valuable – apart from the famous trophy itself, of course, which had, in fact, been both stolen and recovered not long before the tournament.

'Taking the trophy would be a stupid idea anyway,' Patch told himself out loud. 'It's far too high profile. It would be impossible to sell and, knowing my luck, I'd get arrested for trying. I should stick to things I know about, like a piece of Lalique glass or Clarice Cliff pottery. Do you have any suggestions, Drusillaaaa?' he asked, the sprite's name turning into a gaping yawn. He pushed his phone across the table top too hard and had to grab it to stop it falling off the other side. He'd been unusually tired all morning, which was making him especially cranky.

'Me?' Drusilla sounded surprised to be asked.

'Yeah. You've been around the block, haven't you?'

'Around the...?'

Patch huffed an impatient sigh. 'You need to top up your knowledge of common sayings. It means you're old and you've visited loads of places,' he explained.

'Age is irrelevant,' replied the sprite, haughtily. 'But I am well-travelled and have visited many eras and seen events that would both beguile and repulse you.'

'I don't care about the history,' Patch said. He didn't want to find himself entangled in problems he'd be unable to solve, like the Norman invasion of 1066, or the fate of John Lennon. 'I want to find an object to bring back. Something that will make me a sizeable profit to help fund Cass's uni years, but not an item with any notoriety – not the Mona Lisa or anything, you know?'

'How would a sprite know what objects would be of monetary value to a human in the present year? Money is only paper or metal. It doesn't hold the same importance when you realise that's all it is.'

'It can be plastic as well. They make notes from polymers now,' he pointed out.

'Oh good grief, how ghastly.'

'You sound so much like my mother that it's giving me flashbacks,' muttered Patch. 'Ghaaaaastly,' he declared, mocking her accent. His mother had been the kind of woman who pretended to be upper-class despite her humble upbringing. Her father, George Smith, who Jake remembered as a short, bald man whose favourite pastimes were watching cricket and walking his mongrel dog Jip around the local park, had described his daughter Louise as an original fake. He'd insisted on calling her by the nickname Wheezy, which she absolutely hated. Patch smiled at the memory of Grandpa George. What a great bloke he'd been. It was such a pity about the cancer which had ultimately taken him.

'Don't blame me for the voice.' Drusilla sounded defensive. 'I merely chose it from your memory.'

'Yeah, you said. More than once. I suppose it could be worse. You could have chosen Jen's. That would have had me in pieces every time you spoke.'

Silence stretched on for a number of seconds, with Drusilla seemingly uncertain whether to respond to his comment or not. Finally, Patch said, 'Well, my mother was an utter cow, but I guess I can live with you using her voice. Not that I have any choice.'

'Indeed,' replied Drusilla, in a softer tone than Louise Patch had ever used in conversation with him.

Patch picked up his slice of cake and took a bite, chewing it slowly and letting the sugary pillow dissolve in his mouth. It was an exceptionally good cake.

'Well,' he said, licking each of his fingers in turn, 'I'm sure I'll think of something I can bring back and sell. Perhaps I'll collect a whole hoard of stuff and become the Indiana Jones of the antique world.'

'Whoever that may be,' commented Drusilla, quietly.

'Oh, yeah. He's a character in a film series – an archaeologist who collects unique items. I'd rather not get myself into the kind of scrapes he does, though. The idea of ending up face-to-face with Hitler doesn't appeal to me one bit.'

'Now there's a name I've heard,' said Drusilla. 'Hitler, Adolf. Architect of the holocaust and directly accountable for the deaths of millions of humans. I, too, would be quite glad never to meet him.'

'Good. I wasn't planning on travelling abroad to acquire my booty anyway. I'll stick to England, and as close to home as I can manage. I don't want to leave Cass by herself while her father gallivants around the country and hops about in time to bring back treasure from other eras. She might think she's all grown up, but I'm still responsible for her: for the time being, anyway.' He frowned. Cass had grown to resemble her mother more with each day that passed, a fact which made him increasingly protective of her. She was growing up fast, and sometimes he struggled to keep up.

A few months back, Cass had – completely out of the blue – brought a boyfriend home to meet her dad. Noah was a surly boy who made snide little jokes at Cass's expense. Patch thought him a poor match for his daughter and had regrettably voiced that opinion in front of her after Noah left. She'd been angry, defensive and tearful, and told her father to trust her judgement. Then, a few weeks later, she broke up with the boy and wouldn't say why. Patch, although worried what indiscretion Noah might have committed, was so grateful their father-daughter relationship had not been blighted by his knee-jerk reaction to the boy that he didn't press her to talk about what had happened, hoping she'd speak to him if she needed to get it off her chest.

Cass had much to learn, but so did Patch. He'd managed the onset of her periods, on the day after her twelfth birthday, far better, although more by luck than judgement. Six months before Cass "started", he had overheard two mothers at a bus stop discussing their daughters' horrifying experiences, and immediately sought advice on a website aimed at mums. He was ready for the conversation when it came, but she'd already talked with a friend's mother and knew way more about it than he ever could.

When it came to romance, he had assumed, following a few casual comments she'd made rather than awkward in-depth discussions, that Cass would prefer a girlfriend. This would be a far safer bet in her father's opinion: he knew what boys were like. Noah's albeit temporary arrival on the scene left Patch with unanswered questions about his daughter's sexuality which, months later, he still hadn't had the guts to broach. Perhaps he'd have to revisit that website for mothers. Having her mum here would be better, he thought, his heart twisting like a rag being wrung out. Jen had been an expert at dealing with emotional issues.

Shaking off thoughts of Jen and forcing his mind back to his quest for treasure, he said, 'There's always Poole pottery, isn't there? Some of that is worth a fair amount. My first foray into selling antiques was a piece of Poole.'

He hesitated for a moment, expecting Drusilla to ask him about it. When she didn't, he proceeded with his story anyway.

'This great big platey dish thing caught my eye at a boot fair,' he said, demonstrating the size using spread hands, like a fisherman boasting about the size of his catch. 'A charger, they call it, although I didn't know the proper term at the time. I liked it because the colours were so vibrant and the design was different from anything I'd ever seen. The lady wanted a fiver for it. I knocked her down to three, paid and took my find home.

'I noticed it had a dolphin on the underside with the words *Poole England* and I decided to look up the mark on the internet. When I discovered the charger was worth upwards of £200, I put it on one of those selling websites that do auctions and bingo: £220 profit from a three quid outlay, Drusilla. What do you think of that?'

'Yes, I'm sure that's marvellous, Patch,' responded the sprite, sounding distinctly bored.

'Well, money might have no meaning for the likes of you, but I got a huge buzz out of it. I bought Cass a locket from the proceeds and put a photo of her mother in it for her. She wears it all the time. After that, I thought maybe I could keep an eye out for Poole stuff at future boot sales, but I knew there was money to be made from more than just pottery, so I started spending my free time researching antiques and learning more. I made some losses along the way, of course, but I found that if I bought without letting my heart rule my head, I generally made a profit. And the more I knew, the more successful I became.'

He laughed, shaking his head. 'People selling at boot fairs can be so dim, Drusilla, a lot of them haven't a clue what they're selling. Of course there's more tat than treasures, but gems are there to be found for those who hunt hard enough.'

'How clever of you,' Drusilla said.

From her neutral tone, Patch wasn't sure if she meant it or was being sarcastic. Accustomed as he was to that voice having nothing to say by way of praise for his deeds, he had learned not to care too deeply.

He glanced at the time and swore. It was past noon and he'd hoped to travel back to obtain his first item today. Time was fast running out and he hadn't come up with a single iron-clad idea. He said as much to Drusilla.

'Well, it would have had to have been an item you could source locally if you were going to do everything in one morning.'

'True, but it would have been nice to at least have come up with a half decent plan. It's frustrating having this thing,' he flicked a hand towards the clay-clad glass lying on the table before him, 'and not being able to use it.'

'*Thing?*' Drusilla tutted, but when Patch didn't respond, she changed tack. 'Time will wait for you, Patch.'

'The past will wait. The present marches inexorably onward,' he replied, staring into the distance.

'I suppose it would.'

'It's a funny thing, time,' he said. 'It moves at different speeds depending on so many factors – how much fun you're having; how old you are; whether you're in love, or asleep.'

'For me,' explained Drusilla, 'time is like a magic carpet. You can ride upon it and be here and now one moment, and then back a millennium or three in a flash. It isn't linear at all.'

Patch widened his eyes, making his forehead wrinkle like the bellows of a concertina. 'Weird,' he said, pushing his chair back. He crossed the kitchen, deposited his plate next to the sink and filled the kettle to make his customary pre-work coffee. Once he'd made his drink, he left the artefact on the table and wandered into the living room, where he flicked on the TV. His favourite antiques show was on.

Taking a tiny slurp of his scalding-hot brew, he lowered himself into an armchair ready to judge the contestants' poor choice of purchases. No sooner had he sat down than the show switched to the presenter's segment, where the guest host would talk about a particularly interesting item, or visit a location of historical interest.

The Scottish presenter was sitting at a table with a trio of mugs lined up for the camera.

'Coronation memorabilia, although collectable, is rarely valuable,' she said.

Realising he'd left The Infinity Glass on the kitchen table, Patch put his coffee cup on the grubby grey carpet at his feet and went back into the kitchen.

'This piece, however, is different,' the presenter said.

Patch slid back into his seat and placed the time travel device on his lap. 'Is it now?' He reached to retrieve his coffee. 'Why's that, then?'

Minutes later, Patch silenced the TV to allow him to concentrate. His neurons were firing in a cascade reaction of excitement as he frantically searched the internet.

The date of George VI's coronation was simple to find – 12 May 1937. The next part was harder: finding likely shops where the coronation mug featured on the antiques show might have been sold. If those blue, yellow and black-decorated mugs could make five hundred quid or more for an original one pound investment, it would be outright foolish of him not to make a trip through time to find one. Maybe he could pick up a couple while he was at it.

A glance at the time confirmed Patch needed to head off to work. Regardless of the lure of potential profits from what looked to him like a particularly ordinary piece of chinaware, he'd still have to turn up at the supermarket and do his shift or risk getting fired. Trotting upstairs, he reluctantly changed into his blue trousers and navy blue fleece, cussing under his breath at the need to hurry.

Realising the impracticality of taking The Infinity Glass with him to work, he decided, on a whim, to hide it. He opened the rarely used right-hand door of the wardrobe – which he still thought of as Jen's side – and reached a hand onto the top shelf. Extracting a white shoe box, he opened it and shoved the object inside, trying his best not to peek at the cream satin shoes – the ones Jen had worn to their wedding. Then he shoved the box back onto the shelf.

'Am I to be left behind?' asked Drusilla.

'Must you be with the object, then?' he asked.

'Or nearby, yes,' she told him.

'Well then, yes, I'm leaving you behind. But it won't matter, will it? Time isn't linear for you anyway.'

Not waiting for her response, he closed the wardrobe door. Two minutes later, he pulled on his work boots and navy logoed jacket, grabbed his orange and yellow high vis vest and flew out of the door.

* * *

Halfway through his shift, Patch felt his phone vibrate inside his jacket pocket. He pulled over into the rear of a bus stop to check who was trying to contact him.

Dad? Are you OK? Where are you? Cass's message read.

I'm working, he replied, noticing this was the fourth message she'd sent in the last half hour. Her first was a simple *Hey, I'm home,* but each subsequent message sounded more and more concerned at his absence. How had he not noticed the alerts arriving? He glared at the phone.

'Bloody useless piece of junk,' he spat.

Oh, right. I thought you'd disappeared again, despite your promise to be here when I got home, came his daughter's almost instantaneous response, followed by: *Forgot you had work today.*

So did I, he returned, grumbling at himself for being so focussed on concealing his time travelling exploits from Cass earlier that he had inadvertently misled her. *Sorry,*

shouldn't have made a promise I couldn't keep. I'm
absolutely fine, honest. See you in a couple of hours.

She sent him a red heart emoji, which propagated into a bubbling group of them that floated prettily up the screen before disappearing. Patch smiled, and then shoved the phone back in his pocket. While he waited for a gap in the seemingly endless stream of traffic, a pang of guilt hit him for causing her worry.

* * *

When he arrived home, Cass announced she had used his credit card details to order them a takeaway.

'For your birthday,' she said, grinning.

'What? I get to pay for an expensive meal when we have perfectly good food in the fridge just because my age number has moved on by a digit? Anyway, I had my card with me – how did you use it to order?'

Cass blushed. 'Remembered the number,' she admitted, shuffling her feet.

Her eyes glistened with tears, so he said, 'Don't worry, it's fine. You were doing something nice for me, weren't you, and we haven't had a takeaway for months.'

She sniffed and stared at the floor.

'Look,' he said, 'I'm sorry for being grumpy. It's a great idea.'

Cass wiped away a tear with her knuckle and gave a weak smile in response.

'So you *should* be sorry,' she said.

'I'll get us plates,' he offered, trying to show the appropriate enthusiasm for her plan.

After the food was eaten and the plates cleared away, Cass, who normally did her homework in her bedroom, insisted she 'needed company this evening' and installed herself and her pile of psychology books at the dining table behind the sofa. Patch was sure she was keeping tabs on him and he alternated between more guilt and annoyance that he couldn't do the research he wanted with her right behind him, able to peer over his shoulder.

Once she finished her homework, Cass settled into the sofa next to him, pulling her long legs up and wrapping her arms around her knees to stop her feet from sliding. After a few minutes, her chin dropped, and then jerked reflexively straight back up again.

'Why don't you go to bed? You're obviously tired,' said her father.

'I'm watching this,' she protested, waving at the TV screen.

'What, the sports news? You hate cricket.'

'So do you. Anyway, I'm waiting for the weather forecast,' she countered, pouting.

Her father yawned loudly, stretching his fists in front of him as if he were gripping the handlebars of a Harley-Davidson motorcycle. 'Well, I'm going to bed. Don't stay up too late.' He rose from the sofa, squeezed his eyes shut and yawned again.

'Night, Dad,' said Cass, adding very quietly, 'And happy birthday.'

'Mmm,' he grumbled. 'G'night, sweetheart.'

As he traipsed wearily upstairs, he could feel his daughter's eyes following him from inside the living room. Her arms remained folded around her bent legs and her chin on her knees. He wished she'd never witnessed his arrival back from 1066.

Despite his exhaustion, Patch was unable to sleep. He kept debating whether he should tell Cass about The Infinity Glass after all. Knowing he wasn't going to pop randomly in and out of existence would undoubtedly reduce her stress levels.

I'll make one trip back for those mugs first, then, when I have something to show for my troubles, I'll tell her how I got them. Maybe introduce her to Drusilla, too.

Less at odds with his own conscience now, Patch drifted off to sleep.

* * *

He awoke with a useful thought wafting aimlessly around in his brain and it took him a couple of minutes to tether it. He was certain he had an old tin he'd bought as part of a job lot stowed away in a cupboard – a tin which initially appeared only to contain various styles, sizes and colours of buttons, some attached to pieces of card, some in plastic bags and others loose. When he'd tipped the buttons out, however, he discovered bits and pieces of pre-decimal currency mixed amongst them, both notes and coins. This meant he already had what he needed to purchase the coronation mug he'd seen on TV without having to literally go shopping for money first – as long as he hadn't thrown the tin and its contents away, that was, and he didn't recall having done so.

After a few minutes of rifling around amongst the socks and underwear in the bottom of his chest of drawers, he held the battered tea tin aloft in triumph. Although he was eager to discover how much cash it contained, he could hear Cass filling the kettle in the kitchen, so he left it on his bedside table and trotted downstairs.

Cass smiled when he entered the kitchen dressed in his brushed cotton pyjama trousers and a pair of tatty old mule slippers.

'Hey, Dad. Can I make you a coffee? I put enough water in the kettle for both of us.'

'Don't bother, I can do it. I fancy toast, too, so you carry on with your own breakfast,' he replied.

'Any plans for today?' Cass asked, clutching a bowl of sugary cereal and a spoon and sliding onto a high stool at the breakfast bar. 'You aren't working, are you?'

'No, that's right. I thought I might do a bit of bargain hunting,' he said, truthfully.

'Didn't you go the other day?'

'Yeah, but I didn't buy anything. Besides, I have a plan.'

'Pass me my tea, would you, Dad? I left it by the kettle. Are you going to let me in on it?'

'On what?' he asked, having lost track of the conversation.

'The plan you mentioned just now.'

Patch passed her drink over and wrinkled his nose. 'I don't want to tell you yet. Later perhaps – depending how it goes.'

Cass wrapped her hand around her mug and stared into it like it was a crystal ball. 'Oh. Right.'

Patch popped two slices of bread into the toaster and reached for the "Best Dad Ever" mug Cass had bought him for Fathers' Day a few years previously.

'Well,' she said, laughing nervously. 'Enjoy your shopping and don't do anything I wouldn't do.'

'I'll be sensible,' he assured her.

She gave him a sideways glance. 'Promise?'

'Good grief, Cass, I'm a grown adult. Do I need to promise?'

'Not sure.' She shovelled a heaped spoonful of cereal into her mouth and washed it down with tea.

He turned to face the toaster, but could feel her eyes boring into the back of his head. He chose to ignore it.

The sound of the toast popping up finally broke the silence and Patch scraped butter onto one slice, adding crunchy peanut butter to the second.

'I have to go,' said Cass, curtly. She crossed the kitchen and deposited her bowl and spoon in the sink, adding water to the dregs of her tea.

Patch waited for his customary kiss on the cheek, but his daughter walked straight past him without as much as a backward glance. When she reached the door, she hesitated. With a loud tut and a deep sigh, she ran back and kissed him.

'Be *good*,' she told him, pointedly.

Patch smiled sheepishly. 'I'll do my best,' he said. 'If things go to plan, I'll have a particularly interesting item to show you later. Then we can have a chat about stuff.'

'Stuff?'

'Yeah.' He took a bite of his toast, chewing slowly so Cass would get the idea he wasn't ready to have that chat now.

She shook her head and left the kitchen. He had barely swallowed his first mouthful of sticky peanut butter and toast when she slammed the front door shut behind her, making him jump. He couldn't wait to see her face when he presented the valuable coronation mug and told her where – or when – he'd acquired it.

Once breakfast was finished, he trotted back upstairs to fetch the artefact, then returned to the kitchen. Slouching lazily in his chair with his legs crossed at the ankles, he stared intently at his phone screen.

He double-checked the date of the coronation in question, though he was sure he'd correctly recalled it from yesterday: Wednesday, 12 May 1937. He planned to travel back to a week before the historic day to shop for the now valuable mug. The next question was where to find one.

Twisting The Infinity Glass absentmindedly between his hands, he asked himself out loud, 'Where do you find a coronation mug for sale?'

Chapter 7

A China Shop

'How about a china shop?' suggested Drusilla, in a patronising tone.

'A china shop? I haven't seen a specialist china shop for decades,' said Patch. 'But then, we are talking about the 1930s, so your suggestion is probably spot on. Well done, Drusilla.'

'Seemed like the simple answer to a simple question,' she mumbled.

Turning his attention back to his phone, he took to the internet again. Entering *Hastings china shop 1937* into an image search, Patch clicked on the top picture and laughed.

'Bingo! What amazing luck.' He banged the table top with the palm of his hand. Using forefinger and thumb, he zoomed in on the photograph of an old-fashioned shop front with the words *Bell's China* painted in neat lettering above the window. There, in front and centre of the grainy black-and-white photo, sat what looked like the coronation mug he sought.

'This is going to be a simple task, Drusilla. It won't even take me ten minutes. Perhaps I'll have a stroll around while I'm there and see if anything else grabs my attention – or I could go and buy an ice-cream and sit on the seafront enjoying the spring weather. I'll have to think about what to wear, though. I don't want to stick out like a sore thumb and draw attention to myself.'

Quarter of an hour and yet another internet search later, he was ready to tear his hair out. 'I don't have anything like these clothes. The trousers are ridiculous. Whoever wore these awful things, Drusilla?' he asked, gesturing frustratedly at the image on his phone screen.

'Plenty of men dressed like that, dependent, of course, upon social class, the weather and the occasion,' she said.

'You've visited the 1930s?'

'Several times, yes.'

'Why didn't you tell me? You could have saved me searching.'

'You didn't ask me, Patch.'

She was right: he had instructed her to speak only when called by name, although he was sure she'd suggested a china shop earlier without prompting.

A shopping trip would be needed if he were to find a suitable outfit, so Patch favourited a website with a useful variety of photographs from the relevant time period and headed for town. There was a charity shop he occasionally popped into to check its latest stock for unnoticed treasures, and he had seen in passing that it had several rails of second-hand clothing. It was as good a place as any to start.

* * *

Standing in the cramped changing room between the shop and its stockroom, Patch stared at himself in the narrow full-length mirror. He was dressed in beige trousers with a stiff crease along the front of each turned-up leg. The cut was far more generous than he was used to from his favoured skinny jeans. He'd chosen a light-brown checked shirt which he had been reluctant to tuck into the top of the trousers, and his feet were confined in a pair of stiff lace-up shoes which creaked when he flexed his toes. He felt like a hapless soul who had been invited to a fancy-dress party and had come in full costume, only to discover he'd been duped and it wasn't a fancy-dress party at all.

'I look like a bloody mushroom in these colours,' he mumbled, raking his fingers through his long, unruly hair. His hairstyle would be out of place in 1937, but it wasn't something he was willing to compromise over. He'd be a laughing stock at work and the brunt of jokes for months if he turned up all neatly shorn.

Many of the pictures he'd found online showed men from the era in question wearing fedora hats, and he debated the idea of tying his hair back or hiding it beneath a hat. He hadn't looked in every corner, but the shop didn't seem to sell men's headwear. He thought his inability to buy a fedora might in fact have been an incredibly lucky escape – he felt uncomfortable enough as it was. If people gawped at his hair, so be it.

Who knows, perhaps I'll start a fashion trend, he thought.

After changing swiftly back into his own clothes, he went to pay the meagre ticket price for his outfit and left. Once home, he emptied the tea tin to find out how much pre-decimal money it held. He found four oversized pound notes and two red ten shilling notes that were folded in half at the very bottom of the tin. The notes bore no date, but he discarded the ten shilling with Elizabeth II's image, and then quickly checked the internet to see if the others were the right design for the year he'd be visiting. He was in luck. Around half of the coins were from George V's reign, and those added up to twelve shillings and nine pence, plus three ha'pennies. He had to do another internet search to understand that there had been twelve pennies to a shilling and twenty shillings to a pound.

'So two hundred and forty pennies to a pound,' he muttered, hoping he'd remember if the need arose. 'What a ridiculous system,' he remarked. 'Why not use base ten when that's the usual number of fingers people have?'

Patch put two pounds plus some loose change into his wallet and tucked the rest of the money safely away in a drawer, then changed into his costume. Next, he tied his hair into a ponytail and tucked it into the back of his shirt. He deliberately avoided checking himself out in the mirror on his way out of the bedroom.

Time travelling from inside his home wasn't an option for this trip. Although his house was Victorian and would undoubtedly be standing in 1937, it would be someone else's home and he didn't want to be responsible for any heart attacks. Instead, he would walk into town and find a quiet place from which he could surreptitiously disappear.

Given there wouldn't be plastic carrier bags in the 1930s, he cocooned the artefact in a yellow duster from the kitchen drawer and began searching for an appropriate bag in which to carry it. With a vague recollection of having seen something suitable in the cupboard under the stairs, Patch rooted around in the cramped, gloomy space and found a khaki satchel which would hopefully fit reasonably well with the trends of the era.

His preference was to disguise his strange outfit with a long coat, but he'd have to shed any non-period clothing before time travelling, and what were the chances that it would still be there when he returned an hour later? He didn't want to lose his decent long coat, and a jacket wouldn't hide the ridiculous trousers anyway. Eventually, he elected to go as he was, but to take the back roads wherever possible to avoid attention. At least the weather was mild.

Turning the key to lock his front door, he heard a high-pitched peal of a giggle behind him and swivelled round in time to see the taller of a pair of young women across the road lowering an outstretched arm. He guessed she had been pointing at him. The second woman masked her mouth with a cupped hand and whispered in the ear of her taller friend, all the while holding her gaze on Patch and his apparently hilarious outfit.

His face flushed red with embarrassment. This was the precise scenario he had hoped to avoid. His first instinct was to shout at them, but what could he say, beyond his usual string of swear words? This pair of gossips didn't deserve his time and attention, and besides, he wanted to get going; it was already nearly 2pm. For once, he buttoned his lip and strode away quickly, although he growled under his breath when the giggling recommenced.

It didn't take him long to reach the shop – now transformed into a gaudy fast-food restaurant. Nearby, Patch found an alley where a row of commercial-sized wheelie bins would provide him with the cover he needed to disappear without drawing the attention of passers-by. In these insalubrious surroundings, he was glad he had decided against bringing a coat with him. There was nowhere here he could have left it without it getting both filthy and smelly, even if nobody stole it while he was gone.

Sliding a hand into the satchel and snaking his fingers around the metal frame containing the artefact, he said, 'Take me to Wednesday 5 May 1937'. He didn't bother specifying a time – mid-afternoon would be fine.

He screwed his eyes shut in preparation and there was a sound like a thousand people simultaneously snapping their fingers. Patch, despite being prepared for it, flinched.

* * *

Exactly like the previous time, Patch arrived feeling frozen. Goosebumps ran along both his arms, sending a tidal wave of hairs up on end. The unpleasant sensation advanced like a swarm of ants across his back and he realised his teeth were chattering too. He waited impatiently for the chill to abate, and soon warmth flooded back through his body. Opening his eyes, he gave a sigh of relief, having half expected to see his breath appear as frozen water droplets hanging in the air before him.

The wheelie bins in the alleyway were gone. He'd thought there would be some of the old metal-can variety in their place, like those he remembered from his early childhood. But there were no bins at all crowding the alley in 1937 – and no errant rubbish blowing around like ugly plastic autumn leaves either. He wondered how businesses dealt with their rubbish, but wasn't bothered enough to delay his mission to find out the answer.

Out on the street, a grating beep from an approaching vehicle reminded him that this road had not always been pedestrianised and he hopped onto the narrow – bollard-free in 1937 – pavement, giving the driver a friendly wave by way of apology. The car was a bottle-green box of a vehicle with low-slung headlights like baleful cartoon eyes and a pair of wing mirrors which protruded like exaggerated antennae. It chugged past and an acrid odour wafted up from the rear. Patch grimaced at the vile stench of leaded petrol exhaust fumes – it was so strong that he could taste it.

A light drizzle dampened the air and, possibly as a consequence, only a handful of people were walking along the street. Patch noted with considerable relief that the men were mostly dressed similarly to him, but all wore hats and coats and none had long hair. When a man glanced at him from below knitted eyebrows, Patch self-consciously checked his ponytail. It was still tucked away out of sight, so it was more likely his lack of a coat in the miserable weather that was drawing the unwanted attention. The man arranged his features back to neutral and gave a polite nod and a 'Good afternoon' on his way past.

The only two women Patch passed both wore dresses under their coats. What was visible of their hairstyles reminded him of his mother's: wavy and painstakingly pinned in place. There was not a single pair of jeans, trainers or tracksuit bottoms in sight, of course.

At this time of year, he would have expected every door to be open to encourage passers-by to enter. Today, however, every single one was closed and every interior looked dark and uninviting. *Bell's China* was no exception and Patch approached to check the opening hours sign. *Wednesday 9–12,* it said in blue cursive lettering. Where the afternoon opening hours should have been, it said, *Half day closing.*

'What?' he gasped. 'No! It can't be shut, surely.'

'Is there a problem, sir?' asked an older man who, with his black umbrella held aloft above his grey hat and coat, reminded the time traveller vaguely of Gene Kelly in *Singin' in the Rain*.

Patch's anxiety level shot up. The idea of holding a conversation with a stranger from the past rattled him much more than he would have imagined. It would be like talking to a ghost although, this being their time, not his, perhaps it was he who was the spirit here.

'Sir?' The man reached out a tentative hand. 'Are you unwell?'

Patch gulped, his mouth suddenly dry. 'I'm brilliant,' he replied. 'Except for... Hey, why are all the shops closed?'

The man frowned uncomprehendingly. 'It's Wednesday: half day closing.' He pointed helpfully at the sign Patch had already read.

'What, all of them?'

'Certainly. Are you sure you are well? You're as white as a sheet.'

'Yeah, I'm good. I mean, yes, I'm perfectly fine, thank you for your concern,' Patch responded, altering his choice of words to better fit with the stranger's manner of speaking. 'Don't let me keep you. Have a nice day.'

Be polite, not American, he chastised himself. *Pah! Have a nice day, indeed.*

With a gracious – if hesitant – smile, the man continued on his way, leaving Patch gawping helplessly at the coronation mug sitting an arm's length away on the other side of a pane of glass.

He needed to sit down, but could find nowhere in the narrow street to do so. Instead, he made his way to the seafront. Expecting it to be much the same as he knew it, except slightly less shabby and missing the noisy amusement arcades, Patch was surprised to discover how different the seafront was. Two substantial shed-like buildings and another that looked similar to an aircraft hangar stood where fairground rides were located in the twenty-first century. The manmade boating lake was not cordoned off from the promenade by railings in these pre-Health & Safety Executive days and, instead of the familiar fibreglass swan pedaloes, odd wooden boats with numbers hand-painted on the rear and several canoes which could have come straight out of the Disney film *Pocahontas* were tied up at one end, near the 'hangar'. Patch wondered if they were stored in the building overnight. Nobody rode on the lake today – not with the steady drizzle that settled like a spider's web on Patch's arms and the chilly breeze blowing off the English Channel which made him shiver.

Very few pedestrians were braving the seafront today at all. An occasional car chugged along the road and a green-liveried trolleybus glided by beneath overhead wires. Patch, who had been gazing upward at the ornate but most likely inadequate street lighting while crossing the road, had failed to register the rows of parallel wires until after the trolleybus had gone past.

He took cover in a roadside shelter with an overhanging roof and wooden bench seating lining each side. This was still here in his own time, although he hadn't paid the old trolleybus stop much attention, let alone wondered how long it had been there. Leaning forward, elbows on knees and chin on the heels of his hands, he let misery at his failed mission sweep over him. A discarded newspaper fluttered weakly on the wooden slats nearby but he barely noticed.

'Damn it. Why didn't I choose a time in the morning? That one tiny detail was my downfall, wasn't it, Drusilla?'

'It seems so, yes. A pity, for sure,' replied the sprite, who had remained silent until now.

He sprung gleefully to his feet, lifting a triumphant finger. 'But the answer is obvious. I can wait until my hour is up, and then travel back here again, except this time I'll choose 10am and the shop will be open.'

'Ummm...'

'What? Um *what*?' asked Patch, sitting down again and slapping a frustrated hand on the bench seat. 'For pity's sake, don't tell me there are rules against going to the same day twice?'

'Not the same day. The same year.'

Patch would have sworn had a boy of about eight not been walking briskly past. The child wore a heavy jacket, but beneath it he was dressed in short trousers and had long grey socks pulled as high as they would go, leaving his knobbly knees showing in between. There was no sign of any adult keeping an eye on the child.

'Not the same year?' Patch said between gritted teeth. 'I thought linear time had no meaning for you. Why can't I go to the same year twice?'

'It's not my rule. It's a limitation of the device, and I don't know the reason either, so don't bother asking.'

Patch snorted like an angry bull. 'So I'll have to go back with nothing to show Cass. No proof.'

Drusilla remained silent.

The wind direction shifted and the discarded newspaper fluttered more insistently, finally drawing Patch's attention. He whipped it up and checked for a date at the top: Saturday 1 May 1937. It was the *Hastings & St Leonards Observer*, the same local paper Patch was familiar with, but this in a more antiquated, tightly packed format.

He tucked the newspaper under his arm. 'This will have to do for proof. I doubt it has any monetary value, but at least I can prove to Cass that I time travelled to 1937.'

'But no mug,' said Drusilla. 'Such a pity.'

'No, no mug. Not unless I find myself a sledgehammer and decide to do a bit of looting, but I'm not the sort who engages in wanton destruction of property. More's the pity.'

'It's good to have scruples,' said Drusilla.

'Sure. It's great,' replied Patch, dryly. 'Effing bloody marvellous.'

When the time came for his return home, Patch stayed on the bench. Nobody was around to witness his disappearance anyway, so the location didn't matter.

The usual sound marked his return to the alleyway from which he had departed an hour earlier. Arriving seated but without a seat to support him, Patch fell to the ground, narrowly avoiding hitting his head against the brick wall behind him.

He pulled his knees up to his chin and hugged his arms around them, shivering violently. He elected to remain where he was for now, hoping he'd warm up.

'How... how l-l-long will this l-last, Drusilla?' he asked, after a while.

'The chill? I'm afraid I can't tell you.'

'T-t-t-t-t...' Patch swallowed hard. 'Terrific. I have to g-get home and ch-change before Cass arrives. What's the t-t-time?'

'It's 3.27 pm, Patch.'

He growled frustratedly, then stood and brushed off the seat of his trousers. Then, damp, dirty and still thawing out, he retraced his route up the hill to home, the newspaper tucked firmly beneath his arm.

Chapter 8

Coming Clean

'This is great, Dad,' said Cass. 'What a find! The condition is near perfect. Can I keep it?'

Patch hadn't expected his daughter to arrive home while he was still showering, but then he did stand in the steaming flow of water for an awfully long time. Shaking off the pervasive chill from his bones wasn't easy. When he approached the top of the stairs, his lower half swathed in a bath towel, to go and retrieve the newspaper he'd left lying on the chest of drawers in the front hallway, he found her sitting on the bottom step with his second-rate souvenir draped across her lap.

'Look at this.' She pointed. 'The front page is full of adverts. They were selling cotton Union Jacks for Coronation Day – the Queen's father's coronation, presumably, or was it the one who abdicated? – and there was a fashion show going on at some place called Mastins. Isn't there somewhere in Hastings still called Mastins? The name rings a bell.'

Patch loved it when Cass overflowed with enthusiasm like this. She was like a kid trying to choose which present to open first on Christmas morning. He enjoyed being dragged along for the ride with her, too; he didn't know anyone else who could get up a steam of fervour like his Cass could.

'Yeah, the roundabout near the Tourist Information Centre on the seafront is called Mastins, I think,' said Patch. 'You know, where that fountain is. The one people keep putting washing up liquid in, so it bubbles over like a crazy science experiment.'

He had planned to show Cass the newspaper this evening, after dinner, but her discovery of it while he was showering meant events had overtaken him. How should he handle the situation now? Was the time right to tell her about The Infinity Glass? He tried to think fast, but Cass was already speaking again.

'And here, inside, they're already talking about air-raid precautions when the War didn't start until 1939. Seems a bit previous, doesn't it?'

'Mmm, I dunno. They knew war was coming. At least some people clearly did. It would be stupid not to start thinking about defence if you could see the writing on the wall.'

'It's so interesting, though.' Cass's eyes were sparkling with excitement. 'History, Dad. History being made, even in an ordinary seaside town like Hastings.'

'Yes. I guess it's a privileged position to see it all with the benefit of historical hindsight.'

'Exactly. Can you imagine being here back then?' she asked, demonstrating her enthusiasm with sparkling eyes and gesticulating hands. 'Imagine not knowing whether war would definitely come – and if it did, which side would win. Wondering if the Nazis would occupy the UK and Hitler himself would broadcast to the nation from Buckingham Palace. We know what happened, but it was their day-to-day life and they had literally no clue. It puts a whole new perspective on things, seeing this one simple newspaper.'

'I suppose it does. Well, I need to get dressed,' he said, nodding towards the towel around his middle.

'Sure,' she replied, lowering her eyes eagerly back to the page and chewing lightly on her bottom lip.

Strolling into his bedroom, Patch couldn't help but smile at his daughter's ebullience. She liked what he'd brought back from 1937, even though it wasn't a valuable coronation mug. A simple newspaper, though? Patch shook his head. From his point of view, it was a damned poor consolation prize. What would Cass have thought of his intended purchase?

Putting aside profit and thinking about style, he hadn't been impressed at all by the pictures he'd seen of the mug. He found the design busy, the colours boring and the shape bog standard, but then that was his personal opinion. All that really mattered from his point of view was the potential for profit – what somebody else would be willing to pay for it. If he'd had to decide on an item to choose from a shelf full of different commemorative pieces, he wouldn't have had a clue which was the most valuable. He needed to up his game – to fill in some knowledge gaps so he wouldn't miss out on a potential prize antique for want of a snippet of specialist information. Cass could keep the newspaper. He would have only chucked it in the recycling anyway.

He still wanted to tell her about Drusilla and The Infinity Glass, though, and tonight he would do it.

* * *

Patch waited with growing impatience for the right moment to tell Cass about his time-travelling adventures, but the evening stretched into night and the BBC *Ten*

O'clock News came on with him still debating how to tell her in a way that was believable.

He watched her sitting in her usual armchair with her legs crossed and her splayed knees resting on the wide padded arms. Her head moved from side to side like an old-fashioned typewriter carriage as she perused the open newspaper. She had been ensconced like this ever since finishing dinner and her plate lay discarded on the floor, the cutlery askew and a couple of unwanted new potatoes sitting in a congealing puddle of sunflower spread near the rim.

Patch jabbed the remote control to turn off the babbling television. The news was as gloomy as ever and he didn't need to hear the Prime Minister's latest speech about how wonderfully well the economy was growing. It was all self-congratulatory drivel with no real substance, but such was the nature of modern politics. Churchill would turn in his grave if he saw what sorry money-grabbing halfwits passed themselves off as politicians in the early twenty-first century.

Cass carried on reading, oblivious to the fact that he'd turned the telly off.

Patch cleared his throat, hoping to gain her attention, but she did not lift her head. He scratched behind his ear, then took a mouthful of his coffee, to find it barely lukewarm.

'Eugh!'

At last, she looked up, her eyes questioning.

'Coffee's cold,' he explained.

She was about to return to her reading, so he said, 'Um, Cass, you remember the thing that happened the other day?'

Her back straightened. She closed the newspaper and dropped it onto the floor, careful to avoid it landing on her plate.

'Of course. How could I forget? Has it happened again? Are you feeling alright?' she asked.

'I'm fine, don't worry. But it has happened again, yes.'

Cass's fingers flew to her mouth and her eyebrows lifted into steep arches.

'You don't need to worry, Cass. I'm completely in control of it.'

She lowered her hands into her lap and tipped her head to one side. 'What do you mean, in control of it?'

'You know the newspaper from 1937?'

'Stop trying to change the subject.'

'I'm not – hear me out, please, Cass. I didn't buy the paper in an antique shop. I got it from 1937.'

She twitched an eyebrow, bemused. 'You weren't alive in 1937. Grandma wasn't even born until 1939.'

Patch leaned forward, looking her right in the eye so she would see he wasn't lying. 'I time travelled, Cass. I went back to 1937. I found the newspaper lying in a tram shelter on the seafront. I brought it home with me to prove where I'd been.'

She stared at him for a couple of seconds, then made a little guttural noise. 'Yeah, right. Pull the other one, Dad. You'll be telling me next that you met a woman with a police box which was bigger on the inside. Ha ha!'

Patch pressed his lips together hard. Of course she wouldn't believe him. His daughter was a smart girl.

'I'm not pulling your leg. It's real. You can tell when I'm lying – look at me, Cass. When I appeared out of nowhere the other day, I'd been time travelling. I was arriving back from 1066.'

'From *1066?*' she said, smirking.

Patch frowned and Cass tipped her head to one side, as if reconsidering her accusation. Her lips tightened into a thin line.

Patch tried desperately to come up with a more persuasive argument, but Cass beat him to it.

'People don't time travel,' she said. 'It's impossible. Time travel is fictional. If you really believe what you just told me, then you must be having a medical problem that causes hallucinations. You should make an appointment to see a doctor.'

'I know what you're saying. I understand why you think that way, but how else would you explain my appearing right in front of you like I did?' he asked, shaking his head. 'How could that happen unless I'm telling the truth? People don't appear out of thin air, do they?'

'I don't know. It must have been an illusion.'

'What? Come on, think about it!' he implored her. 'Really think about it.'

'Look, you can't tell me you travelled back to 1066 and 1937 and expect me to say, "Yeah, sure, that's chill," can you?' She wrapped her arms around her waist.

'That's why I brought the bloody newspaper back. There's nothing wrong with me, and why would I lie? Come to that, why would I make up such an elaborate story – *and* provide evidence backing it up? Why would I do that, Cass, if it wasn't real?'

'Then show me how. Go on, do it now,' she said, her jaw set stubbornly.

'I can't. The Infinity Glass is upstairs. Besides, I have to decide where I'm going rather than just doing it.'

'Glass? What glass are you on about? Like the thing you drink from, or a mirror? Hey, are you saying you have a magic portal or something?'

Patch held up a hand to tell her to stop. She was asking too many questions.

'Hold up.' He leapt to his feet. 'Let me get it. Let me show you.'

Ignoring Cass's cries of 'Dad! Dad!', he ran upstairs and into his bedroom.

'Drusilla,' he called, fumbling in the shoebox to extract the artefact. 'I'm going to introduce you to my daughter.'

'Ummm...'

Patch took the stairs two at a time and re-entered the living room with the grubby-looking object held high like a trophy.

Cass pulled her chin in and wrinkled her nose.

'What do you call *that*?' she asked. 'It's not even glass.'

Patch stared at the object in his hand and wished he'd cleaned it up. The time travel device was still caked in dried mud or clay or whatever the heck it was, except for the tiny bit he'd chipped off.

'Look. Here, see?' He turned it around so that she could see the object inside.

'Oh. Some kind of glass sculpture, is it? It's kinda fancy, underneath all that muck. Let me see. How does it work?' She tried to take it from him, but Patch held his prize fast, unwilling to give it up, even to her.

'It's complicated. Actually, no, it's easy; it's the rules which are complicated. Tell her, Drusilla.'

'Patch, I can't. She won't hear me,' said Drusilla, apologetically.

'Oh, for pity's sake. Damn and blast, Drusilla, don't do this to me.'

'My voice is exclusively for the custodian. It's inaudible to anyone else,' she explained.

'Who's Drusilla?' asked Cass, scanning around the room. 'Is she here? Can you see her?'

'No. I can hear her, but she's telling me you can't because you aren't the custodian.'

'The custodian. Of The Infinity Glass?'

'That's right. She has my mother's voice.'

'Grandma's voice? Wow, I bet that went down well,' Cass said, sarcastically.

'Yeah, well. I had no choice in the matter.'

'So tell me how it works, then. Show me if it's easier. Set it for a minute into the future and I'll wait for you to reappear.' Her tone of voice told him she still didn't believe a word of his time travel story.

'Can I do what she's suggesting, Drusilla?' asked Patch.

'No, of course not. Backward travel only, excluding return trips, of course,' answered Drusilla. 'Besides, it would be travelling within your lifetime, which wouldn't be allowed.'

'Oh shit, yeah. I forgot.'

'Forgot?' asked Cass.

'Erm, sorry. Drusilla says I can't go forward, only back.'

'Then take me back in time. I could... Dad, please take me to meet Mum,' she said, her eyes pleading and already glistening with tears.

Patch swore. It was as if she hadn't believed him until the moment her mother entered the equation, and then she wanted it so badly that it flipped a switch for her.

'I wish I could,' he whispered. 'I wanted that too, trust me, but I can't travel within my own lifetime. There's no point me meeting your mum when she was a tiny baby, is there? I'm so sorry, Cass.' He stepped forward to wrap his arms around her trembling body.

After a few seconds, Cass pushed him away. She wiped away her tears with a knuckle and glared at her father.

'There is something wrong with you,' she snapped. 'Coming up with this ridiculous story. Making me think I might see Mum then saying it's against the damned rules. You knew I'd want to see her if you told me some crazy-arse story about time travelling. What the hell is going on with you? Why would you lie to me like that?'

Confused, Patch said, 'Cass, I'm not lying, I swear I'm not.' He took a step towards her, but Cass avoided his touch by taking a step back. 'Damn it, Cass, why would I lie?'

She shook her head. 'I've no idea. All I know is that you're showing me a crappy piece of junk which looks like you dug it up in the back garden and you expect me to accept that there's an invisible bloody fairy talking to you and helping you time travel.'

'A fairy?' retorted Drusilla. 'You humans can be so offensive.'

Patch didn't know how to react to Cass's outburst. Then suddenly he had an idea, but he hesitated for a moment before acting on it. He didn't want to appear inside the house. He'd have to pick a date before it was built.

'Take me to – I don't know – to midday on the first of June 1850.'

There was a sound like a thousand people snapping their fingers and Patch was shivering on an unfamiliar hillside.

Chapter 9

Daisy Chain

Barely registering his surroundings at first, Patch could think only of Cass back at home and how frightened she must be after seeing her father disappear in front of her eyes. He wished he had reacted better to her totally understandable disbelief, but he couldn't take it back now. He would be here for an hour whether he liked it or not.

Finally focussing on where he was, he saw the wide dirt track which would become his familiar house-packed road sometime during the next fifty or so years only a few metres away. He high-stepped his way out of the tall grass and gloriously colourful mix of gently waving wild flowers into which he had appeared.

The hill leading towards the sea was lined with trees which rustled like murmuring voices in the breeze. A single house stood on the opposite side of the track around twenty metres away. Patch could not remember for the life of him whether that house still stood in his own time, a question he resolved to answer for himself tomorrow. The only other building visible was a church. He assumed, given its location, that it must be All Saints.

Squinting in the bright glow of the summer sun, he inhaled a lungful of fresh air, grateful the weather was good as he'd brought nothing with him to protect himself from rain. Without a "mission" in 1850, he saw no point going to explore. Instead, Patch sat on the verge and picked a daisy, twirling it absently between his forefinger and thumb. On a sudden whim, he picked another and began constructing a chain of them. When she was little, Cass used to enjoy wearing daisy chains on her head, like nature's own beautiful tiara. He would take one back to her today – a floral gift more than a hundred and fifty years old. Perhaps it would help him win her over for having disappeared the way he had.

It took him longer than expected to make a chain of suitable length. An abundance of daisies grew within arm's reach of where he sat, but his fingers had forgotten how to make the required slit in the stem without breaking it. He was hindered by his short fingernails and the seemingly tougher stems on the flowers compared to modern-day daisies, as well as his unfamiliarity with the task.

He was finishing making the circlet when a rough, rasping cough made him look up. A woman with a striking but gaunt face strolled towards him along the track. She was a little shorter than Cass and wore a long brown woollen skirt and a bottle-green laced bodice. She carried a basket hooked over her right arm. A ragged child with a snotty nose and curly chestnut-brown hair peered from behind her skirts.

The woman gave Patch a nod of acknowledgement as she approached. The child pulled on her mother's arm and gawped shamelessly at Patch.

'Do come along, Annie,' chided the woman, her accent broad Irish. To Patch, she bobbed the slightest of curtseys and said, 'Please excuse my daughter's bad manners, sir.'

'Apology accepted. Would she like this? I made it for my own daughter, but there are plenty of flowers here to make another.'

The woman hesitated then, leaving the child sucking her thumb in the middle of the track, walked the four steps needed to reach Patch and took the chain from his outstretched hand.

'It sits on top of the head, like a crown,' he explained.

'Yes, I know. Thank you,' said the woman, returning to her daughter and placing the daisy chain atop the child's unruly curls. 'Say thank you to the gentleman, Annie.' The child continued mutely sucking her thumb and the woman gave her a sharp clip around the ear as the pair continued on their way. 'Annie Tobin, your father and I taught you better manners than that.'

Patch sighed and commenced work on another daisy chain.

'How long do I have left here, Drusilla?' he asked, once Annie and her mother were out of earshot.

'Sixteen minutes, Patch,' replied the sprite.

'Good. That should be plenty of time to finish this,' he said, wondering why an Irishwoman would be in 1850 Hastings. 'Hey, do you think Cass will forgive me?'

'I have no idea. That's dependant on you and how you handle the situation when we return.'

'Hmmm,' grumbled Patch.

As the time for his return home approached, Patch prepared himself mentally for the chill he would experience when he reappeared in his living room. He hunched his shoulders, stiffening at the mere thought of it. Then he thought about Cass. He didn't want to scare her, so instead he decided to play it cool. He rolled his shoulders to loosen them up and tilted his head from side to side, ignoring the audible *crack* of one of his neck vertebrae.

'Give me a ten second countdown, Drusilla.'

'Oh! Um, six, five, four, three, two, one,' said Drusilla.

At the last moment, Patch plastered a cheesy grin on his face and held out both hands, the floral peace offering draped across them. The finger snapping sound came, accompanied by the inevitable cold, and he was home.

His eyes took a few seconds to adjust to the reduction in light levels. He expected Cass to be standing before him with her hands on her hips and a furrowed brow. She wasn't there.

Where was she and why ever would she leave before his reappearance? His grin melted away and his hands dropped despondently to his sides, although he made sure not to let go of his daisy chain gift.

Then he saw her, curled up on her armchair. Her head was resting in the crook of her elbow, which was balanced on the padded arm, and her hair draped like a curtain across her face. A puff of air escaped her mouth and wafted her hair, making Patch's lips stretch into a soft, lopsided smile.

His first instinct was to awaken her straight away and give her his gift but, being frozen to the bone, he would struggle to maintain the façade that he felt fine. Instead, Patch draped his gift across her knees and padded stiffly upstairs to take a shower.

As he stood in the bath, hot water from the shower running down his body in rivulets, he thought about his daughter. When she was no more than a toddler, she had unwittingly saved his life. After Jen died, Cass was what kept him getting out of bed every morning and dealing with the unwanted continuation of his own existence.

With a single income in the household – and a poor one at that – Patch had been unable to afford childcare, so he'd quit his job and the pair of them had scraped by on government benefits until Cass started school. She had been the single good thing in his life during those difficult years. He owed her more than she'd ever know.

When he returned to the living room about twenty minutes later, she stirred slightly but remained fast asleep. He retrieved the daisy chain, which was already showing signs of wilting, and shook her arm gently.

'Cass? Cass, sweetheart, I'm back.'

Her eyes snapped open. When she pushed her hair back, he saw that dried salty lines like snail trails marked her cheeks. She leapt to her feet and pounded his chest with her fists.

'What did you have to do that for?' she screeched. 'You left me here all alone with no clue when you'd come back – or if. I waited and watched and hoped and worried and nothing. Nothing, Dad. I wanted to call for help, but nobody would believe you'd disappeared back to 1850. Besides, what would they do to help me even if they did? So I waited here alone and I cried and I hoped you wouldn't get yourself killed and never come home. Now here you are, all casual and...' she stared at the daisy chain dangling from Patch's hand. 'What the hell's that about?' she asked, pointing at it.

'I made it. I had an hour to kill, so I made you a present.' He offered it to her, but she didn't take it.

'I'm not six any more, Dad. You can't placate me with a stupid daisy chain.'

'No. I'm sorry,' he said, uncurling his fingers and letting his gift drop to the floor.

Father and daughter stared at each other, neither knowing what to say next.

Cass threw herself into his arms. 'At least you're warm this time,' she said, her voice muffled by his shirt.

'Yeah,' he gave an awkward laugh. He had no intention of telling her he'd been upstairs and showered without waking her first. Hopefully she wouldn't notice his still-damp hair. The steam would most likely have cleared from the bathroom before she went up to bed, since he'd had the foresight to leave the door open and the window ajar.

'What was it like?' she asked, pulling away from his embrace. At least she had to accept his word now.

'Time travelling or being in 1850?' he asked.

'Either. Both.'

'I met a woman on the hill. I made a couple of daisy chains and gave one to her kid.'

'You spoke to someone?'

'Sure. Anyway, she spoke to me first.'

'Ah, OK. Where did you go?'

'Where?' he asked. 'Oh, here. Right here. You always arrive exactly where you left, except if that means you'd be imbedded in a tree or whatnot. Those are the rules. I was right here, only the house wasn't, of course.'

They spent the next twenty minutes talking about every detail he could remember: what he'd seen of buildings, the road, houses, the church; even the trackside wild flowers, which Patch, unable to name them, tried to adequately describe. Cass asked about the woman and the little girl, then insisted they log on to the internet and search the 1851 census to find them.

To Patch's surprise, they were there. Both mother and child were named Annie, and they lived in a road which no longer existed – either that or the name of it had been changed. Annie senior had no husband listed on the census, and her status was listed as "widow". Cass speculated whether the Tobin family might have come to England because of the potato famine in Ireland, a theory which fitted neatly with the dates.

Patch and Cass searched for the two Annies on the next census, too, hoping to learn what had become of the pair, but to no avail.

'Perhaps she remarried,' suggested Cass, hopefully.

Patch merely shrugged. He yawned and checked the time. It was after midnight.

'I need to sleep,' he announced, pushing back his chair. 'And you have college tomorrow. You should go to bed too.'

'But we haven't got to the actual details of time travelling yet,' she protested. 'I want to know how it works. You mentioned rules.' She broke into a cavernous yawn.

'Tomorrow,' said Patch. 'I'll tell you everything tomorrow.'

'But Dad—'

'But Dad nothing. I'm zonked and I'll bet you are as well. I'm going to bed. Don't stay up late.'

'I won't,' she promised, reluctantly.

With a satisfied nod, Patch gave his daughter a peck on the cheek and retired to bed. He was closing the door behind him when she called out, 'No more time travelling without telling me first, though, hey, Dad?'

Patch waved a dismissive hand and left without answering.

* * *

Lying in bed later, unable to sleep despite his exhaustion, he realised he hadn't told Cass his grand plan to bring valuable items back from the past and sell them to swell her uni fund. The news could wait. It would have to. She had shut her bedroom door for the night at least fifteen minutes ago and Cass had always been able to fall asleep within moments of her head hitting the pillow.

Her mother had been the same. Many times, Patch had watched Jen's face – so peaceful, serene and utterly perfect – as she slept beside him. Sometimes he'd kissed her softly and she'd stirred, rolling over to mould her body to his. Six years they'd had. Six measly, short years. A single tear escaped the corner of his eye. He allowed it to fall freely and drip with an audible "plop" onto his pillow, then he curled his legs up to his chest and waited for sleep to come.

Chapter 10

Be Careful What You Wish For

Patch awakened to the shrill *trrrring!* of the doorbell. The time on his clock read 8.55am – it was a good job, he thought, throwing back the covers, that he wasn't on the early shift at work today.

Pulling on long pyjama bottoms, he trotted down to the door and accepted a package addressed to Cass. The packet required no signature and he thought it would most likely have fitted through the letterbox if the delivery driver had bothered trying.

Patch meandered through to the kitchen, tossed the grey plastic-wrapped bundle on the table, and grabbed a mug from the cupboard. He needed a coffee.

He filled the kettle, left it to rumble its way to a full boil and trotted back upstairs to get dressed. As he sat on the bed pulling on his socks, The Infinity Glass caught his eye. He picked it up and a small lump of the clay-like coating dropped onto the carpet. Retrieving the debris, he took it and the artefact back downstairs to the kitchen. He placed them on the table, next to Cass's package and the newspaper he'd brought back from his trip to 1937, and went to make himself a coffee and a slice of jam-slathered toast to accompany it.

He bolted down the toast in a few rapid bites and considered making a second slice, but the time travel device caught his eye once again. Tilting his chair onto its back legs, he reached behind him and pulled open the cutlery drawer, extracting an orange-handled vegetable knife.

'Time for a clean-up operation,' he said, inserting the point of the blade into a crack in the clay-like coating.

'Patch, are you sure that's wise?' asked Drusilla, urgently.

'Did I ask your opinion?' he snapped.

'No, but—'

'Then don't give it. I want to see what it is I have here. Don't worry, I'll take good care of your precious artefact.'

'B—'

'A-a-a! Stop distracting me, Drusilla. If I think there's any danger it'll get damaged, I'll stop, I promise. I wouldn't do anything to risk the object that's going to help me earn money for Cass, would I?'

The sprite huffed, but said no more, so Patch continued the cleaning task he'd set himself.

Ten minutes later, the time travel device sat before him amidst a collection of clay rubble. The glass element was formed into a loose trefoil knot with no visible join – no beginning and no end. At each of the three bends, a fat node contained a blob of some kind of liquid: one green blob, one red and one blue. The liquid inside shimmered and wobbled like a droplet of water in zero gravity. The glass knot was contained within a hinged spherical wire cage decorated with tiny figures of eight. The cage had a slightly flattened bottom – presumably for the sake of stability.

'It's a lovely thing, this,' he commented, appreciatively. 'A few scratches on the glass, but otherwise in decent nick.'

'Scratches?' asked Drusilla, her voice shrill.

Patch picked up the artefact and peered at it closely. 'Keep your hair on – not that you have any – it's a bit of minor surface-level scuffing, that's all. I'm sure it wasn't inflicted by the cleaning either, so don't go blaming me.'

'I think removing the protective layer is a terrible mistake, Mr Patch,' said Drusilla quietly.

'Ah, *Mr* Patch is it now?' he asked, grinning. 'Well I have a professional interest in old things and I wanted to see it. I'm glad I cleaned it. I've never seen anything like it before. There's no maker's mark or anything useful, though, which is a bit disappointing.'

'The Maker didn't create this to sell it, Patch. What would be the point in a maker's mark for a piece as utterly unique as The Infinity Glass?'

'I hoped I'd discover who made it. Perhaps where and when it was made, too.'

'It was made by an extraordinarily gifted craftswoman over a hundred years ago.'

'Interesting. Tell me more about this woman. Who was she? Where did she come from? Was she local to here?'

'I cannot say.'

'The rules again?' asked Patch, rolling his eyes.

'Not exactly.'

'You said it was made by a woman. You must know who she was.'

'I told you, I cannot say.'

'You must know, though,' he repeated, emphatically. 'You're linked to this thing, after all. How did that happen?'

'I *will not* tell you!' The following echo that went with Drusilla's voice was barbed. It filled the whole kitchen, bouncing angrily off the hard walls. Patch imagined the face of his mother, whose voice Drusilla had adopted, her red-painted lips pursed and pencilled-in eyebrows drawn together above the top of her large dark-pink plastic-rimmed spectacles.

'Pah! Fine. Whatever,' he said. 'Keep your secrets. But we both know "will not" is different to "cannot".'

He brushed the clay rubble to the edge of the table and scooped it onto his palm, depositing it in the swing bin before returning to the table. There, he opened out the old newspaper to see if any of the articles would pique his curiosity. He spotted the piece about air-raid precautions Cass had told him about and spent a few minutes reading it.

'Weird thought, that,' he said, his fingers absently tapping on the glass.

'What is?' asked Drusilla, her voice sounding ragged.

'Hastings with bomb shelters. I think they used the caves up on the West Hill for a while — at least I've a vague memory of the tour guide saying something like that when I went there on a school trip as a kid. I wonder what other places they used? I can't imagine Hastings was exactly a prime target for the Luftwaffe. It wasn't strategically important, was it? Perhaps I should go and explore wartime Hastings. Pick a date in 1943 and go.'

A thousand people snapped their fingers and Patch fell onto a hard tiled floor.

Patches through Time

PART 2: THE BARGAIN HUNTER's DAUGHTER

Chapter 11

Human Nature

Cass's bus was late again. Tom, a new student in her psychology class, had been trying to chat her up ever since they left the classroom. She'd made the unfortunate mistake of telling him she was going to catch the number 98 bus and he'd immediately suggested they could become 'bus buddies'. She didn't want to be rude, but her new classmate's obvious attempts at flirting were as bad as any she'd ever heard – and she had heard quite a few. The way he leered at her made her want to throw up. She considered herself an excellent judge of human nature, and classified Tom as a self-centred right-wing misogynist within minutes of meeting him. His deodorant was not the most effective, either.

Being quiet, pretty and clever, Cass often attracted attention from the likes of Tom, and she silently wished her best friend Lola could catch the 98 bus with her. It would be fun to have a bus buddy to sit with every day – just not Tom. Sadly, Lola lived in the opposite direction, in Little Common.

At last, the bus pulled in at the kerb and a wave of students eager to board before the seats were all taken carried Cass forward, leaving Tom behind. When she stepped up from the kerb, she nearly tripped over the ankles of the girl in front of her. Cass waved her bus pass across the dirty yellow contactless pad and scaled the stairs to the upper deck. Half the seats were already taken and, instead of choosing one of a vacant pair, she sat next to Joe Peters who already had his headphones on and was staring blankly out of the bus window, like he always did. At least Joe wouldn't try any of that flirtatious nonsense. He was unlikely to acknowledge her existence, beyond the slightest of involuntary blushes when she took her seat.

Good, she thought. *Peace at last.*

Tom's grinning face appeared at the top of the stairs and Cass pretended to be looking for something inside her bag. Tom chose a seat a few rows away from Cass, and Saffron Jacobson claimed the one beside him. Within minutes, Tom had his arm draped around Saff's shoulder, all thoughts of conquering Cass clearly forgotten.

Cass breathed a sigh of relief. She didn't need another Noah in her life. She was content to be "just Cass" for now, not half of a couple. Love was a complicated concept. Finding the right partner in a world populated by billions of humans was a minefield of unmanageable proportions. Cass, unlike most girls she'd come across, had the whole population to choose from rather than just the males – a fact she had so far kept hidden for fear of negative feedback she did not yet have the confidence to deal with. She had dropped a hint or two to her dad, but he hadn't picked up on it and, although she thought he'd be cool with it, something held her back from starting that conversation. For now, anyway.

After Noah, she'd decided to adopt a wait-it-out-then-go-with-the-flow attitude to life and relationships. This meant she would proceed through college and on through uni without putting any pressure on herself to meet a "special someone", and then see what options opened up to her in all aspects of her adult life after graduating.

Her father's face popped into her mind, as it always did when she thought about leaving home and going to university. Cass loved her dad dearly, but worried how he would manage after she left. She had suggested many times that he should date – and even offered to set him up a profile on a dating app. He always responded by insisting Cass was all he needed, which put her under a kind of pressure she found tremendously difficult to deal with, especially now, in her final year at college.

As if coping with ordinary life wasn't enough, this whole time travelling craziness had been thrown into the mix. It was like the storyline of a fantastic novel. She could picture her reckless father choosing to go back to the time of the dinosaurs and getting himself eaten by a bloody T-Rex or velociraptor. His interest in antiques would never prepare him for visiting a real, dangerous living past.

The bus turned off the seafront and chugged onward along Havelock Road. Joe shuffled uneasily in his seat. He would need to disembark at the next stop.

Cass stood to let him past. Joe neither made eye contact nor thanked her.

She slid into the vacant spot next to the window. Below her, Joe alighted from the bus, swung his bag onto his back and strode away towards wherever it was he called home. She sighed, half wishing she'd tried to engage the painfully shy boy in conversation.

Tom and Saff hurried down the stairs together and disembarked in Havelock Road, too, where the pair stopped to share saliva before the bus pulled away.

'Well,' Cass said, quietly. 'That was certainly fast work, Tom.' She hoped Saff knew what she was doing.

At the railway station, Cass piled off the bus with everyone else and waited for another that would take her to her destination.

* * *

When she hopped off the bus a few hundred yards away from home, Cass swiped her phone screen with her index finger, half expecting to have received a message from her father. She couldn't remember whether he was working today or not. At least he'd promised not to mess about with that time travelling thingamabob. Or had he? Anxiety popped its head above the parapet as she struggled to remember his exact words last night, and she sped anxiously home, her key ready in her hand before she reached the peeling front door.

'Dad?' she called, once inside. 'Are you home?'

No reply came, and the hollow emptiness of the house elevated her anxiety.

'DAD!' she shouted.

When there was still no reply, she trotted into the kitchen, where her father recorded his shifts on a slimline calendar which hung beside the back window. She reached for the grey packet lying on the kitchen table – it probably contained the crimson jacket she'd ordered from an online vintage/second-hand shop a few days ago – but then something lying on the floor caught her eye. It must be The Infinity Glass, only it wasn't caked in grime any more – he had cleaned it up. It looked as if it had fallen from the table and rolled underneath. Cass was tempted to leave it there, in case her dad thought she was responsible for any possible damage. Would he still be able to time travel if it was damaged? Guiltily, she realised she'd be happier if he couldn't.

Feeling a tug of curiosity about the object, she crouched down and used an extended index finger to roll it towards her. She pursed her lips. Her dad wouldn't be pleased – a nasty jagged crack a few centimetres long ran along one loop of the knot, ending at a tiny hole beside the green-liquid-filled node. The protective cage, although it had sustained a couple of minor dents, appeared intact.

Leave it here, or pick it up? Leave it here. No, I have to pick it up! Heaving a frustrated sigh, she scooped the damaged object carefully off the floor.

The moment her fingers closed around the glass knot, a stiffness flowed steadily from her fingertips, through her palm and her wrist and onward towards her elbow. She tried to put the artefact on the table, but she couldn't let go.

'Hey, Drusilla,' she shouted angrily, remembering the name of the sprite her father had spoken to when he first showed his daughter his interesting find. 'Get your annoying time travelly thingy to let go of my hand, will you?'

'I will try,' answered a wavering, echoey voice that sounded distinctly like Cass's grandmother. Cass hadn't expected a response – when her father had spoken with Drusilla before, she hadn't been able to hear the sprite's voice at all.

Not wanting to drop it and make the damage worse, Cass placed the device on the kitchen table and waited, her fingers still stuck firmly to it. A moment later, the creeping paralysis in her arm and fingers began to reverse and she released the object. She stretched her fingers, then balled her hands into fists to check all her joints were working properly again.

'Thanks. Don't suppose you can tell me where Dad is?' she asked.

'You mean when,' corrected the sprite.

'Oh, crap. He isn't time travelling again, is he? Doesn't that thing have to go with him?'

After what felt to Cass like an endless pause, Drusilla replied, 'Indeed it does. There has been… an unfortunate mishap involving a World War 2 bomb.'

Chapter 12

Alone and In Charge

Cass spat out a swear word she rarely resorted to using. 'Is my dad OK? He's not...?' she couldn't bring herself to say what she was thinking.

'I am quite confident he is alive, but I cannot be absolutely sure, Cass. The bomb blast separated your father from The Infinity Glass, and it – along with me, of course – returned here without him.'

'Well, go back and fetch him.'

'I cannot. The device is too badly damaged to enable travel.'

'You managed to get back here, though,' argued Cass, wrapping her arms around her waist.

'Yes. The return journey was what I can only describe as a reflex action on the part of The Infinity Glass and The Essence. Their combined power is substantially diminished by the damage and it won't be possible to time travel again unless someone has it properly repaired.'

'How can I get it repaired? It's made of glass. Plus the stuff inside, which I haven't got the first clue about.'

'It will require an expert craftsperson and I think the glass part may need completely replacing. Remember, you must ensure none of the contents are lost. The three Essences hold much of The Infinity Glass' power, which it amplifies at the appropriate moment.' Drusilla's voice still sounded noticeably distant and wavery.

Cass sat down, crossing her arms in front of her on the table. 'Tell me what happened to my dad.'

'We went to 1943. He didn't even choose a specific date, and it caught us both unawares when we were transported to wartime Hastings. Patch – your father – went into the area known as the Old Town. There was a bomb – we heard aircraft overhead, and then there was a tremendously loud bang nearby. The Infinity Glass brought itself and me back here. That is all I can tell you.'

Cass swallowed back a tear. 'How come you're so confident Dad wasn't killed?' she asked.

'I would have sensed the connection break before we left. We returned instantaneously, but I would have known about it if the connection had been lost. Of course, it was severed upon our return by the distance of time.'

'But the explosion and the return trip all happened in an instant,' Cass said, trying hard to understand and deal with Drusilla's information. 'How could you be sure he's not...' she took a deep breath and finished her sentence through tightly clenched teeth. 'Not dead?'

'As I explained to your father, time is not linear or constant for me in the same way it is for you. I am absolutely certain the connection was not lost until the moment of return,' said Drusilla, adding casually, 'Unless he has died from his injuries since I came back, he is alive in 1943.'

Drusilla's words rolled around in Cass's brain for a few moments. *Unless he has died from his injuries since I came back.* The statement gave her no solace. Her father could still be dead.

Her head drooped towards the table and a tear plopped onto the back of her hand. What if she was alone now, despite what Drusilla said? How would she cope without her dad to support her – both emotionally and financially? How could she be "just Cass" without Jake Patch to watch her back? She tried to imagine the loneliness her father might have endured as he died in a time which was not his own. Unable to bear it, she locked the thought away in a deep recess of her mind.

Another thought buzzed into her head like a meandering fly, and she asked, 'Hey, why can I hear you now when I couldn't before?'

'You are the custodian now. With the link broken between The Infinity Glass and your father, the next person to hold it becomes the new custodian.'

'So I can time travel?'

'Of course. Once The Infinity Glass has been properly mended.'

'I can go back and bring him home?' Cass asked, tentatively.

'In theory, I think so.'

'Well, that's not incredibly positive. Can I or can't I?'

'I'm going to say yes,' said Drusilla, sounding less than confident. 'However, I'm not totally sure about bringing back a second person. In your father's case, however, his natural timeline is here. It should be possible for you to bring him back to the time where he belongs.'

Remembering her father mentioning some troublesome "rules", Cass asked, 'There are no rules against it?'

Drusilla answered straight away. 'No. The sticking point would potentially have been the rule about returning to previously visited years, but you are a new custodian. You can go where you wish, but you must remember you have but one hour in your destination time before you are returned home.'

'You sound like the Fairy Godmother in *Cinderella*,' Cass commented. 'Anyway, I'm going to bring him home, so I need to find myself a craftsperson skilled in making or repairing glass objects. Let's do this.'

Chapter 13

Seeking Help

'Hi. Um, I have an ornament that needs fixing. The glass part is cracked and I need it repaired – or it might need completely replacing, I'm not sure. Yes, it's kind of a family heirloom. I broke it and I don't want anyone to find out, so the copy has to be absolutely precise. There are three blobs of fancy coloured liquid inside and you'd need to be incredibly careful not to lose any of it. Oh. You can't? I'm sorry to have bothered you.'

Cass pressed the "end call" button and took a deep, shuddering sigh.

'Well, that's six who can't do it now, unless I could afford the eight hundred quid that man in Yorkshire quoted me. I do have Dad's credit card number memorised, but the guy wanted an immediate bank transfer and it all seemed pretty dodgy.'

'Humans are notoriously unreliable,' replied Drusilla. 'And confidence tricksters are apparently equally common in any time one visits.'

'I don't think he was that exactly. He was an advantage-taker, for sure, and he obviously caught on to how desperate I am to get The Infinity Glass fixed and upped his estimated price by a few hundred pounds. Whatever you want to call him, it leaves me without a craftsperson to fix the artefact. I'm going to keep trying, though. I won't give up on Dad and leave him in the past.'

'Your father deals in antiques, does he not?'

'What are you getting at? Why does that matter?'

'Well, antiques are old things which must need repair work done to them sometimes. Perhaps your father has a contact who makes or repairs glass items. Does he have a book where he records details of his associates?'

'It would be on his phone if anywhere,' said Cass, raking her fingers through her hair. 'I'd guess that's with him in 1943. He hardly goes anywhere without it, so the chances are he had it when he time travelled. I'll try ringing on the off-chance he left it behind.'

Cass rang her dad's number, but an echoing silence hung in the air instead of the usual ringtone.

'Damn; nothing at all.' She aborted the attempt. 'What now? I'm seriously running short of options, but there's no way I'm giving up.'

'I know a woman who might be willing to help,' said Drusilla, guardedly.

'Really?' asked Cass, her eagerly raised eyebrows reversing into a frown. 'Well, why the hell didn't you say that straight off?'

'I didn't want to have to resort to her. She is not the most reliable.'

'How do you even know her? She must be here in the present day, then, otherwise you wouldn't have suggested her.'

'She is alive now, yes. She has unparalleled skill with glass.'

'That's brilliant, but I feel like you're avoiding my question about how you know her. How could you possibly come across a craftsperson from the twenty-first century at all, let alone one who you think can fix The Infinity Glass?'

'She was... I mean, we have a—'

Cass had an epiphany and interrupted the sprite's dithering. 'Wait. Was she a custodian?'

'She was indeed the previous custodian: the one who left The Infinity Glass where your father found it.'

'And she's an expert in working with glass?'

'Yes. It's why she picked up The Infinity Glass in the first place. She recognised the workmanship and wanted to take a closer look.'

'How come this person isn't the custodian now?'

Drusilla took a while to answer, as if she were chewing over the exact phrase to use. 'She chose to end the bond,' she said, slowly.

'What, just like that?' Cass snapped her fingers.

'Yes, if you like. Just like that.'

'Why?'

'Would you like me to take you to her shop?' asked Drusilla, ignoring Cass's question.

'Oh, she has a shop? Why doesn't she have a website, then? I'd have found it by now if she did, and everyone who wants their business to be seen has a website, don't they?'

'Not Lucia. She prefers to gain customers through word-of-mouth – by personal recommendation, you know.'

'I see,' said Cass, though she couldn't imagine any business succeeding in the modern world without an online presence. 'Where is Lucia's shop, then? Is it nearby? If you tell me the address, I can find out how to get there,' she added, her thumbs already swiping across her phone screen.

'Put that dreadful device away. I can take you there tomorrow.'

'Tomorrow? What's wrong with today? I need Dad back now. He's stuck in the past and needs my help to come home.'

'We can travel to any date and time you wish, remember?' said Drusilla. 'And I'm a little out of sorts, you might say.'

Cass was thinking through possibilities. 'Wait,' she said, 'couldn't we get there early and stop him being too close when the bomb explodes?'

'No – no, it doesn't work like that. The Infinity Glass cannot exist twice in the same time frame. We must arrive after the explosion and after The Infinity Glass returns here.'

'Oh, I suppose I should have realised. Could what I suggested have caused a paradox?'

'No. It's simply impossible, Cass.'

'One of those rules Dad talked about, is it?'

'Yes, precisely that.'

'I want Dad home as soon as possible, though. If we meet Lucia today, we could get this thing repaired and have him home in time for dinner.'

'It won't be a quick fix, Cass. You must be prepared to wait. The glass itself is a special mix of materials – have you noticed the hint of blue within it?'

'No, of course not. Is it magical glass?'

'No, no. There is no such thing as magic.'

Cass blushed at her own foolishness. 'But how else does it work if not by magic?'

'It is advanced science, that is all.'

'From where?'

'What do you mean?'

'Does it come from Earth or from a faraway galaxy or something?'

'It most definitely comes from Earth.'

'Earth of the future?' asked Cass. Leaning forward, she stared intently at The Infinity Glass and noticed, for the first time, the slight blue tinge and the barely perceptible shimmering of the blobs of liquid within the three nodes.

'No. It resides now within its own natural time. If not, it would have to return after an hour, according to the rules, would it not?'

'Ah. I suppose so.' It did make sense, but now another question occurred to Cass. 'Who made it? Who has such advanced scientific knowledge to be able to create such a thing? And why did they make it so fragile?'

'The Maker was a unique individual. I cannot tell you their name; it is privileged information, and maintaining that secret is one of the rules – a part of the programming, to use an equivalent modern term.'

'It's old, though, isn't it?' asked Cass, turning the object around, careful not to shake it or drop it and cause even more catastrophic damage.

'By your standards, yes. Old, but not ancient like myself.'

Cass wanted straightforward answers to her questions but, realising Drusilla was not about to give her those, she returned her thoughts to her father, trapped and possibly badly injured in wartime Hastings. She sighed and closed her eyes. When tears welled up and threatened to spill over, it took a few moments of slow, deep breathing for Cass to regain her composure.

Finally, she opened her eyes, lifted her chin and took a deep breath. 'Well, I'll do whatever I have to do to bring Dad home, just like he would do for me,' she said.

'Of course, Cass. I understand,' replied Drusilla. 'We will go and meet Lucia tomorrow.'

Chapter 14

Lucia's Shop

Lucia's shop barely looked like a shop at all.

Cass found it located in a dismal, litter-strewn backstreet two roads behind a row of charity shops. The front window – a leaded bow that hadn't seen a chamois leather in years – did not boast a glittering, enticing display of glassware, as Cass had expected. In fact, she could not see in through the window at all and wondered if Lucia had installed blackout curtains to deter prying eyes. The only way the property could be identified as a shop was from the faded wooden sign above the window bearing the words "Artisan Glassware" in peeling blue paint. Lucia clearly wasn't seeking passing trade – not that such a thing was likely in this road anyway.

The entrance of the property was as unshop-like as the rest of the exterior and Cass thought its condition was even worse than the Patches' front door back at home. At face height, a messily handwritten note had been sealed into a clear plastic bag and roughly gaffer taped to the door. The plastic bag had failed to keep out the damp, making the words "By appointment only. Knock loudly and be prepared to wait" faded and barely legible. What was left of the original black lettering had bled into its constituent colours, reminding Cass of a chromatography experiment she'd done back in secondary school.

Somewhere nearby, a downpipe gurgled like a swamp beast and the plastic lid from a Styrofoam cup cartwheeled along the road past Cass and dropped through the slats of a drainage grill. The reek of decay caused her nose to wrinkle, and she made a conscious choice not to try to locate the source.

'It says by appointment,' she whispered, although secrecy wasn't needed, given that the road remained deserted.

'She will see us. Well, you anyway. Knock and wait, like the sign says.' Drusilla's voice sounded worryingly apprehensive and it didn't give Cass confidence to do as the sprite instructed.

'Are you sure?' Cass asked.

'Yes, yes. Needs must,' snapped Drusilla, impatiently.

Cass knocked twice, and then twice more with added determination, remembering the instruction to knock loudly.

A minute passed, then another.

'Try again,' suggested Drusilla.

'Perhaps she's out.'

'Possibly. Try again anyway.'

Cass did so, then took a half step back and stared at the first floor window above the shop, where she thought she caught a glimpse of something moving in the shadows behind the net curtain.

'I think she's in. There's someone upstairs – I saw them,' she said.

'Hold up The Infinity Glass,' instructed Drusilla.

'What?'

'The Infinity Glass. Hold it up.'

Cass carefully unwound the cloth in which she had wrapped the object before they left home. She held the device aloft for around ten seconds, unsure whether Lucia was looking at it or not. Then came the *clunk, clunk, clunk* of heavy footsteps from behind the door, as if someone was descending a bare wooden staircase wearing working boots.

The door, swollen in its frame, jerked open to the full extent of the security chain and a brusque, authoritative voice demanded, 'What are you doing with that thing? Take it back where you found it.'

'But I need your help,' said Cass, her mind forming a mental picture of the still hidden Lucia, who she decided was a stern-looking woman in her sixties with short grey hair, dressed in dull, utilitarian clothing – the kind of outfit that would fit this location to a tee.

'I want nothing to do with that troublesome object,' barked Lucia. 'Take it away from here. Leave me alone.'

'My father is stuck in 1943,' Cass told her. 'He's probably hurt. He needs my help and The Infinity Glass is damaged.'

'Hah! The best thing that could happen is that damned thing being destroyed. A pity I had too much respect for the workmanship to do it myself.'

'But what about my father?'

'He'll be fine in 1943, I'm sure.'

'And how about me? If you don't care about him, do you at least give a damn what will happen to me?'

'Your mother will—'

Cass interrupted. 'My mother is dead. Without Dad, there's only me. Please help me, Lucia.'

Seconds ticked past with no word from Lucia, but at least the door remained ajar. Cass chewed on her bottom lip and waited. The sprite also remained silent.

After what felt like an eternity, the security chain jingled and scraped and Cass's heart dared to lighten with hope.

The door swung open, revealing Lucia. Completely at odds with Cass's earlier mental image, she was a woman in her early to mid-forties. Her thick, prematurely grey hair had a flash of fuchsia pink running through the loose waves, reminding Cass of raspberry ripple ice-cream, and Lucia wore it piled up in a messy knot on top of her head. Several wild wisps that eluded her large, sparkly hair clip spiralled languidly around her long neck. Her naturally light brown skin was good for her age, although laughter lines radiated from either side of caramel-brown eyes.

She wore a multi-coloured long-sleeved shift dress in vibrant shades of pink, blue and green. Beneath the asymmetrical hemline, a pair of fuchsia-pink leggings covered her long, skinny legs and upon her feet she wore Dr Martens boots which boosted her height, making her several centimetres taller than Cass. The boots were also fuchsia pink. A substantial collection of gold bangles jangled softly on her right wrist and a pink gem glistened on one side of her nose.

Lucia inspected her visitor from head to toe and back again. Once her eyes met Cass's, they locked with them, and Cass shifted her weight awkwardly from foot to foot, wanting to look away. It was clear the older woman was trying to read her inner thoughts, but stubbornness kept her staring right back.

'You speak to the sprite, obviously,' said Lucia, matter-of-factly.

Cass nodded. 'Yes. She told me to come here.'

Lucia's lip twisted into a sneer and her eyes narrowed almost imperceptibly. 'I'd tell the sodding thing to eff off, but I know it can't do that; not as long as you have that damnable Glass with you. Come inside, then. Perhaps we can leave the thing downstairs while we chat about the sprite behind its back.'

'What a cheek. Don't listen to her,' retorted Drusilla.

Leaving the door wide open in her wake, Lucia swivelled around and marched into the gloomy interior, her bangles jangling like ethereal music with each step. Cass gave a lopsided smile and followed Lucia inside.

The room was not a retail shop but, given the exterior, Cass hadn't expected it to be. It had a feeling about it which was more like a cross between a science lab and an industrial unit. The space they'd entered was a waiting area of some sort. It filled about a third of the open-plan room and was cordoned off from the workspace using barriers like those used to keep roads clear of pedestrians during the London Marathon. On their side of the barriers, a couple of utilitarian red moulded-plastic chairs were pushed against the bare brick wall, with a square white coffee table wedged between them.

Cass stopped to survey her surroundings and wondered where Lucia had picked up the metal barriers being used as partitions. She didn't like to ask.

'Some of my customers like to watch me work,' explained Lucia. 'For a few of them, I swear it's more about observing the process than owning the finished item. On the whole, I don't mind, but I don't want customers getting too close to the action, you know? I used to run lessons, too – that's why I created the waiting area – but I gave it up as a bad idea. People are idiots. You'd be surprised how many don't realise burning gas and molten glass could hurt someone. My insurance company didn't like it and neither did I.'

Cass smirked and blushed, recalling her own penchant for melting plastic pens in the flame of her secondary school chemistry lab's Bunsen burners.

In the area on the far side of the barriers, there were metal benches and shelves packed with tins, jars, tools, rolls of tape and a bunch of things Cass couldn't name. One set of shelves bore long cardboard boxes containing a variety of sizes and colours of glass tubes. In a corner of the room was a desk and office chair, although there was no sign of a computer. Cass decided it must be set up elsewhere.

A high Perspex screen ran along the back of the bench nearest the barriers, and a chunky red cylinder stood to one side. An oversized Bunsen burner was clamped at an angle to the edge of the bench and tools were lined up neatly in a row alongside it. One of them looked similar to a retractable silver cocktail swizzle stick Cass's dad had brought home from a boot fair once, others like an elongated arrow head and a pair of super-sized tweezers. Red-lensed safety glasses lay beside a jumble of short lengths of different coloured glass tubes, like those on the shelves.

Lucia cleared her throat. 'Leave that,' she said, tilting her head towards the artefact, 'on a bench somewhere and come upstairs for a chat. It's this way,' she added, setting off across the room.

'Don't leave me behind,' hissed Drusilla. 'I need to know what's happening, Cass. *Please*.'

Cass ignored the sprite's pleading, placed the time travel device carefully on the nearest bench and trotted after Lucia, who had already ducked past a curtain. Beyond that, a bare wooden staircase led to what Cass assumed must be living space on the upper floors.

'Cass, it's important I'm kept informed. You can't trust her,' shouted the sprite.

Cass snorted. 'Yeah, sure,' she said, wobbling her head and wrinkling her nose. 'You're acting like I can trust you better. Besides, you're the one who brought me here. You told me she was my best hope of saving Dad.'

'Of course you can trust me,' insisted Drusilla, but Cass was already trudging up the stairs. Lucia, who presumably realised it wasn't aimed at her, paid no heed to Cass's conversation.

'Your father trusted me,' called the sprite in a last attempt to stop Cass in her tracks.

'And see where it got him,' replied Cass, not looking back. With a shake of her head, she continued after Lucia.

Chapter 15

What's In a Name?

'So, can you help me?' asked Cass, putting a half-finished mug of hot chocolate on the floor at her feet. She had spent the last fifteen minutes explaining her father's situation along with what sparse background information she had about the circumstances, while Lucia made them drinks in her kitchenette, interjecting with regular questions throughout the story.

Lucia nodded. 'I think so. A copy of The Infinity Glass will be a challenging make and not something I have experience with – obviously – but I'm confident I can do it. I've examined it at close quarters many times and I've worked out how it was made. Given my interest in glass, I'd probably have tried to make myself a copy while I was custodian if not for the fact that I couldn't replicate The Essence – those blobs of liquid in the nodes. Goodness only knows where that came from.' She sighed and shook her head. 'It will take a fair number of attempts, mind you, and I may need more details from that sprite – assuming it will answer questions if required.'

'I expect she would,' answered Cass, wincing. 'She isn't happy about being left downstairs, but I wouldn't have found you if not for her guidance. She must want to help.'

'You keep calling it *her* and *she*. Why do you do that?' asked Lucia.

Cass shrugged one shoulder. 'Drusilla's a girl's name, isn't it? And she sounds feminine to me. She speaks with my grandmother's voice.'

'Drusilla, is it now? It was called Haven when I knew it.'

'Haven? That's not even a name. Is it?'

'Anything is a name if you use it that way,' responded Lucia, taking a sip from her own hot chocolate. 'After all, celebrities give their kids all kinds of weird and wonderful names. I wonder why it chose Drusilla this time.'

'Maybe we can ask her – or it, or whatever the correct pronoun for a sprite might be.'

'I doubt you'd get a straight answer. Be aware that it has its own agenda. It isn't like a genie that has to grant wishes. No, it's altogether a different creature. It's not malicious – at least, I don't believe so – but it isn't human and you should take care not to anthropomorphise.'

'How do you know so much about Drusilla? I've not been able to find out very much yet myself,' said Cass, retrieving her mug from the floor and taking a sip from it. On a side table nearby, a framed photograph of a younger Lucia with a girl of around ten years of age drew her gaze. As the girl's eyes were the same shape and colour as Lucia's, Cass assumed she was the glassmaker's daughter or niece.

'I was custodian of the device for a fair while before I decided I'd had enough of it,' replied Lucia, dryly.

'How long?'

'Oh, I don't know. A year and a half. A little more, I think.'

'Why did you dispose of it?' asked Cass. The glassmaker shot her a sideways glance and Cass added, 'If you don't mind telling me.'

'It becomes addictive – or it did for me, anyway,' said Lucia, staring into the distance. 'A fact it took me far too long to realise. The more times I travelled, the more I wanted to do it and the less of a life I had here and now. I believed I might lose myself if I carried on – like the present would become unimportant – and I couldn't let that happen. My life, I realised, needs to be mine to control, so I broke the bond. It was the hardest thing I've ever had to do.' She glanced towards her feet, then towards the photograph Cass had spotted earlier. Then she gave Cass a weak half smile.

'Did you regret giving it up?' Cass asked.

'Initially, yes, I regretted it terribly, but that was purely because of the addiction. As for now… well, until you walked in through my front door carrying it, I'd have said a huge resounding no, but the pull that thing has on me is incredibly strong, even this long after I broke the bond. Giving it up was the best decision I ever made.'

'You said you feel the pull after this long. How long ago did you do it?' asked Cass, tilting her head to the side.

'Two years ago. Almost to the day,' Lucia replied, quietly.

'Tell me about your experiences of time travelling,' said Cass, settling back into the soft cushions of the sofa.

Lucia shook her head emphatically. 'No, absolutely not.'

'What? Why not?' asked Cass, sitting up straight once more. 'I need to know what to expect once The Infinity Glass is back in working order.'

'You make too many assumptions, including that my workmanship will be good enough to mean the device will still function as it used to.' Lucia stood abruptly and marched to the sink to rinse her mug, leaving Cass trying to stave off a rising sense of panic.

'You said you could do it.' Tears welled up in Cass's eyes. 'But now you're saying you can't.'

Lucia turned the tap fully on and the pressure of the flow sent a fountain of water arcing in and out of the mug, then splashing all over the front of her dress.

'Damn it,' she cussed, brushing droplets from her clothes onto the laminate floor. She glanced up from her wet dress and made eye contact with her visitor. 'Look,' Lucia's eyebrows knitted together and her jaw was set like a stone statue, 'I'll do my absolute best. I wish I could guarantee to make it work again, but I can't promise. It's a strange object and I don't have The Maker's knowledge. As for sharing time travelling experiences, well, I don't know you. This is personal stuff you're asking me to talk about and I'm afraid I choose not to share it.'

Cass shook her head and lifted her hands defensively, aware that pushing Lucia might make her change her mind about helping to fix the artefact at all.

'I'm sorry,' Cass said, wiping her eyes and thinking quickly. 'You don't have to tell me anything you aren't comfortable talking about. I thought sharing might help, and I told you my story. I suppose I thought we were both on the same side.'

Lucia deflated. 'Well, yes, we are,' she conceded. 'Of course we are. Perhaps sometime I'll tell you, but it's all too raw still at the moment.'

After two years? Cass thought, but she kept the question to herself.

'Sure,' she said instead. 'Whenever. No pressure. How about, as a sign of mutual trust, I leave the thing itself here with you until it's fixed?'

'NO!'

Cass flinched and her mouth fell open. She snapped it shut again.

'OK then, no, I won't do that. I'm sorry.'

'It's a nice gesture,' said Lucia, chewing on a thumb nail, 'but I can't have it here. It's bad enough that it's downstairs. Besides, you don't know me well enough to trust me. You're painfully naïve, Cass – people will try to take advantage of that if you don't learn fast. How old are you again?'

'I'll be eighteen soon.'

Lucia nodded. 'Be more wary of people, Cass. If you don't learn that now, it's a lesson you'll end up learning the hard way.'

'That's incredibly cynical of you.'

'Realistic, I'd say. Anyway, I don't need to keep the thing here. I'll need to take measurements, though. You are sure it's attached to you now, aren't you? I don't want it gluing itself to me again.'

'Yes. You saw me holding it before you let me in. I spoke to Drusilla earlier, too, remember?'

'Yes, of course you did. I do remember, but that damned thing has me on edge. I thought I'd seen the back of it and suddenly, here it is again. It does nothing for my nerves. Let's do the measuring now; bite the bullet, as it were.'

'I could take some photos, too, if it would help.'

'I know what it looks like. It's fine; I won't need that, thank you. Let's go downstairs and see how the sprite is doing after stewing in its own juices for half an hour.'

Cass followed Lucia back to the workshop, wondering what Drusilla and her – or rather its – artefact had done to this poor woman to make her so angry. Not that it mattered. Cass had no option but to use The

Infinity Glass herself if she was going to help her father return from 1943, regardless of Lucia's experiences with it.

Thinking back, Cass recalled that the glassworker had been chatty and self-confident after she first let her into her home. It was only when Cass asked the older woman to share her time travel experiences that she had shut down and started acting oddly. Cass decided to question Drusilla about it later, hoping that the sprite would be more forthcoming.

Lucia hunted around in a pine chest of drawers and found a notepad while Cass settled onto a wooden stool which had every appearance of having been reclaimed from a secondary school science lab. The glassmaker began by drawing a remarkably three-dimensional freehand diagram of the glass knot. Then she used a measuring tape and callipers to determine the precise dimensions of the item, although she didn't take it out of its hinged cage housing. Each measurement was checked several times before Lucia wrote it down, and after taking each one, she would suck on the end of her pencil and shake her head, muttering, 'Even more bloody faultless than I'd imagined' or 'Perfect rotational symmetry, even in three dimensions', and once, 'Damn it for being so exquisite.'

Stabbing her pencil into her hair, Lucia said, 'I'm going to have to take it out of the protective cage now, to be sure my measurements aren't off by a significant margin. I didn't want to do that really, but I'm not confident enough in the measurements taken through the housing. I'll be very careful.'

Cass nodded, silently.

Both women held their breath while Lucia carefully worked a knife around the join between the halves of the protective cage, pushing and gently twisting. Drusilla, meanwhile, fussed like a mother hen.

'Oh, do be very careful'; 'Gently. *Gently* now!'; 'Tell her, Cass. Tell her to go slowly.'

Cass chose not to pass on the advice.

After much careful easing, Lucia finally placed the glass element of the piece upon the cloth in which Cass had transported it. She tucked the sides of the cloth underneath to create a dip in the centre to prevent the precious artefact falling from the bench.

Once Lucia had measured it and made one minor adjustment to her initial notes, she placed it back inside its hinged metal cage. Cass and Lucia exhaled loudly – then both laughed simultaneously with obvious relief.

'When will you make the replacement?' asked Cass.

Lucia scratched her head using the end of the pencil. 'I need to buy a particular kind of glass for it. I know what to order, though.'

'Did Haven tell you what the blue colourant is?' asked Cass.

'Of course. The sprite was happy to discuss details with me, but wouldn't tell me about the science behind it. I think the phrase it used was *beyond the comprehension of one without the necessary gift.*'

'Pah!' spat Drusilla. 'There has only ever been a single human who has possessed the scientific knowledge to truly understand how The Infinity Glass works, and that was a most exceptional person. She understood it because she devised it. Whatever knowledge Lucia has, it is no match for that of The Maker.'

Cass ignored the sprite, figuring that it wasn't her job to repeat the words to Lucia, and that Lucia wouldn't want to hear them anyway.

'I have everything I need now,' said the glassmaker, storing her pencil above her left ear after restoring The Infinity Glass to its housing. 'I think you should take that with you and leave now. Come back in a week.'

'A week?' asked Cass, unable to imagine spending that long worrying about her father.

'Yes, a week. They'll have the glass in stock; it isn't particularly unusual – but it's not something I have lying around in the workshop. Once the glass arrives, I expect it will take me several attempts to make it. The shape is going to be difficult to reproduce accurately and I have a feeling the tight bends will be problematic, as will fashioning three identical nodes. I will have to be extraordinarily precise.'

Cass couldn't imagine the process of making an intricate glass knot at all. Working with molten glass was one of those jobs that looked simple in the hands of an expert, but wasn't at all. She would Google it at home later – and maybe check out a video clip or two.

'What about The Essence?' she asked. 'You must need that too. How will we get it out of the old Glass and into the new one?'

'Well, it might be easy or it might be hard, but I think we can work it out between us when the time comes. We're both resourceful women. In the meantime, I'll give it some thought and you can do the same. I'll leave the vessel unsealed, of course, until The Essence is inside.'

'Shall I give you my phone number so you can call when it's ready?' asked Cass, uncertainly.

'Sure,' replied Lucia, grabbing the pencil from behind her ear and poising it above the notepad.

'I could text you and you'd have it. Tell me your number,' said Cass.

'I don't have a mobile phone, they're bloody horrid things. Tell me yours and I'll write it down and call you using a good old-fashioned landline.'

Cass gave her number, adding her address as an afterthought, and Lucia wrote both next to her sketch of The Infinity Glass.

'How much will it cost?' asked Cass, afraid she wouldn't be able to afford it.

Lucia blinked slowly and scratched her chin. 'Not a penny,' she said. 'A youngster like you needs her father, especially when she's lost her mother already.'

Cass opened her mouth to protest. 'But I have to pay you.'

'Rubbish! I offered to do it for nothing and you shouldn't look a gift horse in the mouth.'

Cass hadn't heard that phrase before, but inferred the meaning. She nodded.

'Thank you.'

'Well, goodbye for now. I'll see you in a week,' said Lucia. Cass tried not to let her expression give away how dejected and alone she felt, but she must have failed because the older woman patted her shoulder. 'It will be fine, don't worry.'

'She's lying,' said Drusilla casually. 'She has no idea if it will work.'

Once outside, Cass asked, 'Drusilla, aren't you worried what will happen to you if Lucia fails to replicate the artefact?'

'Not at all. At least if she fails, I won't have to hold these ridiculous conversations with humans any more.'

'Oh? What would happen to you instead?' asked Cass.

Drusilla hesitated, then said, 'Well, I'd have to go back where I came from, I suppose.'

'Have to?'

'Did I say have to? I don't know why I said that. It would be perfectly lovely to go back.'

'Then why did you bother telling me about Lucia at all? If the place you came from is so brilliant, then why are you keen to get this thing working again?'

Drusilla took a few moments before replying. 'There are some things I don't wish to discuss,' she said, haughtily.

'Oh, how bloody marvellous. Now everybody's keeping secrets,' muttered Cass, miserably.

As she wandered back towards home, she decided Lucia and Drusilla could keep as many secrets as they liked. All that mattered was getting her dad home safe and sound.

Chapter 16

Waiting...

The next week dragged by for Cass. It was half-term week, which normally meant meeting up with Lola, but Cass was so miserable that she ignored several messages from her friend. Instead, she binge-watched old episodes of *NCIS* and *The Great British Bake Off* and did her homework as well as she could with a distracted brain. When she realised how little food there was in the house, she arranged a supermarket delivery using the memorised details from her dad's credit card. Life, she concluded sadly, had to carry on regardless of what had happened. Her father was out there somewhere and when he came home, everything would go fully back to normal. Besides, she couldn't forfeit the future he'd dreamt of for her, even if he never returned.

She couldn't face being in the same room with The Infinity Glass itself, so left it on a pillow in her father's bedroom. Drusilla – or Haven, whatever her or its name really was – could stew in its own juices for a while.

On the first night, once she'd extinguished her light, Cass lay awake, staring into the thick, enveloping darkness. A gaping void opened up in her chest like a star collapsing into a black hole, and for a moment she wanted it to consume her. Finally, the knowledge that she was her father's only hope forced her back from the edge of despair.

Then, in a terrifying instant, she became acutely aware of the dozens of people who must have lived in the house she called home before her. If she listened hard enough, she thought she would hear the whispers of the past. Her shoulders shuddered violently and she fumbled to turn the bedside light back on. Ghosts were the last thing she wanted to be worrying about – especially if her father was in danger of becoming one of them.

The next morning, an exhausted Cass called her father's work and explained he had food poisoning. A pang of sorrow overtook her unexpectedly when she said he'd be away for a week, but would then hopefully be fit to return. Would he return? Would Lucia fix the device well enough that time travel would be possible? Would Cass find her father in 1943 Hastings and be able to bring them both safely home, given a single short hour in which to do it? How would it feel to be transported through time? She had no answers, merely a determination to do everything in her power to bring her dad home.

On Tuesday morning, after a surprisingly restful night's sleep, Cass went online while eating her breakfast to research bombing raids on Hastings during World War 2. *There were 85 air raids on Hastings. 550 HE bombs and 16 flying bombs fell on the town, with 154 lives lost, 260 people seriously injured and 439 people receiving lesser injuries,* she read. She made a mental note to ask Drusilla the date of the raid which had left her father stranded in the past. The sprite wasn't sure Lucia would be able to make The Infinity Glass work again. If Cass knew when he was, but then couldn't reach him, it would ramp up her existing level of torment.

'Please be one of the 439 lesser injuries, Dad, not the 260 and definitely not one of the...' A tear dripped onto her thumb. She swiped the page angrily off her screen and placed her phone face down on the table, as if doing so would banish all thoughts of her father's potential death. It didn't work. Unable to face her toast, she tossed it in the kitchen bin and glugged down the contents of a glass of water, hoping to silence her grumbling stomach.

On Thursday evening, six days after her first meeting with Lucia, Cass could wait no longer and decided to phone the glassmaker to ask for a progress report. She picked up her phone, but gave a despairing tut when she realised she hadn't taken note of Lucia's landline number.

If she had a mobile, we'd have exchanged numbers for sure, she thought, angrily. Glancing briefly at her phone, she noticed she'd received a voicemail message. Excited and worried in equal measures, she fumbled to pick it up.

'Hello, Cass, this is Lucia. I think I have what you need. I need the, erm... contents, to finish off, of course, but I can't deal with that until you return with the original item. I can't guarantee any of the replacements will be a hundred per cent identical, but the measurements are looking good, so I think it will be fine. I'm available on Saturday morning, say at ten o'clock, for you to call by. Let me know if that's convenient. Thanks.'

Cass listened to the message twice more, and then wandered into the bathroom. Lucia had been very careful not to mention The Infinity Glass or The Essence by name. It was as if the glassmaker thought someone might listen in on her message and try to acquire the time travel device for themselves. Her caution seemed over the top, although Cass was pretty sure the advertising algorithms on her phone eavesdropped to send her tailored adverts.

'Why can't she see me until Saturday, and why are exact measurements of the thing so important?' she wondered out loud, staring at her reflection in the mirrored door of the bathroom wall cabinet.

'The measurements—' said Drusilla.

'Shit! You frightened the life out of me,' squealed Cass. 'I didn't realise you could hear me. The Infinity Glass is in Dad's room.'

'You are close enough. The wall is irrelevant. Straight line distance determines range.'

'Fine,' said Cass, loading her toothbrush with toothpaste. 'Then what difference does replicating the precise measurements of the object make?'

'The shape and dimensions determine the length of stay in the chosen time.'

Cass scratched her head. 'It would be way easier if you could stay as long as you wanted.'

'Maybe so, but we're talking science, Cass, not magic. Remember? The dimensions and capacity of the object determine the length of stay because of the temporal properties of The Essence and the shape, size and composition of The Infinity Glass.'

'That's not the most helpful to me,' mumbled Cass, irritated by the limitations of the device.

'Well, I could just keep quiet,' snapped Drusilla. Cass doubted it was true. 'Do you want the benefit of my wisdom or not?'

Cass sighed and replaced the lid on her toothpaste tube. 'Yes, I do appreciate your help. I'm trying hard to get my head around all of this. I want my dad back.'

'Mmm, well. Lucia has finished making the replacement, I hear.'

'Yes,' said Cass, displeased that Drusilla was able to surreptitiously listen in on the voicemail message.

'And you're collecting it on Saturday, are you?' asked the sprite.

'Yes, of course. The sooner, the better.'

'I'll be glad of that too.'

'Oh?'

'Yes. I have been what you might call off-colour ever since the damage occurred. We have a close connection, the artefact and I.'

'I take it replacing the glass element with a new one won't mess things up for you?' asked Cass.

'Thank you for thinking of me, but no, I'm confident it will not.'

'How can you be certain, though?'

'I'm not certain, I only said confident. You do ask lots of awkward questions, don't you?'

'And you don't give helpful enough answers,' responded Cass, commencing scrubbing her teeth.

Once Cass finished in the bathroom, she wandered into her bedroom. It was late, but Lucia's voicemail message had only been sent recently. She'd probably still be up. Cass chewed her lip and her pulse rate increased. She was determined not to be overheard by the interfering sprite.

'Hey, Drusilla? Are you there?' she asked, to check she was outside Drusilla's range. When no answer came, Cass gave a nod of satisfaction and called Lucia's number.

Lucia's phone clicked straight over to an answerphone message. 'Hello, this is Lucia Grant. I'm not available at the moment. If you'd like to leave a message, do help yourself after that irritating tone.'

Cass waited for the long beep indicating the recording phase, and then said, 'Hi, Lucia, Cass Patch here. I'll be there at ten on Saturday. Oh, and I would like to pay you. It's not fair to expect something for nothing.

Let me know how much would be appropriate – actually, I have my dad's credit card details so I don't suppose you need... Damn it, the call's cut off.'

Cass's face reddened. 'I hate leaving messages,' she grumbled, tossing her discarded clothes into the wash bin and climbing into bed. 'Why couldn't Lucia have a mobile like everyone else? Texting is way easier.'

That night, she lay awake, unable to turn off the maelstrom of unhelpful thoughts swirling around her brain. It was only now that she realised Lucia had mentioned replacements – plural. She must have spent hours and hours working on it, all to save someone she'd never even met.

A firework exploded and whistled in the distance, directing Cass's thought processes back to more ordinary events. Bonfire night was almost a week away, but the people of Hastings enjoyed a longer firework season because the town council's Hastings Day display took place around the anniversary of the famous battle, in mid-October. At least tonight's firework offering was a lone straggler, not part of a whole noisy display that would keep Cass awake.

She rolled onto her side, pulling the covers up underneath her chin. 'I'll be there soon, Dad,' she promised. It didn't matter when she left to travel back in time, because she could choose her date and appear soon after the bomb blast which had severed his connection with The Infinity Glass, regardless of when she left. But waiting a moment longer than was absolutely necessary still felt like it would be letting him down.

* * *

She dreamt about her mother that night. As a child, she'd had many such dreams. Usually, they consisted of her lovely golden-haired mother lifting an infant Cass into the air and spinning her around while her father watched, smiling broadly. They were a perfect, happy family, like those she'd seen in TV ads.

As years progressed, the dreams had come less and less often, and stopped completely by the time she reached ten. Sometimes she tried to force the dreams to return, concentrating on a mental image of her mother while she lay waiting to sleep. It never worked.

Tonight's dream was different from those she used to have. Cass was not a small child this time, but her present age. She was sitting in the kitchen at home, holding the artefact in her hand.

'Take me to my parents' wedding day,' she told it, firmly.

In an instant, she appeared outside the registry office. A pair of double doors flew open to reveal her mother and father, looking exactly how they did in the photo on her dad's bedroom wall. Her mum clutched a modest bouquet of colourful flowers and a rainbow shower of confetti rained on the newlyweds out of the cloudless sky.

Someone took Cass by the hand. It was her grandmother. The old lady pulled Cass backwards into a crowd of faceless onlookers dressed in suits and assorted elegant dresses.

Cass's mother launched her bouquet into the air and it flew towards her daughter's outstretched hands. Cass caught it and laughed with delight.

'The Infinity Glass can take you to any time you like,' said Grandma, nodding wisely. '*Any time you like,*' she repeated, emphasising each word. 'What an amazing opportunity. Imagine what you could do. Imagine.'

Cass opened one eye. Her left arm was curled over her head and her right was wrapped tightly around her torso. Her brain slowly unfurled from its introspective sleep state like crumpled cellophane trying to return to its natural form. She hauled her knees up towards her chest and closed her eyes, frowning with sluggish frustration and trying her best to force the cellophane back into a ball so she could return to her dream. But the world around her had already emerged from the darkness and become real again, so, instead of continuing her efforts to go back to sleep, she rolled onto her back and focussed her now fully conscious mind on what her subconscious had been telling her.

Oh. Yes, of course! I could meet Mum.

Chapter 17

An Unexpected Change of Plan

'Hey, Cass, where are you? Why aren't you answering my messages?' asked Lola.

Cass had been ignoring her friend, but had woken up that morning thinking perhaps she would send Lola a vague reply to set her mind at rest. Instead, she had become lost in daydreams about her mother and forgotten all about Lola until her phone rang.

'Um, I've got a family problem. My dad has food poisoning,' Cass repeated the lie she'd told her father's work. Staring bleakly into her breakfast bowl, she realised her cereal had turned into a soggy, unappetising mush. It was after ten o'clock and she hadn't showered yet.

'Oh no! Is he going to be OK?' asked Lola. 'Do you need any help? I'm not great with sick people and all that yuck, but I could do your shopping or wash up or something.'

'Nah, don't worry, I'm good, thanks. Dad'll be fine in a few days, I expect.'

'You say that, but my cousin got food poisoning from bad shrimps and had to take months off work – he spent a week in hospital. It was James – remember?'

Cass didn't recall at all, but Lola had a big extended family and was never short of a story about some disaster that had befallen one or another of them. Cass wasn't surprised there had been a food-poisoning incident.

She and Lola had been friends since their second day at college. Cass had been looking for room 21B where there was a lunchtime meeting about diversity and inclusion. She'd exited the stairwell and barely avoided bumping into a tall, slim girl with a short afro and a puzzled frown.

'I don't suppose you know where room 21B is, do you?' asked the girl, glancing at her phone to check the time.

It turned out they were a floor below where they needed to be for the meeting. When they eventually found room 21B, they sat together, expressed similar viewpoints during the question and answer session and left together, having discovered they'd both be in the same History class straight after lunch. They went on to become great friends, and were planning on going to the same university and getting adjoining rooms in halls.

Although she considered herself enlightened, Cass had learned more about diversity and inclusion from being best friends with Lola than from a string of diversity meetings with the well-meaning but ineffectual leadership team at their college. It was disturbing how many people of their age were openly racist, and if Cass hated hearing it, Lola, who had a Jamaican mother and an American father, must find being on the receiving end of such vile behaviour virtually unbearable.

It was partly because of Lola's experiences that Cass kept quiet about her bisexuality. It wasn't because she thought being bi was morally wrong; far from it. But she wasn't yet ready to be open about it – to come out – and deal with whatever nastiness came her way from idiots who thought their morals were better than hers.

'Thanks for offering your help, Lo,' said Cass. 'But honestly, my dad'll be fine.' She coiled her free arm around her middle and paced back and forth in the small kitchen. 'He's thrown up and is pretty washed out, but he's already looking better than he did first thing this morning.'

'You sure?' If Lola was trying to hide the relief in her voice, she was doing an exceedingly bad job.

'Yeah, yeah. But I don't want to leave him by himself today. Hey, Lo, I need to go, he's calling for me.'

'Oh, right. See you Monday, then?'

'Yup, I 'spect so. Thanks for checking on me. See you soon.' Cass pressed the on-screen button to end the call. Guilt ate away at her, both for lying to Lola and for how easily she had done it, but she could hardly tell her best friend the truth, could she? Her dad was stuck in 1943 and she was now giving serious consideration to the possibility of travelling through time to meet her mother. The lie about her dad being sick definitely sounded more credible.

She decided it was time to make a final decision about what to do next. 'It wouldn't be right for me to leave Dad where he is,' she mumbled, her pacing continuing at a faster speed. 'But then again, it doesn't matter, does it? Like Drusilla said, he'll still be there and I can turn up at any chosen moment, regardless of when I leave. He won't know the difference. There's time. Ha-ha. Time.

'On the other hand, I could leave my personal time travel adventure until Dad's safely back, but what if he won't let me go? I'd have to travel without him because I'm not sure we could go together, plus there's Drusilla's rule about not travelling within your own lifetime if he went with me. There's so much at stake with this. I'd never forgive myself if I missed my only opportunity to meet my mum.

'There we are, then. It's decided. Meet Mum first, then go and fetch Dad back from 1943. Assuming The Infinity Glass will be fully functioning again after tomorrow. Everything is riding on Lucia's skills now.'

If she was to meet her mum, what date should she choose? Her parents had married on 10 January 2001; her dad said it was her mum's way of helping him remember their anniversary – making it 10/01/01 with all the zeros and ones would, according to Jen's logic, make it the date more memorable for him.

Cass imagined herself turning up at her parents' wedding, like in her dream. She didn't have an invitation, of course. She'd be out of place there, a stranger in the midst of her own family. Questions might be asked to which she had no reasonable answer. Her brow furrowed and her nose wrinkled. No, she needed to come up with another date when she could guarantee knowing where her mother would be.

One of her dad's favourite stories to tell at bedtime when Cass was little had been about the day he first met her mother. It happened on Mothers' Day, 2 April 2000. Jen was lonely and miserable because her previous boyfriend had dumped her the night before. Jake Patch had been walking along the promenade with a bouquet of flowers to give his mother, who always insisted on flowers for Mothers' Day, when he saw the lone woman sitting on the beach with shoulders hunched and knees drawn up to her chest. The Mothers' Day bouquet was a few flowers short that year.

Cass knew the exact time and place where her parents would be when they met. In actual fact, she knew the whole story so well that she could have told it to her dad instead of him telling it to her: it was 11am, on the beach opposite the statue of Queen Victoria in St Leonards.

'Perfect,' said Cass. 'I could be there at half past ten and pretend I'm in the same boat she is – that I've been dumped, too. No, wait. I can't do that. What if I'm still there when Dad goes past? I could put him off going to give her the flowers – or I could change something so that Mum leaves before he gets there. I'm going to have to wait until after they've met. Jeez, I could have seriously screwed things up. What if I'd stopped them from meeting at all?' She shook her head, angry at herself for not thinking things through properly. She'd seen the *Back to the Future* films several times. Messing around in your parents' past wasn't smart.

But imagine being there when my parents meet, she thought. *What an opportunity that would be. I could stand by the railings and watch them when they look at one another for the first time. Then, after Dad leaves to deliver the bouquet to Grandma…*

A thousand butterflies fluttered in Cass's chest. She was about to do the impossible. Cass Patch was going to meet her mother.

Chapter 18

Failure

'Drusilla, we're leaving now. It's time to go to Lucia's.'

'I am well aware of the date and time, Cass,' snapped Drusilla. 'I am, as you well know, a—'

'Sprite. Yes. Good for you,' mumbled Cass, wrapping The Infinity Glass in a towel and shoving it into a tote bag. 'I've been meaning to ask: why does Lucia call you Haven?'

'Haven was the name I chose to use with her.'

'And it's Drusilla for Dad – and for me now, too?'

'That's right.'

'What's your real name?'

'Sorry?'

'Your real name. What is it? If you chose to be Haven for Lucia and Drusilla for Dad, who are you really?'

'I am a sprite,' said Drusilla, sounding confused.

'Good grief, I know that. A sprite named what?'

'Currently called Drusilla. Previously called Haven, Cleopatra, Sonora, Johannes, Aegeus, Stark, Griffin, Amari. Shall I continue?'

'No. Why have you had so many?'

'A different name for each custodian. One that fits the chosen voice.'

'So Grandma felt like a Drusilla to you, did she? Her name was Louise.'

'I wouldn't wish to be mistaken for the ghost or spirit of the person whose voice I had chosen to adopt. It would surely confuse matters. I chose Drusilla because the name lived somewhere in your father's subconscious and you chose to keep calling me by the same name after he was left behind in 1943. Was Drusilla a poor choice on my part?'

Cass shrugged. 'It will do, since you don't have a name of your own. There's a zoo called Drusilla's. Dad used to take me there when I was little. Your name probably came from that.'

'Names are not relevant,' insisted Drusilla, 'unless one is a human. Labels are not required. I am not a city or a road or a mountain, so why give myself a name by which to define myself?'

'It's what people do, isn't it?' asked Cass, puzzled.

'Exactly. It is what humans do. Sprites do not.'

Cass's mind switched to more important matters. 'I hope it went well with making the replacement Glass,' she said, trotting down the stairs.

'We will find out soon enough. However, the existing Infinity Glass will not last long in this condition. Its structural integrity is failing.'

Cass giggled, despite the seriousness of Drusilla's comment. 'You sound like something from *Star Trek*.'

'*Star*...?'

'It's a film – and an old TV series,' explained Cass.

'Oh, good gracious. You people set so much store by fiction.'

'Why not? It's fun. Perhaps a little fun would make your existence better too. You should try it.'

'I think not, thank you. The world is not a frivolous place.'

'That's the point I was trying to make.'

Banging the swollen front door shut behind her, Cass set off for Lucia's shop.

* * *

By the time they arrived at Lucia's, the fine drizzle which had fallen in a silent curtain since the start of their journey lay on Cass's hair like frosting.

'What a vile day,' remarked Lucia, glancing skyward and allowing Cass to pass her in the doorway. Today the glassmaker sported patchwork trousers, a garish pink top and the stack of bangles she'd worn previously.

Cass went inside and went to sit on one of the red plastic chairs in the waiting area.

'Don't be daft, come on through,' said Lucia. She pulled at the closest of the barriers and it squealed across the tiled floor, making a sound like a metallic version of chalk across a blackboard. Cass followed close behind her.

On Lucia's workbench sat a line of five unfinished glass knots.

'Why did you make so many?' asked Cass.

Lucia selected the glass object closest to her.

'This one is a failure,' she said. 'Look, the tube here collapsed in on itself and sealed up. I meant to throw it away.' She tossed the offending item into a metal bucket on the floor where it clattered, but didn't smash. 'There were several other failures, too, but those were more – well, catastrophic, let's say.'

'What about these?' asked Cass, pointing towards the remaining four. 'They aren't failures, too, are they?'

'No. These are all pretty good. I'm guessing some are better than others, though.'

'But they all look the same to me.'

'Do they?' asked Lucia, incredulously. 'I suppose you don't have my eye for glass.'

Cass shrugged. 'I guess not. How do we choose?' she asked.

'We try one at a time to see which, if any, works.'

'You mean I'm going to have to time travel immediately – from here in your workshop?'

'How else can we test it?' asked Lucia.

'But I'm not prepared. My clothes and make-up are all wrong for 1943 and I haven't properly thought through a plan yet.' *Besides, I want to see my mum first*, she thought, panicking.

'Don't worry, you aren't going straight to 1943; you're going to 1997. If you travel back to mid-April of that year, I was away on my honeymoon.'

'I didn't realise you were married.'

Lucia frowned. 'I'm not. Not any more. I lost David five years ago. When I say lost, I mean he died.'

Cass opened her mouth to offer condolences, but Lucia cut in first. 'No, don't be sorry, it's fine. I'm resigned to it now. Anyway, like I was saying, I've been here since 1996, but the place was empty while David and I were away on our honeymoon. You'll travel to 1997, wait an hour, and then The Infinity Glass will return you here.'

Cass thought through the logistics of the proposed trip and asked, 'How can I be confident that being able to travel backward through time will mean I can return safely afterwards?'

'Ah, well. Because if you'd got stuck in the past, you'd have had to break a window or door to escape onto the street. Everything was secure when we returned from our honeymoon,' said Lucia, happily, 'so you must either have not succeeded at all or succeeded both in travelling and returning.'

'Break a window? Aren't there latches to open them from the inside, or keys sitting around on windowsills?'

'No. David was always very careful about things like that. You'd have definitely had to break your way out.'

'Wow, you've given this a lot of thought, haven't you?'

'Of course. Details are important. I need The Infinity Glass now, please. I'm going to break it into this,' she lifted a metal bowl with one hand, 'using this,' she added, lifting a claw hammer from the seat of the chair with the other. 'Haven – Drusilla, or whatever you want to call yourself – be prepared. I've no idea what will happen to The Essence, but I have beakers ready, one for each colour. Although... well, we'll see how it goes. Are you ready, sprite?'

'I'm ready,' proclaimed Drusilla, confidently.

'She says go ahead,' reported Cass, handing the artefact to Lucia and taking a step back in case of flying glass.

Lucia put on a pair of red safety goggles and nodded towards a spare pair lying on the workbench. 'Use those, please. I don't need to have to take you to A&E with glass in your eye. There's enough going on as it is.'

Cass nodded and put the goggles on.

Lucia tried once, twice, then a third time, hitting the artefact with increasing ferocity. Her jaw set determinedly, she tried a fourth time and it finally broke. Instead of breaking into long shards, the whole thing shattered into tiny fragments which tinkled musically when they rained down onto the workbench. Cass gawped at the globules of Essence, which hung in the air in the exact spot they had inhabited before Lucia smashed the glass. Lucia swore and swiftly scooped the shimmering glob of blue Essence into a beaker, turning

149

the container upside down on her workbench to stop the contents escaping. Then she repeated the process with the red one while Cass captured the green.

'That stuff is seriously weird, isn't it?' Cass commented, registering that the colours of the three blobs, which should have looked different when viewed through the red safety glasses, remained unchanged.

Lucia nodded and stared first at the shattered glass, then at the blobs of Essence floating ethereally a centimetre or so above the workbench. The glassmaker's chest was rising and falling heavily.

'Are you OK?' Cass asked.

Lucia didn't respond.

'Lucia?'

'Oh, I thought you meant the sprite. I'm fine. A bit — what might you say? Weirded out, perhaps, but I'm fine.'

'How about you, Drusilla?' asked Cass.

No reply came.

'Drusilla!'

Still nothing.

'Lucia, Drusilla isn't replying. What does this mean? Has it all gone wrong?' asked Cass, desperately.

Chapter 19

A Difficult Make

Silence hung in the air like an over-inflated balloon ready to burst. Cass stared at Lucia and Lucia at Cass.

The glassmaker spoke first. 'All we can do is finish constructing the new Glass and see what happens. I have to admit, I didn't foresee completely losing the damned sprite.'

'If Drusilla's gone for good, will The Infinity Glass still work – will I be able to time travel?' asked Cass, winkling out the single most important question from those swimming around in her mind. At least, after her previous conversation with the sprite, she could be sure Drusilla hadn't died when the glass broke.

'I don't know whether it will work or not, to be totally honest. Time travelling glass artefacts with sprites attached aren't exactly something there's a precedent for,' said Lucia, shaking her head.

'Couldn't you at least lie and say you think it will probably be fine?' asked Cass, wrapping her arms around her middle and realising she was trembling.

'OK then, I think it will probably be fine,' the corner of Lucia's mouth twitched up in an uncertain half smile beneath lowered eyebrows.

'That's not even funny.'

'No.' Lucia's shoulders slumped and the half smile melted away. 'Well, let's move on rather than getting ourselves stuck here trying to solve impossible riddles, shall we?'

Cass nodded.

Lucia selected the closest of the newly crafted glass objects, turning it over and around to check it from every possible angle.

'How are you going to get the liquid balls inside?' asked Cass.

'No clue. I'm just going to wing it. I left a way in for the Essence in each object I made, and one of the three tubes is straighter than the others so there's some room to manoeuvre, but it's still going to be awkward. I expect a solution will present itself to us one way or another.'

Lucia lifted the beaker in which the blue sphere hovered. She manoeuvred the new Glass directly above it, then tilted the beaker slowly backwards. The sphere didn't move.

'Oh,' said Lucia. 'I thought it would, you know, go upwards into it. Perhaps it needs encouragement.'

She prodded the blue blob with one of the open ends of the curved glass tube. As soon as the blob touched the glass, it morphed from a sphere to a cube, and then into a long, thin cylinder. Once its shape matched the container, it slipped inside, drifting smoothly along the tube until it reached the nodule furthest from where it had entered. Lucia blocked the other open end of the glass with a finger, perhaps for fear that The Essence would go straight through and spill out of the other side. Instead, it came to a halt, morphed back into a sphere, and wobbled gently. Cass's instinct told her it was "waiting" for the other colours to take their places.

Lucia repeated the process with the green and red spheres. 'Well, that went better than I imagined,' she said, once all three spheres were in place. 'Closing up will take a while. The shape isn't precisely right yet, because I had to leave the ends accessible for filling, which means it lacks the perfect uniformity it needs. Do you want to watch me work?'

'Yes. No. Oh, I don't know; mightn't I put you off?'

Lucia shrugged. 'I'm used to it. You are at least two shades paler than you were when you arrived, though. If you'd prefer, you could go upstairs and make us drinks.'

'Yeah, alright.'

Lucia told Cass which cupboards and drawers to find things in in her kitchen and Cass sloped dejectedly up the stairs.

When she returned with a pair of steaming mugs, she asked, 'How's it going?'

Lucia shook her head frustratedly. 'We're one down already,' said the older woman, her hands on her hips. 'Thankfully, I prepared for the possibility of failures.'

Three upturned beakers were lined up on the workbench, each containing a coloured ball of Essence. 'What happened?' Cass asked. She had been naïve to assume that this would be a straightforward ten-minute visit with the glassmaker.

'It imploded: pressure issues. Heat and cold while sealing objects can cause problems – you have to be careful,' explained Lucia. 'To be honest, I made what I consider a damned foolish mistake. Thankfully it was a simple matter to recapture the blobs of Essence. I'm going to try the second Glass now. Why don't you take a seat?'

Cass, who was hovering near the red chairs in the waiting area, put the drinks on the table and perched on the front edge of a seat, but then realised she couldn't see over the barriers from that low position. All that she could see were Lucia's head and shoulders and, because the glassmaker had donned the red safety goggles, Cass couldn't even read her facial expression. Not wanting to be any bother, she sipped at her hot chocolate, burning her tongue. She replaced the mug on the table to allow the drink to cool, then slid back in the chair and waited, her hands in her lap and her fingers laced together.

Alone with her thoughts, she wondered what Lucia would think of her plan to meet her mother. Lucia's clever idea of a test run to 1997 meant Cass would know whether the device was functioning properly without going straight back to 1943. Once it was back in her possession, she could return home with it and make whatever trips she chose without scrutiny.

After a few minutes, Cass decided she'd like to see what was going on, despite not fully understanding the process, so she rose slowly from her seat.

Lucia glanced up at her. 'Don't worry; even if all of these were to fail – which I don't think is likely, I might add – I have plenty more glass. We'll get there.'

Cass smiled weakly. She knew that if not for Lucia's help, her dad would have no hope at all of returning home. Deciding to let Lucia work without being observed, she sank back into the seat.

Cass had drunk about half of her hot chocolate by the time Lucia said, 'Success! I have to let it cool a while and fill the hole, then we can try it out.'

'Hole?' asked Cass, springing to her feet.

'Yes. Don't worry, it's a hole I made on purpose. Part of the process, not a mistake.'

Cass sat back down, wishing she'd brought a book with her so she could engross herself in a story to take her mind off what was happening. As it was, she flipped between worrying about the consequences if the new Infinity Glass wouldn't work, wondering what could have happened to Drusilla, and daydreaming about how it would be to actually meet her mother. But the most important thing was finding her dad and returning him to his proper time, and all her options for time travel were dependent on the skills of the glassmaker.

'There,' said Lucia, sounding comfortingly positive. She pushed open the barriers and came to sit on the other chair. 'How are you doing?' she asked, wrapping her slender fingers around her mug. She wasn't wearing her bangles any more. Cass guessed she must have taken them off to work.

'How am I?' asked Cass. 'Well, I'm worried about whether the damned thing will work, of course – although don't get me wrong, I know you are the best person possible to be working on it – and I'm stressed at having no control over any of this and terrified that I won't be able to find my dad and bring him home with only an hour to do it in. Apart from that, I'm good.'

'I'm sorry, Cass. I wish I could go instead of you. I've travelled using The Infinity Glass before, after all. Not that it's something I would want to do again, with the benefit of hindsight.'

Cass gave a half-hearted shrug and stared at her fingers. 'You're already doing the most important thing you can do,' she said.

'Yes. I suppose so.'

Neither spoke for a while, then Cass said, 'Hey, I haven't seen any of your stuff.'

'My stuff?' asked Lucia.

'The objects you make – from glass. Can you show me some of it?'

'Erm, well, I don't keep things lying around. They're commissions, so I post them to whoever ordered them. I have several things I've kept for personal use. Didn't you notice them upstairs?'

'I had my mind on other things. Sorry.'

'Perhaps I'll show you later, then, after we're finished here.'

'I'd like that,' replied Cass, managing a weak smile.

Another long silence followed.

'Hey, would you like me to be there with you when you leave on your mission to find your dad?' asked Lucia.

'Oh.' The offer was unexpected. 'Um, that's kind, but I'll be OK. I've been there when Dad left on one of his journeys and I was there when he returned from another, so I have first – or rather, second-hand – experience of what I can expect to happen. Plus I'll have had the practice run, thanks to your brilliant idea.'

'You know about the extreme chill travellers experience, do you?'

Cass recalled her father having to take a hot shower after returning from 1066. She'd been asleep when he returned from 1850.

'Oh, that's normal, is it?' she asked.

'Oh yes, definitely. It's rather unpleasant, but I suppose there could be worse side-effects.'

'Right. OK. Thanks for the warning. Is there anything else I should know?'

'You're aware of the rules, are you?'

'Yes, ish.'

'Ish. Great.'

'Do you know all of them, then?' asked Cass.

Lucia shrugged. 'I doubt it,' she admitted. 'The damned sprite only tells you when you try to break one of them, but I know a few. Travel is through time, not space;

no travelling within your lifetime; no requesting an early return; and no travelling to the same time twice.'

Cass nodded. 'Yeah, I had those. Let's hope there aren't any more. Drusilla said I ought to be able to travel back with Dad even though The Infinity Glass usually only allows a single traveller. I hope she – it – was right about that, otherwise all this has been...' she took a deep, shuddering breath, closing her eyes to hide the tears welling up.

'Oh, goodness me, I should be there when you leave. Cass, let me be there, will you? You'll need someone if things don't work out.'

Cass turned her face away from Lucia and wiped a tear with her knuckle. 'I'll manage. Thanks for the offer, though. Hey,' she said, deciding to change the subject, 'won't the new Infinity Glass have cooled by now? Let's go and try it out, shall we?' She stood and Lucia followed her through the barriers, checking her watch.

'It's been more than ten minutes. It will be fine.'

'Let's test it, then, shall we?' asked Cass, reaching for the glass knot.

'Hang on, you can't use it as it is. I need to put it in the metal housing.'

'Oh. Right. Can I do it?' asked Cass. 'You've done all the rest. It would be good to have been part of the process and this is all that's left.'

Lucia nodded solemnly and handed Cass both the housing and – with significantly more caution – the new Infinity Glass.

Cass took both items carefully and pushed the device into its housing. 'It seems the tiniest bit tight, I think,' she said, grimacing. 'Still, at least it closes.'

Lucia stared at the completed artefact. 'Try calling the sprite,' she suggested.

Cass had all but forgotten about Drusilla. 'Oh, of course. Drusilla, are you here?'

Lucia's eyes widened as she waited expectantly for Cass to acknowledge a response.

'There's no reply,' reported Cass, despondently.

'Well then. Perhaps the link with the sprite was permanently broken when I destroyed the original Infinity Glass. The object itself might still work. Tell it you want to go to 16 April 1997.'

'OK.' Cass stiffened. 'I'd like to go to 16 April,' she closed her eyes, '1997.'

Chapter 20

Trial Run

'What a pity,' said Lucia. 'Let's try another.'

Cass opened her eyes and passed the failed device back, fresh tears spilling down her cheeks. 'Would The Infinity Glass have done that thing where it sticks to me if it was working properly?' she asked.

'That's a difficult question and I'm not at all sure of the answer. Maybe yes, and maybe no, but if it *does* attach to you, only a sprite can unbind you from it, so you'd better hope Drusilla comes back. Come to think of it, it's a good job I wasn't the one who put it inside the housing. What if it had attached to me?'

'But you're The Maker now,' said Cass. 'Surely it wouldn't stick to you?'

'It's not a chance I'm willing to take. After I've transferred The Essence to the next glass and sealed and cooled it, you can put it into the housing again.'

'Can I watch you work?' asked Cass.

Lucia passed Cass the spare pair of safety goggles she had worn earlier. 'Put these on and stand well back,' she instructed.

Soon, Lucia's second attempt at making a new time travelling Infinity Glass was ready to test. Cass called the sprite, but again received no response. She tried asking the device to take her to 1997, but with no success.

Swallowing hard, she passed it back to Lucia, who said, 'Don't worry. I told you we'd make it work and I intend to keep my promise. It has to be exactly right, that's all. Like Thomas Edison and the lightbulb, we'll keep on trying until it's right.'

Cass got the impression Lucia's singsong tone was a poorly disguised attempt to convey a confidence that the glassmaker didn't feel, but she said nothing. Their efforts would either work or not; it was as disturbingly simple as that.

Once the third try was safely enclosed inside its housing, Cass, forgetting to call for Drusilla first, immediately blurted out, 'Take me to 16 April 1997.'

There was a sound like a thousand people simultaneously snapping their fingers and Lucia disappeared. So did the workbench and the barriers separating the two areas of the workshop.

Cass shivered violently, clutching the artefact to her chest so as not to drop it.

'Drusilla?' she called quietly, not confident enough that she'd time travelled as planned and eager to avoid being caught trespassing if she'd arrived in the wrong time.

'I'm here, Cass,' said the sprite.

'Oh, thank goodness. Is this 1997?'

'Yes. This is 16 April in that year.'

'Good. Great. And you – are you OK?'

'Thank you, yes. I am fine. I was unaffected by the breaking of the glass, but it did, rather surprisingly, mean I could no longer communicate with you. I have been watching, however, and hoping one of Lucia's replacement pieces would function adequately.'

'So, I have an hour here?' asked Cass, swivelling around to take in the entire room. Apart from the viewing area being missing and the workbench repositioned, the most obvious change to the room was a shelving unit full of beautiful, brightly coloured objects. They were either vases or lamps, although she wasn't sure which, and were lined up proudly in the front bow window. The filing cabinet stood against the same wall it occupied in Cass's time, as did a couple of other shelf units. The workbench bearing the torch now stood several feet away from where it would be in the future; here, it abutted the white wall in what would become the viewing area.

'You don't have an entire hour, I think, but very close,' said Drusilla. 'By my calculations, fifty-seven minutes and fifteen seconds in total. The glass object is not quite precise enough in its dimensions.'

'At least it works,' mumbled Cass, caustically. 'Don't knock it.'

'Oh, I'm not. Lucia has great skill when working with glass. She is simply not as skilled as the original Maker.'

'Well, she *is* The Maker now, isn't she? Of this version of The Infinity Glass, at least.'

'The metal element is important, too, though, so strictly it would be more accurate to call her The Co-maker.'

'Fine, Co-maker it is, then, since you have to be so precise. Oh!' she exclaimed, the sensation of warmth flooding back into her veins taking her by surprise. 'What a bizarre sensation. At least I'm warm again.'

The sprite did not respond, but Cass realised Drusilla had no reason to care about the custodian's physical comfort, or lack of it.

With a little under an hour to kill, she considered going upstairs to have a nose around. Her destination had been Lucia's idea, and yet Cass was a trespasser here. Going into the glassmaker's living space would be a violation. The much younger Lucia who lived here had not given permission for Cass to invade her home and workshop. Indeed, the Lucia who lived here in 1997 had never set eyes on the time travel device.

Instead, Cass rooted around on the glassmaker's desk and found a blank sheet of paper. She wrote "CP 16/4/1997" on it and wedged it behind the filing cabinet, wanting there to be proof that she'd been here. Then she sat cross-legged on the floor and thought about meeting her mum and saving her dad.

'Would you like a countdown to your return time? Your father found it useful,' suggested Drusilla later, when the moment of return finally approached.

'Oh, OK. Sure,' replied Cass, standing and brushing her dusty jeans with the palms of her hands.

'One minute to go. I shall count from ten seconds.'

Cass counted backwards from sixty in her head, but her timing was off and she'd only reached fourteen when the sprite began at ten.

'Three, two, one.'

Cass closed an eye and hunched her shoulders.

There was a sound like a thousand people snapping their fingers and Lucia reappeared, with a startled expression on her face.

Cass shivered, feeling so bitterly cold that she thought she would exhale a cloud of frozen water vapour or maybe produce a string of icicles from her fingertips.

'You can shower if you need to warm up,' said Lucia, patting Cass's shoulder.

'Th-th-thanks, but n-no. I-I'll be fine in a few m-minutes. Ch-check behind the f-filing cabinet, near the b-bottom. I left you a note.'

Lucia retrieved the scrap of dirty paper. 'Nice. Shows how long it is since I reorganised in here, doesn't it?'

'At least it's proof that I time travelled.'

'I saw you disappear,' said Lucia, smiling, 'and then come back again. It was clear my glass had worked. You've returned early, though. I set a timer and it's only coming up to fifty-eight minutes now.'

'Drusilla says your version of The Infinity Glass isn't accurate to the original.'

'Do you want to try another?' asked Lucia.

'No need. This works. Who knows if the others would or not and I can't take a chance for the sake of less than three minutes. Thank you, Lucia. Now I'll be able to try to save my dad.'

'If you have any problems when you reach 1943,' said Lucia, 'my grandmother lived here back then. If you need somewhere to shelter, I'd bet money on her taking you in. Her name was Rose Preston. It's best you don't mention that her granddaughter sent you, though – that would freak her out.'

'I'll have less than an hour. There won't be time to faff about making social calls,' Cass pointed out.

'I get that. I meant in case you get stuck; in case something goes wrong,' said Lucia, frowning.

'Failure isn't an option.' Cass spoke with a confidence she didn't feel. 'Didn't you ever time travel back to see your grandmother when you were custodian? You had the artefact for a fair while, after all.'

'Yes, I did visit her, and Grandad, as a matter of fact. It was nice to see them, but it was all a bit pointless without being able to explain who I was. I figured they wouldn't get it and it would spoil things. At least I was lucky enough to know them as old people. They both died when I was a kid, though, so my memories aren't all that clear.'

163

Cass tried not to show her disappointment at Lucia's negative experience. 'Oh. That's a shame,' she said.

Lucia tilted her head to the side, but took a deep breath and smiled ruefully. Her eyes narrowed, as if some previously unthought-of possibility had just occurred to her.

Hoping the glassmaker hadn't figured out her plan to meet her mother, Cass said hastily, 'Um, well, I think I should go now. I'll come back and tell you how it went. I'll bring my dad with me; he'll want to say thanks.'

Lucia wafted a hand at her. 'No need for that. You can if you want, but I just hope you find him fit and well and succeed in getting him home. That's why I did this, after all. But Cass, if it doesn't go well – if you have to return alone – I want you to come back here anyway.'

Cass shook her head angrily. 'It has to work,' she said, making her way to the front door.

'One more thing,' called Lucia.

'What's that?' Cass glanced back expectantly.

'Be careful.'

Chapter 21

Bees and Lightning

Cass walked home feeling like a person out of place in the world. She had time travelled. Who of all the strangers she passed on her route back home could say they had done the same? Not one of them. She and Lucia were the only living people who had used either the original Infinity Glass or its replacement to travel into the past. Her father didn't count in her tally because he was still in 1943. The uniqueness of her situation made her feel both exceptionally special and totally alone.

Sitting cross-legged on her bed a little later, she gazed into The Infinity Glass, taking in the curve and colour of the glass, and then focussing on one of the globules of Essence. Concentrating on the liquid, she noticed a low-level buzzing sensation gradually filling her whole body as if she were a hive full of bees. A sense of calm washed over her and she raised her hand, imagining a thread of almost tangible time extending from the encased glass knot to her fingertips – a thread that joined her present time with every other moment that had ever been. She could picture it in her mind's eye: a writhing green strand both static and flowing; both electric and neutral; both transient and eternal.

She clenched her fist and the moment passed.

'Was that normal?' she asked Drusilla.

'Was what normal?'

'I can't describe it. It was weird, like bees and some kind of weird lightning all at once.'

'Bees?'

'Yes, bees. Buzzy, you know?'

'Are you quite well, Cass?'

Cass couldn't believe Drusilla hadn't noticed what had happened and worried suddenly there could be a problem with The Infinity Glass. 'I thought the artefact was doing something. Didn't you notice anything strange at all?'

'I did not, but then I don't experience the chill that custodians feel when they travel either. I've never heard any previous custodian mention bees and lightning, though. Perhaps you should see a physician.'

Shaking her head, Cass said, 'No way. I'm fine now, and you and I have things to do.'

'Do I take it you are ready to travel?'

'Not yet, but soon. I thought I'd check fashion trends and stuff to make sure I don't look out of place. I'm a bit scared – I don't want to mess anything up.'

'I can describe what the young women were wearing when I travelled with your father, if it would help,' said Drusilla.

'With my...? Ohhh. We aren't going back for Dad yet. I have another trip I need to make first.'

'Your mother?' asked the sprite.

'How did you know?'

'Your father wanted to see her again too. Unfortunately, it was against the rules for him.'

Cass stiffened. 'And for me? Is it against the rules for me?'

'As long as you travel to part of her life which was not within your own lifetime, no, it is not against the rules for you.'

Cass clapped her hands like a fluttering oyster shell. 'Brilliant. I'll be ready soon. As ready as a person can be, at least.'

'Jolly good.'

'Aren't you bothered that I'm leaving Dad for now?'

'No. It's your choice, not mine, and I have no strong feelings for your father.'

'Seriously? That's pretty cold of you.'

'I'm not subject to human sensibilities.'

'Terrific. But you wanted me to have The Infinity Glass repaired. Was that not so I could save my dad?'

'No. I explained that I have an attachment to The Infinity Glass.'

'I see. It was to help yourself, then' said Cass. She wasn't convinced that the sprite had no empathy for her father's situation at all, but decided it wasn't worth an argument. Instead, she decided to try a slightly different tack. 'Why are you so attached to the object? Or attached to it at all, come to that? Why would you want that – are you kind of along for the thrill of the ride?'

'Being with The Infinity Glass is, for want of a better term, my job: to act as an intermediary between it and the custodian. I am not a thrill-seeker, Cass.'

It was an unsatisfactory answer, but Cass thought it unlikely she'd extract a better one. 'OK, sure, whatever,' she said. 'Well, I'm going now. I'll get back to you once I have the info I need.'

She scooped her phone up from the bed and, leaving the time travel device on her pillow, trotted downstairs. She realised that if her father had travelled back to 1943 from anywhere except inside his own house, The Infinity

Glass might have remained unfound upon its return to the present day. With the artefact damaged and no handy human to get it fixed, the sprite would probably have eventually returned to wherever it originated and Cass would have been left fatherless, but with no clue what had happened.

Taking to her favourite seat in the living room, she swivelled around sideways and hooked her legs over the arm of the chair. Using her phone to access the internet, she read an article entitled "Fashion dos and don'ts from the turn of the millennium".

Cass discovered that 2000 was the year when The London Eye took its first paying passengers and something called the Millennium Dome opened in London too – she looked it up and discovered it was what she knew as the O2. Anti-capitalist riots had taken place in London during May and the Queen Mother celebrated her hundredth birthday in August.

'Goodness, the Queen's mother?' said Cass. Her mind still trying to envision the Queen having a mother at all, she scrolled on to the information she'd visited this website to learn.

Once she'd found the fashion details she wanted, she scanned the page, grimacing at the idea of micro miniskirts, red leather trousers and wearing a dress over a pair of jeans. She didn't own a frock with a handkerchief hemline, but thought some of the ones shown were pretty, if in a Tinkerbell-ish kind of way. The low-rise jeans pictured had way too low a waist band for her liking.

After much thought, she reached the conclusion that regular people wouldn't have worn these super-trendy items every day and, as long as she stuck with clothes considered basic staples, she would probably fit in fine. She found a pair of plain jeans, a tight short-sleeved grey top, added her newly arrived red vintage jacket in case it was chilly and got changed. Next, she slid quietly into her dad's bedroom and opened a drawer. Rummaging around, she found a wind-up wristwatch with a delicate oval face and a filigree gold strap. She corrected the time, wound it and put it to her ear, smiling to hear the *tick, tick, tick* of the mechanism. The timepiece had been a birthday gift from her father to her mother the year they married. It felt fitting for her to be wearing it, and it pleased her how well it fitted her wrist.

Still admiring how attractive her mother's watch looked on her, Cass fetched a pair of red canvas shoes from the front hall and sat on the bottom of the stairs to pull them on. She tied the laces, double-knotting them for good measure, then froze like a statue at the enormity of what she planned to do. It was one thing to travel to a place she was sure would be empty, but quite another to meet Jennifer Cassidy on the day she first set eyes on Jake Patch. Her resolve wobbled. Perhaps it would be safer to go straight back for her dad.

'No!' she exclaimed, slapping her hands on her knees. 'Come on, Cass, there will never be another chance for you to do this. You'd hate yourself if you didn't try – if you could have met her and you chickened out.'

Her eyebrows knitted together and her jaw set determinedly, she jumped to her feet and stomped upstairs to fetch The Infinity Glass.

'Did my father ever time travel from somewhere outside of this house?' Cass asked Drusilla.

'Once, yes. When we went back for the mug.'

'For a mug?'

'Yes, a commemorative mug. He intended to acquire it for a pound and sell it for five hundred. He was most keen to obtain money to help you through university.'

'Oh. I knew he was trying to save up a bit to help me out, but he didn't say anything about the mug.'

'He was most frustrated when all he could bring home was a newspaper.'

'I'll bet he was.' Cass remembered her reaction to the souvenir. At least she'd been enthusiastic about it. The social history held within a single newspaper was astounding. It made her think about all the social history she could, using The Infinity Glass, see for herself. There were so many years she'd like to visit if she had the chance: she could watch the moon landing in 1969 live on TV; go to Queen Elizabeth II's coronation; see an original performance of a Shakespeare play; march with the Suffragettes; or stand in the crowd of onlookers when Amelia Earhart landed her plane in Northern Ireland after her solo crossing of the Atlantic.

And yet she had chosen to meet her mother, and then save her father, who would most likely have a stern talk with her if she told him she wanted to gallivant around in time when she ought to be studying. Lucia's warning about time travel being potentially addictive was still fresh in her mind, too. The future was important – she didn't want to lose the life she was supposed to have.

'Anyway,' she continued, 'the reason I asked was to find out a good spot to travel from. He must have had to find a quiet, out-of-the-way place relatively near where he wanted to be and I'll need somewhere similar.'

'You are correct about your father. He found an alley. Would you like me to direct you there?'

'An alley? Sounds charming.'

'It served a purpose.'

'A bit yucky, though.'

'Less than salubrious, indeed, but it was quiet and near his intended destination for finding the mug.'

'Oh. What part of Hastings was it in, then?'

'Near the beach, at the bottom of the long hill.'

'OK, so in the Old Town. Closer to St Leonards would be better, but I'm a fast walker. I need to travel from a place that will be quiet today and back in 2000 as well. So stinky alleyway it is, then. Hey, it's not too secluded, is it, Drusilla? I don't want to end up getting murdered or anything.'

'Let me think. It was directly off a shopping street. Even if someone was in there, you could very quickly run back to a busier area. You would be as safe as one could reasonably predict.'

'Then there's no reason to delay for a moment longer.'

Chapter 22

Mothers' Day

The alley her dad had used for his own departure through time was pleasingly deserted.

'I didn't know there'd be bin storage here,' said Cass, wrinkling her nose at the fetid stench of decaying food hanging in the air. 'I'm guessing those are for a restaurant or café. Ugh!'

'Your father thought it useful to have the bins here, so there would be somewhere he could conceal himself from view when he left.'

'But the bins wouldn't be here any time prior to about 2010, would they? I mean, they wouldn't still be here when he arrived in his chosen time.'

'Yes, that became apparent. But we had no issue with observers. This is not – nor ever has been, I think – a busy area.'

Cass nodded. 'Well then, here goes.'

She had given long and hard thought to the exact arrival time to ask for during the walk from home. She wanted to get to her parents' meeting place early enough to see them meet. Her dad had said they only talked for a few minutes before swapping phone numbers, so there should be time afterwards for Cass to make her way from the promenade onto the beach to meet her mum before The Infinity Glass returned her.

She reached into the tote bag in which she'd brought the time travel device and ran her fingertip over the smooth metal of the hinged container.

'Take me to 10.40am on the second of April 2000.'

There was a sound like a thousand people simultaneously snapping their fingers and the black roll-top waste bins disappeared, as expected, to be replaced with a row of smaller plastic bins.

'Brrr!' Cass rubbed her arms vigorously. Although she was glad she was wearing a jacket, it couldn't stop the chill that came with time travelling. Hopefully it would at least help her warm up more rapidly. 'We are in the year 2000, are we, Drusilla?' she asked, trying to stop her teeth from chattering.

'Yes, exactly as you requested. You needn't check every time you travel; The Infinity Glass will not misdirect you.'

'It's not the original object, though, is it?' Cass pointed out. 'I want a little reassurance before I go wandering onto the street and find people wearing Victorian clothes. Although, plastic bins, Cass, duh!'

'As you wish. Consider yourself reassured.'

Cass saw a teenager stroll past the end of the alleyway wearing jeans, trainers and a white T-shirt beneath a red and navy checked shirt. It all fitted the era. She'd made it.

Nervously, she sidled towards the exit from the alleyway.

'Stroll out confidently,' suggested Drusilla. 'If you act furtively, people will assume you are up to no good.'

Cass thought the sprite had a point. She took a deep breath and strode straight into the path of a boy on a bicycle. The gangly youth swerved, barely avoiding a fall.

'Stupid tart,' he shouted, but he didn't stop to confront her.

Several faces turned to see what was going on and an older woman with kind eyes gave Cass a supportive smile, but said nothing.

Pressing her fingers to her thumping heart, Cass waited a few seconds until the bicycle and its rider had disappeared, and then turned to head in the same direction he had gone – to the left, towards the town centre. She couldn't afford to waste any time.

With that in mind, she asked, 'Hey, Drusilla, what's the time?'

'It's 10.41, Cass.'

She set the hands on her wristwatch accordingly. 'I have a little over fifty-seven minutes in total. I arrived at 10.40, which means I'll leave at 11.37. Drusilla, I'd like a countdown. Tell me when I have a minute, then thirty seconds, then do a count from fifteen seconds. Can you do that?'

'Of course. You have no need for a timepiece.'

'Well, not strictly, no, but I can't keep asking you how long I have. Someone might hear me and it's easier not to have people think I've gone a bit odd and started talking to myself.' As if to prove her point, a man going the other way raised a quizzical eyebrow at her.

'I'm not going to talk to you again unless I absolutely have to, Drusilla.' Cass tried not to move her lips while speaking. 'Not until we're back. The watch will help me with the time until you give me the countdown I asked for. OK?'

'Very well.'

Little was different in this part of Hastings from the place Cass frequented. One or two shops which were boarded up in her own time were open and bustling with

Mothers' Day business and there was no sign of graffiti here, but the familiar mechanical windmill on the Crazy Golf course still turned on the seafront, although the pirate course had yet to be built. Most of what she saw was so familiar that Cass had to remind herself this was not her own time.

Not very far away, at the top end of Harold Road, her paternal grandmother still lived. Not only would Cass's mother be here, alive and well, but her father, too, unaware of the future that lay ahead in which he would become a father, lose a wife and, much later, discover the unique object now concealed in Cass's tote bag.

Here in the year 2000, she had unique knowledge about future events – not just in her family, but in the world – and it saddened and frustrated her to realise that, in an hour's visit, she couldn't do anything about climate change, Brexit or anything else of wider significance. She had come here to meet her mother, and there was scarcely time to do that.

She checked the time regularly. After about ten minutes of walking, she concluded she'd underestimated how long it would take her to get to her destination. She broke into a trot and wished she'd bothered to check the distance on her phone instead of guessing.

I can't mess this up for the sake of a few minutes, she told herself, angrily.

She arrived opposite the statue a little out of breath. Her chest heaved and she wasn't sure whether it was because of the running or her excitement at what was about to happen. She scanned the beach to find her mother, but the only people around were a man walking a pair of dogs on the wet sand and some hardy soul wading thigh-deep in the English Channel wearing nothing but a scant pair of blue swimming trunks.

Where is she?

Cass set off, picking a direction at random and hoping for the best. Glancing at her watch, she realised her limited time here was fast ticking away.

A familiar figure strode past her from behind, cradling a bouquet of flowers in his arms. It was her father. Cass felt a pang of remorse, as if someone was kneading her heart. He was stuck in 1943 and she'd left him there to come and do this – but she was here now, so it was too late to change her mind.

Glancing sideways towards the beach, Cass caught sight of a blonde-haired figure leaning against a breakwater. Her father had passed by without noticing her.

Cass thought quickly. 'Ouch!' she cried, crouching and grabbing her ankle.

The younger version of her father turned and hurried back to help. 'Are you OK?' he asked.

Cass sat on the lower promenade and stared up at her dad. He looked back at her as if she were any random stranger and she felt it like a stab through her heart, even though she knew that a stranger was precisely what she was to him here in the year 2000. He'd probably say she was not even a twinkle in his eye.

Well, his damned eye would never twinkle unless he fell in love with Jennifer Cassidy, would it?

'I'm fine; I twisted my ankle is all. I'll sit here for a few minutes and massage it out.'

Jake Patch nodded. 'If you're sure.'

On the beach, Jen gave a mournful sob and Jake Patch turned to see where the noise was coming from. Cass was relieved not to have to draw his attention to the forlorn figure with her head in her hands and her knees drawn up to her chest.

'Bloody hell!' exclaimed Jake. 'Now there are two ladies in distress.' He chewed his lip, clearly torn between whether to go to the woman on the beach or stay with Cass.

'She sounds miserable. Perhaps you could...' Cass wished she didn't have to prod him into doing what would be instinctive to her.

'I'll go and ask if she's OK, shall I?' asked her father. 'Do you think I should? Maybe she'd prefer to be alone.'

'No, I don't think she would,' reasoned Cass. 'She's crying on a beach. I wouldn't want to be alone if it was me.'

Jake nodded, his eyes meeting Cass's for the briefest moment. He was so young that it made her strangely sad. His hair was shorter and tidy for once, the frown lines she was accustomed to seeing wiped away as if by photo editing software.

'Go and talk to her,' Cass told him, firmly.

'Right.'

'Perhaps a flower would cheer her up,' she added.

Jake smiled. 'Good idea. Thanks.' He stepped onto the pebbled beach, approached Jen and leaned forward to speak to her. Their words were carried away on the breeze, so Cass could only watch her father's back and her mother's left shoulder.

The pair talked quietly for a couple of minutes before Jake drew several flowers from the Mothers' Day bouquet and handed them to Jen. The soft tinkle of Jen's laughter floated up the beach, sending Cass's pulse rate soaring.

A few moments later, Jake patted his pockets in turn, finding a pen but no paper to write on. With a familiar nonchalant shrug, he scribbled instead on the back of his hand, and then dropped down to sit on the pebbles beside Jen.

Cass's mother cautiously offered her own fist and he wrote on it. They were exchanging phone numbers the old-fashioned way, Cass realised, smiling and wiping away a single tear.

'None of this would have happened if not for me. You'd have flounced straight past without noticing her. There's a bloody paradox if ever there was,' said Cass said out loud, her eyes fixed on the young man who would one day be her father. 'And you never mentioned someone else having suggested you give her the flowers, although it was a much more romantic story the way you told it, I'll give you that.'

'Are you hurt, miss?' asked a gruff voice. A middle-aged man with a grey-sprinkled beard and a bald head was staring at Cass with a concerned expression.

'I twisted my ankle, but I'm fine, thanks.' She leapt up and put her weight on both feet to prove her point. 'Thanks for stopping, I appreciate it, but I don't need any help, thanks.'

The man nodded curtly and continued on his way. She turned to see what her parents were doing now.

Jen sat on the beach, staring at the phone number written on her hand and sniffing her flowers. Jake was crunching his way back across the pebbles towards the promenade. Cass thought he might be coming back to check on her, but she didn't have time to hold another conversation with her dad if she was to meet her mother, so she walked briskly away in the opposite direction. After a few steps, she stopped and sneaked a backward glance to see where he was. He was heading away from her now, presumably taking the remaining flowers to her grandma.

This was her chance. She'd witnessed their first meeting – made it happen, even – and now she would finally meet her mother. She walked shakily towards the seated figure, who had turned towards the sea to watch the man swimming in the cold, calm waters.

'Erm, hello,' said Cass, nervously.

Her mother pushed a strand of perfect long mid-blonde hair behind her ear and blinked her ice-blue eyes. Her skin was pale and flawless, her lips full and her eyebrows dark, as if she coloured them, exactly like Cass did with her own.

'Are you OK?' asked Cass, certain her heart would stop if her mother didn't speak soon.

'Yeah, I think so,' her mum replied, her voice soft and wistful. 'Hey, did you see that guy give me flowers?'

'I did. It was a sweet gesture.'

'I can't decide whether it wasn't a bit weird. I mean, he acted genuine enough, but you have to be careful, don't you?'

Cass was surprised to realise she would have to help again. 'Did he seem OK?' she asked. 'He seemed perfectly nice to me – I twisted my ankle up on the prom and he asked if I needed any help. I thought he was just a pleasant, decent man.'

Jen nodded and shrugged at the same time. 'I gave him my phone number, but now I'm wondering if that was a mistake. I did get – you know – that magnetic pull you feel when you *like* like someone. But I've just been dumped, for goodness' sake. Maybe I should tell that Jake guy I'm not interested. Although he probably won't call me anyway. Jeez, why am I telling you all this stuff?' She threw her hands up, and then raked her fingers through her hair.

'I don't mind at all,' said Cass, sitting on the pebbles. 'Sometimes it's good to have a stranger to talk to – better than a friend who'll say what you want them to say instead of being honest.'

'Yeah, I s'pose. Oh, my name is Jen, by the way.'

'C-Caroline,' said Cass, smiling.

'Well, what do you think, Caroline? Shall I agree to see him if he calls me?'

'Well,' Cass wrapped her arms around her legs, mirroring her mother, 'you did get that immediate physical attraction you mentioned.'

'Yeah, I did,' Jen chewed her bottom lip. 'Maybe I will, then.'

'Sure, do it. You should meet somewhere public and take sensible precautions just in case, but I have a really good feeling about the two of you.'

'You do?'

Cass nodded eagerly. 'Sure. He's got to be better than the jerk who dumped you.'

Jen rolled her eyes. 'Sam? I don't want to talk about him. He's a jerk, like you said. I don't know why I ever went out with him. My best friend Alice tried to warn me off him, but I was too dumb to take her advice, even though she dated him about a year ago. She was absolutely right about him. I definitely owe her an apology.'

Cass had never heard her dad mention anyone called Alice. Perhaps she was one of the nameless guests in the wedding photos. The wedding that would never happen if she couldn't persuade her mum to give Jake Patch a chance.

'She'll understand, I bet she will.'

'I s'pect so. She's a decent person, Alice.'

A comfortable silence fell and Cass wished she could stay here all day so that the two of them could chat about nothing in particular and everything important in the world. Before she'd come here, the idea of "meet, chat and leave" had been so simple, but now it was clear how damned hard the leaving part was going to be.

'Are you seeing anyone, Caroline?' Jen asked.

'No. I was, but he was a nightmare,' she said, adding, 'Actually, I'm bi, so I'm not restricted to seeing just boys anyway.' Cass's admission surprised her more than it did her mother. She had never revealed that to another human being before, not even Lo, but now she'd outed herself – and pretty abruptly, at that – to her mother. 'Oh, crap. I mean, I'm not trying to pick you up or anything. I've never told anyone else what I just told you. I don't know why I said it.'

Jen smiled. 'Don't worry, Caroline, it's cool. I'm not shocked or offended or anything. If you haven't told anyone else, I'm flattered you chose me to open up to. I don't expect it's an easy topic to broach in casual conversation.'

'You're right there. I haven't told my dad. I think he's kinda guessed, but I want to tell him properly.'

'Nor your mum?'

Cass shook her head. She had told her mum, but it didn't count because Jen had no idea she was speaking to her future daughter.

'Mum died when I was tiny.' Her fingers reached automatically for the locket which hung around her neck, containing a tiny photograph of her mother.

'Oh, I'm sorry. Well, don't wait for your dad to bring up the subject of your sexuality,' advised Jen, her eyebrows knotting together. 'Do it on your own terms, Caroline.'

'Yeah. Yeah, you're right.'

'You don't think it will bother him, do you? He won't disown you or anything, will he? If he does, you can come to mine. I have a flat in the Old Town.'

Cass smiled. 'No, Dad won't throw me out. I'm sure of it.'

The pair smiled at one another. Jen laid her hand gently on Cass's arm and Cass broke into goose bumps.

'You were right about chatting with a stranger,' agreed Jen. 'It can help a lot.'

'Yep.' Cass glanced at her wristwatch, aware that she still needed to find a quiet place from where she could disappear back to her own time without drawing attention. She certainly didn't want to flick out of existence in front of her mum.

'Somewhere you need to be?' asked Jen.

'What?'

'You were looking at your watch.'

'Oh, um, yeah. Soonish, but not immediately.'

'Perhaps we could meet for a coffee sometime,' suggested Jen.

Torn, Cass couldn't decide whether to agree to the offer, knowing she'd have to let her mother down, or say no straight off. She didn't want to hurt Jen's feelings either way.

Saved by a flash of an idea, she said, 'I'm sorry, I don't live locally. I'm here visiting a friend.'

Jen deflated. 'Oh. Pity. I felt like we could be good friends, you and I.'

'Yeah.' Cass bit back tears.

Jen stood up. 'I think I'll go home now. It's been a bit of a day, hasn't it? But it was lovely meeting you, Caroline.'

'You too,' said Cass, squinting into the glare of the sun. She wanted to say, *Do you have to go? I'm your daughter from the future and I want to learn literally everything there is to know about you,* but, of course, she could not. 'You going to go out with Jake?' she asked instead. Unsure whether they'd mentioned his name, she panicked that her mother would pick up on her mistake. Luckily, she didn't.

'If he calls, yeah, I will. But I'll be careful, like you suggested.'

'Great. I really hope you guys get on and all.'

'Thanks. Erm, bye.'

'Bye, Jen,' Cass gave a feeble wave and Jen turned and walked away. 'Love you, Mum,' Cass whispered.

Tears flowed hot and fast now and she didn't try to stop them. When Jen's back was nothing more than a barely distinguishable blob in the distance, Cass swiped her face dry with the back of her hand.

'Damn. I meant to tell her to take special care crossing at traffic lights – to say I'd almost been k-killed myself and that drivers are all maniacs. That people sometimes talk on phones when they're driving and that she has to be ultra, ultra-careful. I might have saved her life. How long do I have, Drusilla?'

'About three minutes, Cass,' said the sprite.

'I'll never catch up to her now. What an idiot.' She added a string of swear words, which didn't help at all.

'We should find a quiet place to travel back from; a public lavatory, perhaps,' suggested Drusilla.

'God, no. Anyway, what if it's shut in 2019?' Cass stood and hurried back to the prom. Scurrying into the lower prom area known as "Bottle Alley", she ducked into the first of the exit stairwells leading to the upper level.

'One minute to go,' warned Drusilla.

Cass backed against the wall and waited. After the longest forty-five seconds of her life, the sprite commenced the countdown.

'—three, two, one.'

Snap!

Cass appeared back in the alley, beside the black bins.

Leaning against the wall, her teeth chattering, she said, 'I did it. I met her.' But all she could think about was that she'd lost her mother again, and this time, she was old enough to feel the trauma of it.

Chapter 23

Paradoxically Speaking

'How did that work – that thing I did?' Cass asked Drusilla later, after they'd returned home and Cass had taken a shower to fully revive herself.

'Which thing are you enquiring about, specifically?' asked Drusilla.

'I made my parents meet. They might never have crossed paths at all if not for me, but I could only be there because they had met, on the beach that day. If I hadn't been there, they wouldn't have met and I wouldn't exist. It's a whole circular paradox, isn't it?'

'It does seem that way, yes.'

'So how does that work? How is it possible?'

'Why would I know?' said the sprite, haughtily.

'Well, you're the expert on time.'

'I am—'

'A sprite? I know.'

'I wasn't going to say that.'

'Oh. Sorry. What then?'

'Of course, I am an expert on time, but this is outside of even my vast experience. I have never been a party to the creation of a circular paradox before.'

'So you're no better than me,' said Cass.

'I wouldn't go that far,' Drusilla replied, tightly.

Cass wiggled an eyebrow and gave a self-satisfied smile, pleased to have found a time-related question the sprite couldn't answer. She wondered if Lucia might be able to shed any light on it.

'—and don't have the obvious limitations of being a linear-living human,' Drusilla was saying.

'Sorry, what?'

'Oh, never mind. You wouldn't understand anyway.'

'Don't you have any theories about how a paradox can happen?' asked Cass, climbing onto her bed and crossing her legs.

'I don't indulge in theories.'

'Oh, come on, everyone indulges in theories. Oh no, wait. You're a sprite and sprites don't do dumb human things like guessing, am I right?'

'Precisely so.'

'Hey, I can't have damaged reality by doing what I did, can I? I mean, I haven't caused, like, a tear in the space-time continuum, have I?'

Drusilla gave a loud sigh. 'Time cannot tear, Cass. Has this notion come from a fictional work again?'

Cass blushed. 'Maybe. Anyway, how do you know it can't? You said this was outside of your experience.'

The sprite tutted. 'The truth about time is more complex than you will ever imagine. Your writers could never do it justice, nor hope to understand a tenth of it, let alone write about it with any accuracy.'

'Dad says time is a human construct,' said Cass.

'Hah! What a narrow-minded statement. The way each living thing perceives time is different. I could not hope to explain it to you; you lack the language to describe it, and also the depth of thought required to assimilate the information.'

'You mean I'm stupid?' asked Cass, bristling with anger.

'Merely human.'

'Oh. Great. Thanks for that assessment.'

She leapt off the bed and ran downstairs to find her dad's laptop and its charge cable.

'More research?' asked Drusilla when Cass returned.

'Not this time. I want to record everything that happened today. Every single minute detail I can remember. Oh, wait.'

She disappeared again, but this time only into her dad's room. Returning clutching her parents' wedding photo, which she had taken from his bedroom wall, she wiped the surface dust off it using a corner of her duvet cover, then leaned it carefully against her pillow before opening the laptop. Soon she was deep in thought, her fingers flying across the keys as she typed and typed.

Occasionally she paused, staring either at the photograph propped up on her pillow or at the blank lilac wall, before tapping away again. She wrote about her day as if it were a witness statement, full of facts but few emotions, because if she didn't shut her feelings away, she would start sobbing and be unable to write. She included everything. The precise spot where her mother had been sitting; how far out the tide had been; every tiny detail of what her mother had been wearing – and her dad, too. Everything down to the colours of the flowers her dad had given her mum went into Cass's account. She wanted to remember it all, and not let any of it become lost. It was too precious a memory to lose an iota of it.

By the time she'd finished, the sun was setting and the glow from the computer screen puddled around her, while the rest of the room sank back into the gloom of twilight. Cass read through her work and made a few minor adjustments before saving the final version, uploading it onto *the cloud* and closing down the laptop. Then, she picked up the photo of her parents and lay on the bed, hugging it to her chest in the darkness.

'Do you plan travelling back to find your father now?' asked the sprite, startling Cass. 'I wouldn't recommend it, given that you have travelled twice today already. It is a draining experience, physically, or so I am led to believe.'

Cass nodded, realising Drusilla was right. She ached everywhere – more like a septuagenarian than a teenager. Her shoulders drooped wearily.

'I am tired. It's been a great day, but also an emotionally difficult one. Even if I wasn't tired, my emotions are all over the place and one more trip – let alone to Wartime Britain – doesn't feel possible. Besides, it's getting late and I haven't remotely sorted out what to wear: I'm certain jeans and a jumper won't hack it in 1943.'

'You would look out-of-place, yes. Do you wish me to tell you what the people your father and I saw were typically wearing?'

'No, not now. I need to sleep. I'm going to have to make something to eat first, to stop my grumbling tummy keeping me awake, but I'm not doing anything else apart from the necessities today. As you keep reminding me, Drusilla, I'm only human.'

Chapter 24

Forties Fashion

Cass reached for her mobile phone to check the time, but instead knocked it onto the floor. Groaning, she leaned over the side of the bed to retrieve it. The time on the screen read 11.13am.

'Urggh!' she moaned, turning onto her back. Sunday was half gone and she still had another time travelling adventure to plan, and hopefully complete, before returning to college on Monday.

She had spent the night dreaming about her last jaunt through time. Instead of being full of lovely memories of her chat with her mother on the beach, the dreams had been deeply affected by worries about damaging time. In the last dream, which eventually woke her up, a great gaping, jagged tear appeared in the sky above where Cass and her mother sat on the beach in St Leonards. The pair huddled together, terror-stricken, and suddenly an enormous hand reached through the tear and grabbed Cass within its strong fist. Up, up, up it carried her, through the rip and beyond into a shadowy, timeless oblivion. The reassurances from Drusilla that time could not tear had clearly not reached Cass's subconscious mind.

Now she was awake, an alternative solution to the paradox conundrum popped into her head. She wished she could have thought of it last night and avoided the sleep-disturbing nightmares.

She called out to Drusilla, eager for a second opinion. 'Hey, Drusilla, I think there's an answer to the paradox problem.'

'Oh?' replied the sprite, in the tone a parent uses to a child who they think is about to suggest something foolish.

Cass ignored the tone and continued. 'Yes. Perhaps my being there distracted Dad from what he would have done if I hadn't been there. It doesn't take much to change the course of history. Isn't there something called the Butterfly Effect, where a small change can lead to big consequences? The whole thing is really difficult for me to get my head around, but I suppose it would be – paradoxes are all about contradiction.'

'Your hypothesis is not impossible.' The tone this time was one of surprise. 'Although...'

'You mean I may not be stupid after all?'

'That was your choice of word, not mine. And yet, you are still human.'

'Sure,' said Cass, exasperated by Drusilla's rigid opinion of humanity.

* * *

After doing last night's washing up, Cass made herself a slice of toast using bread a day beyond its use-by date, poured herself a glass of disappointingly flat lemonade and took a seat at the dining table. Retrieving her phone from her pocket, she called her dad's work to reassure his boss that he was getting better and would hopefully be able to return in a couple of days. After she'd hung up, she realised her fingers had been crossed throughout the call.

'Right then, time to think about clothing.' She typed the words *UK fashion 1943* into the search bar on her phone's browser. A few minutes later, she was scrolling through an article about wartime wardrobes.

'What? Clothes were rationed? I thought it was only food,' she said. 'It says here people were allocated clothing coupons and the number of coupons they were entitled to decreased as the war progressed. Jeez, imagine that. Need a coat? Save up your tokens and hope you can get it in time for the onset of winter. Crazy.'

She read further. 'And here it says fabrics were limited and clothing designs had to be altered to use less material. Socks. They limited the length of men's socks, for goodness' sake. That's madness, isn't it, Drusilla?'

'I have no idea. The length of men's socks isn't a matter of enormous importance to me,' replied the sprite.

Cass raked her hand through her hair. 'I suppose not. I thought austerity was a modern thing, but apparently not. I mean I should have realised – it was wartime, for goodness' sake. At least this *make do and mend* scheme they talk about wasn't introduced until September 1943, so it won't limit my choices even more. Imagine mothers trying to make flour bags into boys' shorts. Those must have been horribly scratchy, don't you think?'

'I couldn't say. I am non-corporeal. Neither scratchy trousers nor short socks have any impact upon me.'

'Oh, right. Daft question,' said Cass, adding in a low mutter, 'But then, it *was* rhetorical.'

After a few more minutes of browsing, Cass suddenly asked, 'Hey, you can tell me what date and time he went to, can't you? I mean, there's no rule stopping you, is there?'

'No, there is no rule stopping me. Your father didn't ask for a specific date, but The Infinity Glass took us to 23 May 1943.'

Cass heaved a sigh of relief. 'How about the time?'

'It was 12.37pm.'

Cass nodded. 'A bit random, but OK. Was it a warm day? Cold, wet, blowing half a gale?'

'Moderate. Some patchy cloud, but no rain and no strong winds either.'

'Great. No coat required. Damn, it looks like most women and girls wore dresses. I don't own anything like any of these.'

'The women we saw were dressed like those in your pictures,' said Drusilla, unhelpfully.

Cass ignored the sprite and tried to think back to her school history lessons in an attempt to find an alternative. A smile spread across her face.

'Land girls.' She typed the words into her browser and asked it for images. 'Damn. It says the uniform they wore was a green jersey and brown breeches and I don't have anything like that either. Oh, but see here, several of these pictures show land girls wearing dungarees and shirts. I have a pair of beige dungarees I ordered on a whim last spring. I hope they fit; I don't think I ever tried them on. I'll go and check in a minute. I can borrow a belt from Dad's drawer. I'll check out the shirts. And the shoes, too.'

'I hate to put obstacles in the way of your idea, but why would a land girl be walking around in the Old Town area?' asked Drusilla.

'Oh. Well, they had to live somewhere,' said Cass, zooming in on a photo of a group of land girls to check what they were wearing on their feet. 'They can't all have lived on farms, surely. Some must have travelled rather than living on the job. Anyway, I only want to try and get the basic era right clothing-wise. As long as I can wear clothes that don't stand out like a sore thumb, I think it will be fine. I have limited options.'

'Given the bombing raid and all that went along with it, I imagine you could go dressed as a pantomime horse without anyone caring too much,' said Drusilla.

Cass smiled, despite the seriousness of the situation which lay ahead of her. 'Maybe so, but I'm not taking chances. I want to blend in. I wonder if I can find something to tie around my head. I used to own a cloth hair band a bit like this one – although I think this picture is from a BBC drama rather than being a real photo from the forties, but oh well. Perhaps I've still got that hair band. Ooh, maybe I should Google the date in May we'll be going to and see what comes up, so I can be as prepared as possible. If a bomb was dropped on Hastings, surely there'd be record of it online.'

She typed in the date and added *Hastings* after it.

'Shit. Shit, shit, shit, shit! This is a problem. A huge problem.'

'What is it?'

'Twenty-five killed, eighty-five injured. Second biggest bombing raid on Hastings, in terms of casualties. The Swan Hotel in the High Street destroyed. Were you and Dad in the High Street, Drusilla?'

'Describe where it is and I can tell you.'

Cass gave her directions to get to the High Street. 'And there's a garden with a plaque. I'm ashamed to say I've never read it.'

'I didn't see a garden, but apart from that it sounds, from your description, as if that's where we were when the explosion happened,' said Drusilla.

'Wait.' Cass scrolled down the article. 'That's what the plaque is there for. The gardens are where The Swan Hotel used to stand. Hold on, here's a casualty list.' Cass read the list of names, unable to breathe. Jake Patch was not on the list and there were no unidentified bodies either. 'His name's not on here, although I don't imagine he has any ID on him.'

'I already told you he didn't die.'

'You said he didn't die before The Infinity Glass returned you here. You said you weren't sure. This is the official casualty list and he isn't on it, Drusilla. He's still there somewhere, even if he's injured. I should be able to find him and bring him home.'

'Of course. As I said. I do think it would be sensible to avoid the precise location, however. Or you could choose to arrive the following day – the area ought to have been made safer by then.'

'But Dad wouldn't be there the day after, would he? I know I can't chance getting myself killed by turning up during this – what did they call it? – this *tip and run raid*. We have to arrive when the raid is over, but not too long afterwards. It makes sense.'

A few minutes later, Cass stood facing the full-length mirror in her room, nodding as she took in the new her.

'This would be a great outfit for a fancy dress party. I do look the part, don't you think, Drusilla?'

'You do, Cass,' admitted the sprite. 'I'm impressed.'

'Really?'

'Yes, you have made yourself into a perfectly acceptable facsimile of the girls in the photographs.'

Cass took a deep breath. 'Then I'm nearly ready to go and save my father. We can leave from the alley in the Old Town again. Did Dad do that?'

'No. He was here when we left.'

'Here in the house? Why'd he...? Oh, never mind. I think it would help to devise at least some kind of plan of action before we leave.'

PART 3: THE BARGAIN HUNTER
Chapter 25
The Swan

Jake Patch pushed himself up onto his knees using his good arm, his eyes wide with terror and his pupils dilated. His heart thumped hard, as if it were being beaten with a blacksmith's hammer. A bead of sweat trickled into the hollow of his cheek and he scowled at his right arm, which hung stiff and useless like a lump of lead. The mere weight of it caused him pain and he tried his best to support it with his other hand.

It was actually more impaired than it had been on the day he'd first encountered Drusilla and The Infinity Glass. This time, though, there was no grime-encrusted artefact, nor the associated sprite who spoke with his mother's voice. With the time travel device gone, Patch was well and truly stuck in 1943.

'Oi, mate, this way.' The voice, which must have been nearby, sounded oddly muffled, as if heard under water. Patch struggled to clamber to his feet, but fell back to his knees. His head throbbed, his arm was still not functioning and his shoes crunched through something gritty when he adjusted his footing. He tried vainly to remember why he was here, and indeed where here was.

'This way,' said the voice again.

Patch forced his eyes to focus. A plump man dressed in what appeared to be a dark blue boiler suit approached. The outfit had a badge above the left breast pocket bearing the letters ARP. A light-coloured satchel was slung across the man's shoulder and he wore a brimmed tin hat with a prominent letter "W" on the front, like the air-raid warden in a comedy film Patch had seen, based on a TV series he was too young to remember properly. He dashed forward and grabbed Patch by his good arm, yanking him to his feet.

'Come on,' he said, firmly.

The weight distribution of his injured shoulder shifted, making Patch wince from the pain. 'A… a bomb?' he muttered, his foggy brain finding the word from nowhere. The number 1943 drifted into his consciousness and meandered away again before he could catch it.

'Yep, tha's right, there was a bomb, mate. A bunch of 'em, in fact – the incendiary type. The planes have all gone now, though, and I need to go and help – see if any poor soul is alive in the ruins of The Swan. I have to admit it doesn't look hopeful. You OK? You're a bit wobbly on your pins. I thought you were a goner when I first clapped eyes on you, lying face down on the ground.'

'I'll be fine. My other arm hurts and I can't move it, but I think it will be OK.'

The air-raid warden let go of Patch's elbow and Patch cradled his right arm once again. The pain subsided, but only marginally.

'At least you're alive, and you can walk,' said the warden. 'Get yourself away from here and have the arm sorted out. Walking wounded to the RESH – if they've got room for one more today. If they haven't been hit too. Oh, and the government recommends you carry a gas mask, mate. You appear to have left yours behind today. Not the smartest idea.'

Patch nodded, trying to invent a plausible excuse for his lack of gas mask, but then a siren broke into a solemn wail nearby, increasing in volume to a steady drone.

'Shit!' exclaimed Patch, glancing skyward for any sign of German planes.

'Don't panic, son, it's the all-clear,' explained the warden, reassuringly.

All the while they'd been speaking, Patch realised, the warden had been staring past him, over his shoulder, his greying bushy eyebrows lowered and drawn together. Patch swivelled around to see what the older man was looking at.

'Crap!' he cried. His knees buckled and the man grabbed him to stop him falling.

The building Patch had been walking towards what felt like mere moments earlier – a hotel, was it? – had been reduced to still crumbling remains amidst an enormous pile of rubble and wood which spilled across the narrow road, totally blocking it. What remained of the ground floor was incredibly precarious, as if it might collapse and join the rest of the rubble at any moment. The fragments of the ruined hotel were alight with angry licking flames and a plume of swirling smoke trailed upward into the sky. Patch gasped, only now registering the awful acrid stench hanging in the air, the heat of the fire on his skin and the shattered glass crunching underfoot. The windows of several surrounding buildings had been blown completely away by the blast and someone stood beside where a second-storey window had once been opposite the ruined hotel, their hands covering their face. Several men clambering across the rubble were searching for survivors, but they were held back by the heat of the blaze. The warden was right: it was extremely unlikely any soul had survived the bombing of The Swan.

As the all clear droned on, a memory of another siren swam to the front of Patch's mind. *A siren*, he thought, still gawping at the unbelievable devastation while desperately trying to recall what had happened and what he had seen. Yes, he'd heard a siren before. His memory of recent events started to come back to him.

First came the loud, dull, wailing note of the warning siren, similar to the all-clear except that it undulated in a droning wave. The mere memory of the sorrowful tone made goose bumps rise along the length of his spine and all the way up into his hairline. He had recognised the sound straight away and instinct told him to get off the streets, but he didn't know where to go. Then he remembered that the caves on the West Hill, transformed into a tourist attraction and re-named *Smuggler's Adventure* in Patch's time, had been used as an air-raid shelter during the war. A passageway between the tightly packed houses would lead him straight up to the West Hill and he had run in that direction, still clutching The Infinity Glass.

But then the planes had come, emerging from the clouds and dropping to barely above roof height, their engines a low, ominous growl and their spinning propellers nothing but a smudge against the sky. Patch had seen similar ones at an air show once, years ago, but today they had a far more deadly purpose. They swept over the rooftops, ten or more of them, several firing machine guns – as if bombs would not suffice. Terror filled him from head to toe and his feet turned momentarily to leaden blocks. In the second it took him to decide on a direction of flight, it happened. Oddly, he couldn't remember the explosion which knocked him off his feet.

How long ago was that? He couldn't recall. In his mind, it could have been seconds or hours, although it was probably only a minute or two.

Remembering the device that had brought him here, he frantically checked the ground around his feet for remnants of it. He realised he'd never be able to tell the pale blue glass from all the fragments of shattered windows strewn around, so he searched instead for the metal casing and tell-tale blobs of coloured liquid. There was no sign of it at all. Was that good or bad? It wasn't here, which must mean it had survived the blast. But its absence also meant he couldn't return home.

Suddenly, he had a memory of a woman. She'd been on the High Street, too, running hand-in-hand with a child of around five or six. Someone had called to her from the doorway of the hotel while the sirens were blaring and the thrumming aircraft engines grew closer. She went inside – with the child.

No!

At the thought of a mother and child lying mortally injured beneath the rubble, Patch gave serious consideration to the idea of staying to help search, but his arm was useless. He'd only be in the way of the able-bodied rescuers who were already congregating and assessing how best to approach what remained of the building across the huge and unstable pile of rubble.

So instead, Patch stumbled away.

The RESH the warden had referred to was the Royal East Sussex Hospital, which had closed before Patch turned twenty, sometime during the early 1990s. It was a long way to walk from here to the hospital and he decided medical help would most likely be available if he went to the caves, as he'd originally planned. The obvious route now blocked, he tried to find an alternative, thankful that the wailing sirens had stopped and the planes had moved on, their pilots having turned homeward to report on their success.

Strange how death can be a matter of perspective during wartime, he thought.

A string of weary-looking people were emerging from a passageway further along the High Street. They gathered on the road, staring open-mouthed at the obliterated hotel and leaning on one another for both moral and physical support. They were probably Old-Towners who had sheltered in the caves or some other safe place and were now returning home after the all-clear.

Patch went to wait at the High Street end of the passageway, only now taking the time to assess his injuries. His right shoulder roared with pain and his fingers were numb and pale. The heels of both hands were badly scraped and cut and he could taste blood on his bottom lip. Other than that, he'd got off lightly. He couldn't help but wonder how many souls had been lost in The Swan. If he ever found a way to return home, he'd look it up on the internet. If he didn't, the local paper would tell him, assuming it was still being printed during the war.

Patch realised he was shaking. What if he was stuck here permanently? What if destiny meant him to remain in this time he had accidentally visited? He surely wouldn't live long enough to see his daughter again.

'Deal with the things you can fix,' he told himself, sternly.

Chapter 26

St Clement's Caves

By backtracking along the now straggly line of locals going the opposite way, Patch discovered a closer entrance to the caves than the one he was familiar with. The authorities must have opened a lower entry point to make the shelter more accessible to people in a hurry to find cover, he thought.

It was odd visiting the caves again. He'd last visited when Cass was about seven, and then they had been full of interactive tech and tales of piracy. He vaguely remembered navigating low, claustrophobic tunnels and entering a sizeable cavern described as "The Ball Room". The cavern he entered now bore little resemblance to his recollections of the twenty-first century tourist attraction.

A string of bulbs was festooned across the ceiling like oversized fairy lights and a variety of metal-framed beds, some single and others bunkbeds, stood in neat lines. Being as it was the middle of the day and not long after the all-clear, all were unoccupied, except for one where a boy of about seven sat on the edge with his feet swinging, scuffing the concrete floor. His arms were crossed defiantly and his chin rested on his chest. A woman Patch assumed was his mother perched beside him with a tight-lipped expression on her face.

'Jimmy, you're going to have to go back to the schoolroom else Miss Eldridge will have your guts for garters tomorrow,' she said as Patch passed.

'Don't want to,' huffed the boy.

'If your father was here, he'd take you by the ear and make you, my boy. Don't think I won't do it, either, because I will.'

Patch pitied both boy and mother in equal measures. There had been plenty of days when Cass was that age when she hadn't wanted to go to school. He'd been considerably less forceful about it than Jimmy's mother, though, figuring his daughter knew herself and her own needs better than he did.

At a table positioned directly below one of the hanging lights, a couple of grey-haired men were playing cards, giving an occasional angry glance towards the still warring mother and son. The loud conversation was probably distracting them from their game.

'Tea?' called a cheerful voice.

Patch's eyes adjusted to the dull light level. Beyond the beds, he found the source of the voice: a grey-haired woman of around sixty, sitting at a table which bore a cylindrical urn and an assortment of tin mugs. She wore a man's black coat unbuttoned over her dress.

'The all-clear sounded a while ago,' she added, 'so you could go about your normal business now, but tea's available if you're interested.'

'Erm, yes. Why not? Two sugars,' said Patch, approaching the table unsteadily.

The woman tipped her head to the side and raised an eyebrow, evaluating her visitor with piercing, intelligent eyes.

'Sugar? Not unless you've brought your own. There's a war on, unless you'd forgotten,' she said, haughtily.

'I'm sorry, I...' The room swam slowly around him and Patch reached for the nearest bed frame to sit down. A tingling sensation ran up his right arm and into his neck. 'I don't know if I can...'

The woman rounded the table fast. 'Rose!' she called. 'We have an injured man here.' To Patch, she said, 'You weren't near The Swan, were you? I hear it's bad there.' She crouched in front of him. 'Help's coming, sir. Rose, are you coming?'

A woman appeared out of the gloom and approached, but Patch barely registered her presence. Blackness closed in around him and his eyes rolled back.

PART 4: THE BARGAIN HUNTER's DAUGHTER

Chapter 27

Rescue Mission

Cass sat cross-legged in the living room, wearing her land girl outfit.

'If a bomb exploded near my dad, there are a few logical choices for what he'd have done next,' she said. 'If he was hurt badly, he'd have been taken to hospital. If he had a minor injury, then he might still have gone to get treatment, so again he'd be at the hospital. If he wasn't hurt, he might have helped people who were, in which case he could be getting them to the hospital. Looking for him at the hospital has to be the most logical choice. One thing Dad certainly won't be doing is standing around waiting to be rescued. He won't have realised that's a possibility, will he? Poor Dad. Imagine believing you're stuck in the past.'

'Are you thinking aloud, Cass, or would you like my opinion?' asked Drusilla.

'Both.'

'Well then, your logic seems sound. It's unlikely your father would stay in the High Street, but if it transpires he's not at the hospital either, how will we find him?'

Cass sighed. 'I'm not sure. We don't have long and we'll only get one attempt.'

'Because you can't go to the same year twice.'

'Exactly; the bloody rules. Anyway, it would be easy if he'd left us a trail to follow, but he won't have done that. Like I said, he'll have no clue The Infinity Glass came back here at all, let alone that I got it repaired and now we're mounting a rescue mission.'

'We – or rather you – could ask around in the area of the High Street. Enquire whether anyone saw him and knows where he went.'

'Maybe.' Cass wrapped her arms around her middle. 'Is it likely, though? There would be better things for people to do than watch the movements of a random stranger.'

'But asking around would be a more logical method of finding him than going to search a single possible location on the off-chance he will be there.'

'You said yourself he wouldn't be in the High Street, though,' commented Cass, angrily. 'How about I arrive as early as I possibly can – after the bomb, I mean? To retrieve him before he has a chance to go disappearing off anywhere else.'

'You cannot afford to put yourself in a place where the danger level is high. There is a risk both of you could become stuck – or worse.'

Cass heaved a heavy sigh. 'You're right. He's depending on me. I can't fling myself into the middle of a bombing raid.' She remained silent for a time while she thought the problem through. 'Well, I have less than an hour to find him. If I think he's in the hospital – and I honestly believe that's the most logical place to look for him – I should travel from somewhere close to the old hospital site, so I won't have to waste a chunk of my time walking there. The hospital used to be located just outside the town centre. There's housing there now, but Dad often talks about when it was still a hospital. He spent hours with Grandma in the waiting room there the day he fell out of a tree and sprained his ankle. Thank goodness he shared those childhood stories with me, hey?'

'And if he is not in the hospital?'

Cass shrugged. 'I don't know. Try to get across to the Old Town fast enough that there's a chance of finding him before the artefact brings me back home.'

'I fear your strategy could fail and time will expire before Patch is found. You should be prepared to face that possibility.'

'Thanks for sharing your wisdom,' said Cass, sarcastically. 'Maybe it's a shot in the dark, but I literally have no choice. I have to pick somewhere to start, and the hospital seems like a decent idea. No Old Town alleyway for me this time; we'll find a quiet location much closer to where the Royal Sussex – no, the Royal *East* Sussex – used to stand to save time that I can't afford to waste. Given it's a housing estate now, there must be somewhere I can stand for long enough to, you know...' she gave a single loud click of her fingers to demonstrate.

'You are the custodian,' said the sprite. 'The choice is ultimately yours to make.'

'Then I'm going to make it. We're starting at the hospital. I'm going to ask to be taken to two hours after he left.'

'Oh? Why so long?'

'Because it would take a while for him to travel from the Old Town across to the hospital. If he was taken by ambulance – did they even have ambulances? Was 1943 pre-NHS? Probably.' Cass shivered. 'Anyway, however he travelled there, it would take time.'

'Won't you risk missing him, though? Couldn't he have been treated and left again within the space of two hours?'

'No, I don't think so. There was a bomb explosion. There was definitely a whole bunch of wounded. It would take quite a while to treat them all. If he's badly injured, he'll have been admitted. If not, he'll be waiting in a queue of other people needing to be seen less urgently. We'll find him, Drusilla.'

Cass tried hard to blank out thoughts of how it would be if he couldn't be found, but a black hole opened up inside her, right next to the one which ripped open when she had to deal with losing her mother for a second time. She couldn't lose them both.

* * *

Cass approached the hospital site via what she assumed had been the original steeply sloping access road, now blocked to traffic by a pair of offset railings. The modern buildings had been constructed before she was born.

She'd always considered her father's story, recounting his childhood visit to the hospital, to be nothing more than a mildly amusing anecdote. He was thrilled to share elements of his childhood with her and she could repeat most of his stories word-for-word. Cass smiled, remembering how animated he became when telling her about things that had happened before she came along, even the stories that riled him most: those involving her grandmother.

Impulsively ducking in behind a line of black wheelie bins parading on the pavement ready for collection, Cass immediately regretted her choice. The smell of rotting kitchen waste made her wrinkle her nose.

'Ugh! There must be cleaner places than bin areas for a person to time travel from.' Her unexpected exclamation sent a fat tortoiseshell cat scurrying away from between the bins to hide beneath a nearby car.

Cass extracted The Infinity Glass from inside the satchel. Unbeknown to her, it was the same one her father had used when he time travelled to 1937. Peering above the top of the bin, she checked there was nobody else around. Almost retching when the latest in a string of unpleasant odours reached her nose, she stood up.

'Sod this,' she said, grimacing as she strode away from the bins into the open. 'There's nobody here anyway, so I'm gonna do this somewhere less stinky. Take me to 2.30pm on 23 May 1943.'

Chapter 28

Matron

There was a sound like a thousand people simultaneously snapping their fingers and a red brick wall appeared inches from her nose. Cass reached a tentative hand to touch it, part of her expecting her fingers to sink into the surface as if it were a shimmering magical pool.

'Are we in the right place at the right time, Drusilla?' she asked, realising that if she had arrived a metre further forward, she'd have been staring through one of the tall windows and might have given someone inside a nasty shock. Two metres would have taken her inside the hospital.

'Yes, it is the time and date you requested.'

'Thank you. Then there's no time to waste.'

Slipping The Infinity Glass back inside the satchel, where it lay nestled in a bed of distinctly modern bubble-wrap, Cass tried to work out how to get into the hospital. When no entrance was immediately visible, she chose to go to her left, where a driveway swept around the building like a long, protective arm.

Turning the corner, she came face to face with a startled man. His short coppery-brown hair stuck up in tufts above a bandana of white bandage wrapped around his head, and his right arm was encased in a plaster cast and secured with a sling. The man sucked on a cigarette and puffed a cloud of smoke, which Cass found way worse than the stench of the bins. He wore long, plain pyjamas so she assumed he must be a patient who had popped outside for a smoke.

'You look lost,' observed the man, staring at her intensely.

'I'm not lost,' she retorted. 'I'm just not sure where the way in is.'

He grinned and jerked his head to his right, the same way Cass had been going anyway.

'Main entrance is round that way, love. I s'pose you wouldn't want to share a fag before you go, would you?' He took the cigarette from the corner of his mouth and offered it to her.

'No.' Cass side-stepped him. 'I don't smoke. But thanks for the offer.'

Continuing around the building, she passed several more of the tall windows. She peeked quickly in through each of them, hoping to spot her dad, but wary of being noticed in case people inside reported her as a trespasser. She didn't want any trouble; nobody here could vouch for her or verify her identity. Even her grandmother was only four years old in 1943.

Cass soon happened upon what appeared to be an entrance to the hospital, standing at the top of a dog-legged stairway with more than a dozen steps up to reach it. The stairway would be more appropriate outside a stately home than at a hospital, she thought.

'What the hell?' she heard herself say. 'That's not the most accessible, is it? How the heck do they get people inside from an ambulance?' Her dad regularly complained about health and safety having gone mad in the modern world, but having to climb stairs to access a hospital felt utterly counter-intuitive.

'Ambulance entrance is round the back, love,' said a voice. She turned to find the patient she'd met a couple of minutes earlier standing right behind her, grinning impishly from ear to ear.

She took a swift step back and the smile melted from his face.

'Sorry, miss. I didn't mean to scare you. I'm harmless, honest I am. The entrance for emergencies is round the far side of the building. Are you looking for someone? There were loads of casualties from that bloody air raid earlier. I hear the staff were worked off their feet.'

'I'm trying to find my father. I think he was in the Old Town when it happened.'

The man gave a slight grimace. 'Well, I hope you find him. Would you like me to come with you, show you the entrance? I promise to behave better. I'm terribly bored stuck in here, that's all.'

'No. I'm good. I'll find it. Thank you for your help.' Cass hurried away. She had more important things to do than discourage the flirtations of a man technically old enough to be her great grandfather.

* * *

Cass hurried around to the far side of the hospital and was startled by a tinny jingling sound approaching rapidly from behind. She turned in time to step out of the path of a dark-coloured truck with the words "ARP AMBULANCE" in bold lettering on the side.

The vehicle overtook Cass and came to a halt near the hospital building. Two women climbed from the front seats wearing military-style jackets and trousers. Each wore a hat bearing a silver badge. The pair, focussed on their task, didn't spare Cass a glance as they sped towards the rear of their vehicle, presumably to offload another patient destined for the emergency department.

Confident this was the right door, Cass pushed it open and went inside the building.

She expected to find an administrator or triage nurse on a front desk – someone she could ask about her father – but instead walked into a scene that might just as easily have been a hastily set-up field hospital. Everyone who wasn't a patient was hurrying here and there around the room, and the patients themselves filled most of the available floor space, either sitting on metal chairs or lying on stretchers or the floor.

A red-haired nurse in her early twenties brushed past Cass with an abrupt, 'Excuse me.' She was dressed in a blue uniform with a blood-spattered apron and a stiffly starched white hat.

'I'm looking for my father. Who can I ask, please?' enquired Cass, nervously.

The woman stopped for a moment and stared at Cass, her thin lips pressed tightly together. Then her expression softened.

'Everyone they brought in after the air raid is either here or in the corridor over there,' she explained, waving to her left. 'Except the dead; most of them are in the mortuary already.'

Seeing Cass's horrified expression, the nurse patted her arm, but didn't offer any empty reassurances. Cass decided the nurse had witnessed too much death to throw around pleasantries for the sake of it.

'Have a look around,' said the nurse. 'But don't be getting in the way, and be quick else Matron will chuck you out. Oh, and please don't tell anyone I spoke to you. I'm already on a warning.'

Cass nodded, biting her bottom lip, and the nurse hurried off.

Nearby, someone groaned loudly. A man on a chair sat cradling his arm, blood seeping through a small hole in his shirt. An older man lying on a stretcher a few metres away cried, 'Where's that bloody morphia you promised, nurse?' The young nurse stopped and spoke softly to him before continuing on her way.

It hit Cass how woefully unprepared she had been for the horrors of wounds caused by bombs, bullets and falling masonry. She wrapped her arms around her middle and hoped she'd been wrong after all and her father wasn't here. This was a far cry from the Conquest Hospital A&E where the worst she'd ever encountered in two visits was a man with a bloody nose weaving around and swearing loudly, clearly high on recreational drugs. Wartime wasn't simply a matter of British families erecting corrugated iron air-raid shelters in their gardens or having to "Dig for Victory" and "Make do and mend" while enduring food rationing. This was life and death on the receiving end of German bombs and guns. This was fear and pain and suffering, all while having to carry on with everyday life as well as was humanly possible. History was so easy when you could learn about it in a classroom instead of encountering the practicalities of it face-to-face.

'Time, Drusilla?' asked Cass, quietly.

'Thirty-nine minutes and a few seconds left, Cass,' Drusilla told her.

'He'd better be here,' Cass mumbled. She systematically checked each chair and stretcher, hoping to see that one familiar face she'd come here to find, while making sure to stay as far away from anyone in a uniform as possible for fear of running into Matron.

She made slow progress – the room was packed tightly with barely a centimetre of floor space in which to manoeuvre. The search proved unsuccessful and she realised she'd have to try the corridor the young nurse had mentioned. She pushed open the door, but it hit a heavy-set middle-aged nurse standing on the other side.

'Sorry, Doc— Who are you? What do you think you're doing here?' asked the nurse, scanning Cass from head to toe and frowning. 'This area is not for the public. Leave now.'

'But I urgently need to—'

'I don't care what you need. Get out or I'll escort you on the end of my shoe!'

Cass nodded, gulped and stepped backwards. The nurse – Matron, Cass guessed – pushed the door shut in her face.

'Did you see him? Was he there?' asked Drusilla.

'I'm not sure,' admitted Cass, forcing back tears. 'I couldn't really see anything because that woman was standing in the way. I understand she has a job to do; I know I shouldn't be here – in more ways than one – but I have to find him. What am I going to do now?'

'Windows?' suggested Drusilla.

'Yes, windows. Thank you,' said Cass, hurrying towards the exit doors.

'You're welcome.'

* * *

Cass peered cautiously through the window straight into the corridor from which she'd been ejected. Her father wasn't among those patients she could see, but the nurse she'd had the brush with was standing with her back to

217

the window, directly between Cass and a couple of other patients. She had to check them all, every last one.

Ready to duck back out of sight should the nurse turn her head, Cass waited. Seconds felt like an eternity and she half wondered if she'd be pulled back to her own time before Matron cleared her field of view.

Then it happened. A female patient lying on a stretcher pointed straight at Cass and Matron swivelled round to face her. Only thirty centimetres and a pane of glass separated them. Blood rushed to Cass's face and Matron puffed up to double her normal size.

'Get away from my windows,' barked the woman.

Cass lifted her chin defiantly. 'No, I will not,' she shouted back.

The woman turned a dangerous shade of purple, then swivelled on her heels and strode towards the door, just as Cass had hoped she would. At last she could see the remaining patients. Both were male. Neither of them was her father.

Then she ran.

Chapter 29

Backtracking

Cass sped past several uniformed nurses chatting in a group, but they were engrossed in conversation and didn't so much as glance at her. She flew past window after window. Her priority right now was escaping the dreaded Matron, who'd put fear into Cass's heart as much as she clearly did to the nurses who worked for her.

Once she was as sure as she could be that she was safe, her mind drifted back to the problem of finding her father.

He must have escaped being badly wounded, but he's not here. Damn it, he's not here.

'Time?' she said, panting and leaning against the wall of the building, her hands braced on her knees.

'Twenty-four and a half minutes,' replied Drusilla.

'Is that all? I don't have a plan B. I didn't look up the local air-raid shelters.'

'How about my plan? Ask in the High Street. Find out if anyone saw him.'

'But with twenty-four minutes left, it's hopeless. If we had that many hours, maybe we'd find him, but minutes?' She shook her head despairingly.

'One can only do what one can do,' said the sprite.

Cass rolled her eyes. 'Well *duh*, of course. But the thought we might have to leave him here in the middle of wartime is horrible. He might be OK at the moment – and that's just an assumption, by the way – but there's still a couple more years of this shit to come. Who knows if he'd live through the next air raid or the one after that?' She pushed away from the wall and tried to remember the way back to the steep access road, but she was so flustered that everything looked different from when she'd walked up it such a short time ago.

'That way, I think. Yes, it must be. There's no point wasting time talking, Drusilla. Every second could count. We're going to the High Street.'

* * *

In the town centre, it was immediately apparent that the air raid had extended far beyond the Old Town. A clear-up operation was already in progress, and small groups of regular civilians were talking quietly while wearily surveying the terrible damage done to their town.

Cass registered the impressive spired clock tower in the centre of the Memorial which appeared – miraculously – to have survived entirely unscathed. Although the area in the centre of town was always referred to as 'the Memorial', it had never occurred to Cass that there must be a reason for the name as the building was long gone by the 21st century.

A car turned on its roof came into sight along the road leading to the seafront. Luckily, nobody lay wounded inside what remained of the vehicle, but a cluster of people loitered nearby and a woman sobbed. Cass guessed some unfortunate person or people had died here. She swallowed hard, trying to force the lump from her throat, but failed.

She rushed past the upturned car and tried not to look at it, instead focussing intently on her goal of reaching the Old Town and finding her father. Frustratingly, her progress was significantly impeded by rubble, which slowed her enough that she caught part of a conversation between two women standing near what would become a pedestrian underpass in decades to come.

'—Norman saw them, so low he could see the pilots' evil faces. I'm lucky I didn't lose him today. They hit the Denmark Arms and The Albany as well. Someone said The Swan in the Old Town has gone, too.'

And this is just Hastings, thought Cass. *Imagine what it must be like in London and other cities across the country.* She frowned, took a deep breath and, reminding herself of the urgency of her father's situation, surveyed the way ahead to determine the best route through the debris. Then she hurried steadfastly onward.

When she reached the turn into the High Street, she asked Drusilla, 'Time?'

'Seven minutes, Cass. I'm sorry.'

'Seven? No. Oh, my goodness.' A short way ahead of her, a pile of rubble entirely blocked the road. An ambulance waited with open doors and, beyond the rubble pile, water sprayed into the air as firefighters struggled to extinguish fires blazing in the wreckage of the hotel.

'Hey! I mean, excuse me, sir,' she said to a man wearing a tin hat with a W on the front. 'Have you seen a man with shoulder-length brown hair and narrow black trousers around here today?'

'Yes, Miss. I did.'

'What?'

'I said yes, Miss.' He smiled kindly. 'You know him, I take it?'

'Yes. Yes, he's my father. Was he hurt? Did you see where he went?'

'He was stunned, I think. He was close when the bombs hit The Swan and was thrown to the ground. He'd hurt his arm or his shoulder, along with some lesser injuries. I told him he should get himself to the hospital, so I expect he's gone there.'

Cass shook her head. 'I came from there. He isn't at the hospital. Where else might he have gone?'

'Any of the shelters. There are a few around here.'

'Where?'

'Well, I know he left the High Street, Miss. Perhaps he went to the caves.'

'The caves?'

'Yes, St Clement's. On the West Hill.'

'I know it. Thank you, I'll go and see,' said Cass. She'd never make it to St Clement's Caves in the few minutes that remained. Instead, she trotted towards the alleyway she and her father had both used for previous time travel trips. Leaning against the wall, she let tears flow hot and fast down her cheeks. He was here, nearby, but her attempt to find him had failed. If she'd come to the High Street first, she might have reached him.

'Ten, nine, eight,' counted Drusilla, quietly.

'Shut up,' muttered Cass.

A few seconds later, she arrived back in the road from which she had left. Forgetting there would be no wall to lean against when she arrived, she fell back on her bottom and cried out. The fat tortoiseshell cat she had encountered earlier, which was washing its whiskers atop a nearby wheelie bin, glared at her and jumped off.

Numbed by the events she had lived through, Cass took several minutes to find the motivation to move from her arrival spot, and it was with leaden feet that she made her way back through the Memorial-less town centre.

Then she remembered Lucia. Could the glassmaker offer any advice – any ways of circumventing The Infinity Glass's rules to enable her to retrieve her father from 1943? Cass suspected not, but vowed to try.

Chapter 30

Plan B

By the time she knocked on Lucia's door, Cass had formulated a plan, although it was reliant on a lot of goodwill and co-operation. She had chosen not to share her idea with Drusilla, and had made a detour home to drop both sprite and Infinity Glass off before paying this visit to the glassmaker. Deep down, part of her blamed the sprite for The Infinity Glass having pulled her back to her own time before she could find her father; it didn't matter that Drusilla wasn't responsible for making the rules.

Cass's grand plan was based on two facts: firstly, the rules said a custodian could not visit any given year more than once, so she could not return to 1943 to search for her father again. Secondly, Lucia had detached herself from the device somehow, and it had subsequently bonded with another custodian. In theory, that meant Cass could do whatever Lucia had done to remove herself as custodian.

Next came the most important part: the part that made her nerves jangle at the prospect of suggesting it. Could Lucia re-link with the artefact and go back to 1943 to find Cass's father?

'Nice outfit. Land girl, is it?' asked Lucia, although she didn't step aside to allow Cass to enter.

Cass nodded and drew her arms around her middle.

Lucia pursed her lips. 'Oh. You've already been. You didn't bring him back,' she said, stating facts instead of asking questions.

Pre-occupied with working on her plan all the way here, Cass was brought back to earth with a bump by Lucia's blunt statements. She shook her head at the dreadful reality and her bottom lip quivered. She bit on it, both to stop it wobbling and to hold back the flood of tears welling up ready to fall.

'Can I come in?' she asked, shakily.

The glassmaker hesitated and glanced backwards towards the stairs.

'Oh, I'm sorry. Is there someone else here? I can come back. When would be good for you?'

Lucia tipped her head to one side and took a step backwards to make way for Cass to enter. 'My daughter is here, but you obviously need to come in. Mia won't mind. I've told her all about you.'

'And about my, erm, problem?'

Lucia nodded. 'Yes. That too.'

'Why would you do that?' asked Cass, frowning.

'Because she's my daughter. We talk. She knows about me and The Infinity Glass and about Haven-slash-Drusilla. We don't often keep secrets from each other; not now, anyway.' Turning to face the stairs, Lucia called out, 'Mia? We have a visitor. Cass is here again. Put the kettle on, would you?'

Cass was unsure about going inside. She felt like Lucia had broken a confidence by telling her daughter about her. They hadn't strictly agreed upon secrecy, but Cass had assumed it was a given.

'Maybe I'll come back another time,' she said, her feet stubbornly telling her to stay.

Lucia stared at her from beneath knotted eyebrows. 'Don't be daft; you clearly need to talk and I'm the obvious choice, aren't I? Come on up. Close the door behind you. Give it a good hard shove, it tends to stick.'

Questions whirled around in Cass's head as Lucia ascended the stairs without a backward glance. What good would it do to leave – where would she go? Home to cry in the empty house? That wouldn't help anybody. She couldn't talk to anyone else about what had happened – even her best friend, Lo, would never believe her, let alone volunteer to become custodian to go and retrieve Jake Patch from 1943.

Cass's hastily constructed plan of persuading Lucia to bring her father home was still her best – and only – choice, assuming this Mia girl didn't convince her mother not to do it.

* * *

Mia was filling the kettle when Cass and Lucia reached the top of the stairs. The glassmaker's daughter was about nineteen or twenty, Cass guessed. Slender with long, wavy chestnut-brown hair, Mia had not inherited her mother's taste in garish clothing. Instead, she wore straight-legged jeans, a ribbed red top and a long black and red striped cardigan with enormous deep pockets and a fringed bottom edge.

As Mia bustled around the kitchenette, Cass decided to get straight to the point and tell Lucia what she wanted her to do.

'I didn't find him. The only way to get him back now is for someone else to bring him, and the one person I can think of to do that is you, so—'

'Stop right there,' interrupted Lucia, raising a hand. For a split second, Cass thought the glassmaker was going to strike her, but the hand stayed stationary like Lucia was making a pledge of allegiance. 'I can't do what you're asking of me.'

'Please, there's nobody else.'

'I don't mean I won't,' explained Lucia, shaking her head. 'When I said can't, I meant can't: the rules, Cass. Nobody can be custodian twice.'

'What? Is she right, Drusilla?'

'Well, of course. There would be no point her lying, would there?' said the sprite. 'If you'd asked me, I would have told you.'

'No-no-no-no-no,' muttered Cass, lowering her head onto her hands. 'You were my last hope – *his* last hope. I did think about asking my friend, Lola, but I decided against that straight away. It wouldn't be fair of me to ask her. But you've travelled before. Plus you're older, so you have a better idea what it was like back then.'

'Seriously?' said Mia, who had remained silent until now, although she had balled her hands into fists when Cass asked Lucia to become custodian again. Mia tutted loudly, rolling her eyes for good measure. 'She's not that old, for goodness' sake. You'd have to be in your eighties or older to have any memory of World War 2, you know.'

'I didn't mean it that way. I meant... well, never mind.'

'She means,' said Lucia to her daughter, 'that I at least have a link to that time. Of course my grandparents talked about living through the war. It was such a big deal, after all. I wouldn't be going there without any inkling what I was letting myself in for. But like I said, I can't go. The rules won't allow it.'

Mia's mouth twisted and she turned away.

Cass stared at Lucia through a film of tears. 'I can't leave him. What if he gets caught up in another bombing raid and isn't so lucky this time? Did I tell you I spoke to a man who had seen him? He thinks my dad went to the air-raid shelter inside the caves on the West Hill. Not that it matters if...'

'I'll go,' whispered Mia.

'What?' said Lucia and Cass simultaneously.

Mia turned back to face them. 'I said I'll go.'

Lucia reached out and took hold of her daughter's hand. 'I won't let you do that, Mia. Besides, you don't have any knowledge about wartime in Hastings. It could be dangerous.'

But you didn't think it was a problem for me to go, thought Cass, bitterly.

Mia met her mother's eye. 'Your grandparents were my great grandparents. We discussed the war when I had that history project in year seven. You remember? They told me what it was like during wartime. We chatted for hours and hours... about how Grampy Rodrigo was an Italian prisoner of war who met Grammy Rose at the hospital after being injured, and how he stayed in England after the war and they got married. You're named after his mother. After they both died in 2012, the year after I did the project, I was so glad I'd had that conversation with them. They were both in their nineties and I was so young; I'd only ever thought of them as old people up until then – as if they'd been born that way. You must remember that conversation, Mum. I know way more than you think I do.'

'I do remember, of course,' said Lucia. 'But one cosy chat with your great grandparents doesn't mean you're equipped to go back in time to find Cass's dad. It's too dangerous.'

Mia gave a long blink. 'Not true. We have the date, the time – and now the exact place – where I'd need to go. I can arrive after the air raid, so there'd be no danger from that. As long as Cass can show me a photo of her dad, and as long as he is where she thinks he is, it should be a simple thing to do.'

Her mother shook her head. 'I'm not having you go off with that damned sprite.'

'Charming. What did I ever do to her?' commented Drusilla.

Cass ignored the remark, but wondered why Lucia had such a huge problem with Drusilla.

'If not me, then who?' asked Mia. 'Or are you OK with Cass's father being stuck in 1943 when I could easily get him back?'

'I don't want a fight over this, Mia,' said Lucia, sternly. 'Trust what I'm telling you. Cass, I'm sorry, but Mia won't be going back for your father. That's my final word on the matter.'

Cass picked up the bag containing The Infinity Glass and ran to the front door. Yanking it open, she flew outside onto the pavement, unsure whether her overriding emotion was anger or despair. The door refused her effort to slam it, instead sticking in the frame, so she left it partly open, figuring someone would realise eventually and come to shut it. Not that she cared. If Lucia was happy to let Cass's dad rot in World War 2 Hastings, why should she care about a dumb door?

* * *

Cass paced back and forth in her living room while the time travel device lay on the sofa. She'd been so angry, she was tempted to smash it, but it was still her only hope of bringing her father home safely, even now that she couldn't complete the mission herself.

Snatching up her phone, she sent a message to her best friend.

Hey, Lo. I have a biiiiiiig problem. Need your help. I wouldn't ask, but there's literally nobody else I trust enough. Can we meet up?

Fifteen minutes passed and turned into thirty with no answer from Lola. Had her friend not read the message yet?

Finally, Cass's phone alert pinged and she almost dropped it in her hurry to read Lola's response.

I can do it. Meet me at the café inside the railway station tomorrow morning at 9am and we'll talk. But it wasn't from Lola; it came from an unknown number.

Cass raised her eyebrows and replied with a curt, *I'm sorry, I think you have a wrong number.*

No, definitely not. This is Mia Grant, Lucia's daughter. Will you meet me?

Stunned yet excited, Cass had to ask, *Did your mum change her mind? She seemed so negative when you suggested it.*

Of course she didn't change her mind. Luckily, she left a piece of paper with your number on it next to the phone. See you tomorrow? Oh, and don't bring The Infinity Glass.

Cass thought about it. Lola might be persuaded to go, as long as she believed her friend's unlikely story. The two of them were such good friends that Cass couldn't imagine Lola being able to refuse if she pleaded strongly enough. But Mia already knew about the artefact and the sprite. Besides, how would Cass detach herself as custodian without knowing how Lucia did it?

Do you know how your mum detached herself from being custodian?

I do. Look, I'm your best hope. You know that, right?

Yes, I do. OK, I'll meet you.

She didn't care that she'd be missing college tomorrow.

When Lola replied later, apologetic for not seeing the message immediately, Cass sent her, *No worries, Lo. Situation sorted. I won't be in college tomorrow, but don't worry, it's just a dad problem that I need a day to deal with. Thanks again, lovely xx*

Chapter 31

An Unexpected Ally

'Why?' asked Cass.

She and Mia were sitting in the station coffee shop and Mia had just returned to the table carrying two mugs of steaming, frothy hot chocolate. The glassmaker's daughter leaned forward and gazed deeply into Cass's eyes. Cass found herself wondering if a younger Lucia had been as attractive as her daughter. Her face reddened, but she resisted the urge to look away.

Compelled to fill the charged silence, she asked again, 'Why have you offered to do this?'

Mia blew gently across the top of her drink before taking a tentative sip, finally breaking eye contact.

'Jeez, Mia, say something. Otherwise what are we doing here?'

'I'm thinking,' replied Mia. 'Give me a sec, will you?'

'What is there to think about? I don't understand. I think I should go home now. This was a mistake. I should have stuck with asking my friend.' Cass shoved her chair backwards so violently that she needed to grab it to stop it falling over. A few other coffee shop customers' faces turned towards them to see what the commotion was about.

'Sit,' hissed Mia, sharply. 'I'll tell you. It's knowing where to start that's giving me a problem,' she explained, shaking her head.

When Cass remained standing, Mia tried again. 'Please. Sit down.'

Righting her chair, Cass sat. She rested her elbows on the table and glowered at Mia with a mixture of anger and expectation. She'd come here for answers, but so far all she'd got was a distinctly uninspiring chocolate drink.

'I nearly lost my mother because of that thing,' said Mia, bitterly. 'Hey, you didn't bring it with you, did you?'

Cass shook her head. 'What do you mean you nearly lost her?'

Mia picked absently at the skin beside her thumbnail. 'She told you it was addictive, didn't she? Time travelling, I mean.'

Cass nodded.

'I bet she didn't tell you how addictive. She'd be gone for days.'

'Days? You're lying. It takes you for an hour at a time, not days.'

'Yes, but she'd go straight into the next trip moments after returning. She was losing weight and didn't care about anything except the damned Glass. Haven encouraged her – it was enjoying the adventure way too much.'

'Did you know about The Infinity Glass from the beginning? From whenever it was she found it?'

'I did. I was there when she first disappeared. She'd told me she was hearing a voice nobody else could hear and I thought she needed psychiatric therapy of some sort. Then – the next day, I think – we were talking about her parents and when they met, and *pop!* She was gone. Do you have any idea how scary that was?'

Cass nodded vehemently. 'My dad appeared back from a time travel trip right in front of me. One moment he wasn't there, and the next he was. Somehow, I persuaded myself it hadn't happened the way it looked – that I'd got it wrong. It didn't make sense and it was too weird for me to process it logically, I suppose. Then a few days later, he explained where he'd gone and showed me how time travelling works. He said a date and disappeared. I was so shocked, I swear my heart stopped for a few seconds. I had no idea when he'd be back or anything. I was livid when he arrived back, and he thought he could appease me by bringing me a daisy chain.'

Mia grinned. 'A daisy chain?'

'He used to make them for me when I was little. I think he decided it was a mum-thing to do. He often did that – tried to make up for my mum being gone.'

'Yeah? That's sweet.'

'Mm-hmm. It took me years to realise that was what he was doing, but yeah.'

Realising how much personal information she had shared with Mia in the space of a few sentences, Cass felt the heat rise in her cheeks again. She took several sips of her insipid hot chocolate, hoping Mia would blame the heat of the drink for Cass's pink face.

'Did you know her? Your mother, I mean,' asked Mia, softly.

Cass couldn't help a hint of a sly smile from forming on her lips. 'Not really. At least, I didn't.'

Mia's eyebrows lifted. She blinked a long, hard blink.

'But you've met her now, haven't you? You used The Infinity Glass to do it.' She leaned forward, her pupils dilating.

'Wouldn't you have done the same?' Cass challenged.

234

'In your position, I probably would have, yes. What happened? Did it go well? If you don't mind me asking, that is.'

Cass told Mia all about the meeting with her mother. Once she'd finished relating the events, she added, 'I wanted to be able to bring her back with me. I hated returning to the present knowing she'd still be gone. I should have done something to save her.'

'You shouldn't mess with time,' said Mia, reaching across the table and taking Cass by the hand. 'You don't know what effect it would have. She belonged where she was, and besides, bringing her here would definitely be against the rules. No forward time travel allowed.'

'Oh. I'd forgotten that. Damn those stupid rules.'

'And she wouldn't have been able to stay either. One hour. Less now the device has been re-made.'

Cass slumped dejectedly. 'I forgot quite a lot, apparently.'

Mia released her hand and gave a sympathetic smile. 'Understandable under the circumstances.'

A long pause hung in the air and the young women took simultaneous sips of their drinks.

Cass broke the silence. 'Anyway, you were talking about your mum. You said she was gone for days at a time. What was that about?'

Mia scratched her head and her mouth twisted into a grimace. 'Yeah, things became pretty serious. She reached the point where she'd only stay in the present when she was so exhausted, she had to sleep. In fact, once she rematerialised properly unconscious. I thought she was dead for a few moments – I was petrified.

'That was the day I finally convinced her we needed to have a serious conversation. I helped her to her room so she could catch up on her sleep first, but while she slept, I took The Infinity Glass away and hid it. She was incensed when she discovered it was gone. She actually threatened to hit me if I didn't give it back.

'Once she calmed down and realised what she'd done, we talked properly at last and she agreed to get rid of the thing. She asked Haven how to detach herself from it and Haven didn't want to tell her, of course. When she told it she was never going to time travel again whether she remained custodian or not, the sprite gave in and revealed how to break the bond – on condition we didn't damage the device. Mum kept her promise and didn't harm the artefact, but instead she coated it in a thick layer of plaster of Paris. Hiding it in the antique shop was my idea – and not the best one, either, since your father found it there. We should have buried the damned thing in the middle of the woods.'

'Where was your mother travelling to? Was it to random dates or did she have a specific purpose in mind?'

'I asked her that. She was pretty elusive. I suspect she had some sort of a plan, but it couldn't have been working or she'd never have given up being custodian.'

'She said you didn't have secrets, the two of you.'

'She said that?' asked Mia. 'It isn't true.'

Cass wondered how she would ever know who to trust if everyone told lies.

'I expect she would have given up time travelling anyway – for your sake,' she said.

'You think? I'm less certain.'

Frowning, Cass placed a hand on top of Mia's. 'I'm positive she would have.'

'Erm, anyway,' said Mia, suddenly sounding flustered, 'I came close to losing Mum to that thing and you *have* lost your dad. Temporarily, of course. Mum can't travel back for you – I wouldn't want her to anyway

– and you can't go either. I want to do it. I want to find your father and bring him home for you.'

'How about the addictive element? Aren't you worried about using The Infinity Glass and losing yourself to it?'

'You seem OK.'

'Hah! You say that, but it was me who was compelled to go and meet my mother. I've been weighing up whether to go again, too. I thought I could at the very least have a bit of a *Time Traveler's Wife* thing going on with her where I visit at various points in her life, but perhaps if I'm not going to be allowed to save her, it'd make me too sad to keep popping in and out. She'd work out something was going on. It would get weird.'

'Hmm. Well, personally I'm not worried about becoming addicted to time travel,' said Mia. 'I'm forewarned, after all. Think about this, though: if you ever want to visit your mother again, I can't go and try to retrieve your dad. Or I'd at least have to wait until after you'd seen your mum again. Because you can't be custodian twice, once the bond between you and the device is broken, that would be it.'

'Oh, of course. I hadn't thought that through. So you're telling me I have to choose between visiting my mother, who I never knew until The Infinity Glass came along, and saving my dad, who has been with me, like, my entire life.'

'Or leaving the trip back to 1943 until after you've visited your mum again, yes.'

Cass inhaled deeply. 'There's no question which is the right thing to do. Yes, you could travel back and fetch Dad home at any point, because we get to choose the destination date and time, but it wouldn't be right for me to swan around indulging myself in making daydreams come true while he's stuck in 1943.'

'So you want me to go?'

Cass nodded firmly. 'Yes. Yes please.'

'Well then. We're about the same height and I think I'm a bit thinner than you, so that attractive outfit you were wearing yesterday ought to fit.'

'Attractive? The land girl outfit?'

Mia smiled a one-sided smile. 'Yeah, it looked amazing on you.'

Cass smiled back. 'Thanks. Sure, borrow whatever you like. When do you want to do it?'

'There's no time like the present,' said Mia. 'If that's not too painful a pun.'

Chapter 32

Rules Are For Breaking

'Are you at uni?' asked Cass while the pair of them waited near the row of bus stops outside the railway station.

'Taking a gap year,' replied Mia. 'I thought I'd travel, but I never thought it would be through time.'

Cass frowned. 'I don't want you to feel obliged to help me – us, I mean.'

'Oh, don't worry, obligation has nothing to do with it. I want to do it, like I told you earlier.'

'Yeah, you did say. I just don't get why.'

Mia shrugged one shoulder and kicked a loose stone across the pavement. She changed the subject.

'Mum said you're seventeen. Are you planning on going to uni at all?'

'Yes. Can't wait to be in London. Me and Lo have such plans.'

'Lo? Your boyfriend?'

Cass snorted. 'Lo's a girl; it's short for Lola. She's great – you should meet her.'

'Oh. Girlfriend, then?' asked Mia.

'No, best friend,' responded Cass, casually. She scrolled through on her phone to find a selfie of her and Lola and showed it to Mia, who smiled and nodded in response.

'I hope you have photos of your dad, too,' said Mia. 'I'm going to need to know what he looks like. Perhaps you can send a couple to my phone.'

Cass nodded and sent over the clearest photos of her dad.

Mia zoomed in on one of the pictures. 'He seems like an OK kind of person.'

'Worth saving?' asked Cass, only half joking.

Mia nodded vigorously. 'Oh, definitely.'

One of the waiting buses honked its horn to indicated it was about to reverse, making Cass jump. 'Oh. Ours is about to arrive, once this one has freed up the stop.'

Moments later, the pair boarded their bus. Mia followed Cass to the upper deck where they sat together in the front window seats.

'I like the front seats,' Mia commented. 'You can see the world from here, but it's freeing at the same time, as if you're invisible to everyone else.'

'Yeah. I've never been a back-seat-of-the-bus kinda person,' agreed Cass.

By the time they arrived at their destination stop, roughly ten metres away from the house, Cass had learned a great deal of background information about the glassmaker's daughter. Born and raised in Hastings, Mia was a keen amateur photographer and also had what she described as an 'unnatural interest in geology, for some reason'. She had tried glassmaking, but had not been drawn to it in the same way her mother was and reported that no, her mother was not the least bit disappointed by her lack of interest. It was geology that she hoped to study at university and her ultimate ambition was to work for NASA, 'Or anyone else who'll take me to Mars'.

When Cass apologised for the dilapidated state of her home's front door, Mia simply grinned and said, 'You've seen ours, right? Mum always says it's the love inside that matters, not how fancy your front door is.'

Cass giggled. 'Dad says something similar. Do you think they'd get on?'

Mia rubbed her chin. 'That would be interesting. Let's be sure to find out. I love a nice romance story, don't you?'

Cass couldn't meet Mia's eyes.

'Anyway,' Mia crouched to untie her shoe laces, 'let's get him home before we go mapping out his whole life, shall we?'

'Come on in. Don't bother taking your shoes off, we aren't house-proud here,' Cass told her, heading straight for the stairs. 'You wait in the living room,' she pointed to the doorway, 'and I'll go and fetch the land girl outfit.' Noticing Mia's shoes, she pursed her lips. 'I don't think those will hack it in 1943. What size do you wear?'

'Seven, but don't worry, I brought a pair with me that I thought would work,' said Mia, patting the tote bag slung over her right shoulder. 'They're my mum's, but I'm sure she won't mind that I've borrowed them.'

Cass went to retrieve her outfit.

'Ah, you're back. Where have you been?' asked Drusilla, haughtily. Cass still hadn't told Drusilla about her meeting with Lucia and Mia, nor about Mia's offer of help.

'You'll find out soon enough,' Cass said.

'Oh, very mysterious,' responded the sprite. 'I've been thinking about your problem. We could go back to 1944 to find your father. A few more months most likely won't hurt and you aren't precluded from visiting 1944 because you haven't already been there.'

Cass stopped in her tracks and sat on the edge of her bed. 'You know, that's not the worst idea.' That way, she could remain custodian and retain the ability to visit her mother again. But anything could happen to her father in the space of a few months, couldn't it? History knew what damage the Luftwaffe would cause to the town, but her father was a man out of time. She could check casualty lists, but Jake Patch could choose to use a different name in 1943, and besides, how would it feel to be there without hope of rescue?

'No, I can't leave him there in the hands of fate. Besides, how could I hope to find him when he could be literally anywhere? I'm going with a different option, thank you,' she said, gathering together the dungarees, white shirt, belt and hair band.

'What are you going to do?' asked the sprite, anxiously. 'I can help with the planning if you share your idea with me.'

'Yes, I expect you could, but you're going to have to wait until I see fit to tell you what we've decided to do.'

'I sense our relationship has been adversely affected by recent events,' said the sprite, cautiously.

'Oh, do you?' Cass hesitated in the doorway. 'Well, I know what happened wasn't your fault. You suggested I should go straight to the High Street, and I chose the hospital instead. But I always have to battle to get a straight answer – no, not a straight answer; a complete answer – from you. This time, for now, I'm leaving you in the dark until I need you, Drusilla. Sorry, but that's how it is.'

Drusilla made a noise that sounded distinctly like a sniff.

As Cass descended the stairs, the sprite said, 'You obviously do your best, but humans are incapable of appreciating the complex limitations in force; people can be such frustratingly contrary beings. Anyone would think rules were meant for breaking.'

Chapter 33

All Saints

Mia changed in the kitchen while Cass waited in the living room, her arms hugging her middle and her fingernails digging into her skin. What if she couldn't detach herself from being custodian of The Infinity Glass? What if her instincts about Mia's trustworthiness had been coloured by her attraction to the glassmaker's daughter and she'd unwittingly made a dreadful misjudgement? What if Mia had her own agenda and had no intention of bringing Cass's father home from 1943? What if Mia tried, but couldn't find him? More and more negativity spun around her head, making her dizzy with worry. What if, what if…?

With a theatrical flourish, accompanied by a hearty 'Ta-da!', Mia re-appeared, now dressed in the land girl costume.

Shaking herself out of her ruminations, Cass reacted with a spontaneous, 'Wow.'

Mia beamed. 'See,' she said. 'I told you it was attractive.' She turned side-on to Cass and gave a seductive pout, adding a double-lift of her eyebrows.

Cass laughed awkwardly. 'Lovely. You'd give Vera Lynn a run for her money in that get-up. You'd have all the soldiers chasing after you.' She was fishing for an answer to a question she daren't ask.

'Not interested.' Mia waved a dismissive hand. 'Hey, what about the shoes?' she asked, pointing a toe forward to show them off. 'I think they work great, don't you? My mum wears them for gardening, not that she has anything but a postage-stamp-sized lawn, a few potted shrubs and a distinctly cherry-less ornamental cherry tree.'

'They are a bit the worse for wear,' commented Cass, frowning at the mud-encrusted brown rubber slip-ons and waiting for her speeding pulse rate to calm back down.

'Precisely. I think they're older than I am, which is quite fitting, don't you agree?'

'I guess so, yes. I've no idea whether that precise style works for the era you'll be visiting, but I doubt anyone will notice. Not with the mud.'

'Nobody pays attention to shoes anyway,' said Mia with a shrug. 'Especially not people dealing with living through a world war.'

'No, I guess not. How do I detach from the artefact, then?'

'Oh, that's easy. You tell Haven – Drusilla or whatever – that you don't wish to be custodian anymore. It doesn't work unless you truly mean it, though. I imagine that's to stop coercion.'

'What? That's ridiculous.'

'Stopping coercion?'

'No, not that. It sounds far too easy, that's all. I thought there'd be special words, like a spell maybe.' She blushed. 'Now I've said that out loud, it sounds awfully childish.'

'It's not childish at all. This whole thing is completely unprecedented. It might have required eye of newt and wing of bat, a special dance around a campfire, burning incense – or anything imaginable, come to that. You weren't to know how easy it could be.'

'Shall I go and fetch The Infinity Glass, then?'

'Yes. Let's do this.'

* * *

'I want you to tell me what's happening,' said Drusilla, tartly.

Cass hitched the satchel containing the artefact onto her shoulder.

'I sense something is going on and I won't give you my full co-operation unless you tell me what it is,' whined the sprite.

'I thought you had to help,' said Cass. 'Your role is to be the intermediary between The Infinity Glass and the human custodian, isn't it?'

'Yes, but I do have free will. I'm not technically bound to assist. I'm not enslaved.'

Cass frowned, shocked at the thought that Drusilla wouldn't help. She sat on the side of her bed, temporarily lost for words.

'But neither am I your enemy,' the sprite conceded, its tone now more conciliatory. 'I've never been your enemy, nor your father's. Not even Lucia's.'

At the mention of the glassmaker, Cass said, 'Lucia told me you can't be trusted and Mia thinks the same, but according to you, it is Lucia who's untrustworthy, if I remember correctly. How am I supposed to know whose side to choose?'

'I'm not sure you have to choose, but you do need to accept that a human and a sprite have different perspectives.'

'And priorities.' Cass stood and put her hands on her hips, fumbling to keep hold of the time travel device. She tightened her grip on it, uncertain whether Lucia would do another re-make for her if it got broken again. 'I'm not like you at all, Drusilla. I am a simple, ordinary human.'

'Yes, I am aware; as a human, you have limited knowledge of time and the consequences of travelling through it in a non-linear fashion, which means you need my help. You need me on your side. Tell me about your plan so I can be of assistance.'

Drusilla's voice was as smooth as black silk. Cass felt like she was staring into the hypnotic eyes of a snake, and yet nothing the sprite had told her was unreasonable. She took a quick deep breath.

'We will tell you in a moment, downstairs,' she said, holding her ground.

'We?' barked Drusilla. 'We who? Lucia? Is she here?'

Cass ignored the string of questions from the riled sprite. Returning to the living room, she found Mia scrutinising a framed photo of Cass with her dad at the Old Town's May Day festival, *Jack in the Green*.

'Ohhh,' said the sprite, her tone a mixture of surprise and foreboding. 'I see. You're going to send Mia back to 1943. I understand. An ill-advised choice, I think. You'd be better off remaining custodian yourself and going to 1944, as I suggested.'

'We know what you think and we've already rejected your idea. Mia will go. You can't change our minds.'

Mia turned around to face Cass. 'Is it trying to dis our plan?' she asked.

Cass nodded. 'It guessed you're going instead of me. It's trying to convince me to stay custodian and go to 1944 to find Dad, but it doesn't realise – or perhaps doesn't care – that he could be dead by 1944, or he might have moved away from the area or anything. Your plan is still the most sensible.'

Mia nodded. 'Tell me the date and time I need to visit.'

'She can't be there at the same time you were,' said Drusilla, urgently. 'The Infinity Glass cannot exist twice in the same moment in close proximity. Dire consequences could result for Mia, for your father and for me. Tell her to go to a time after you returned. Trust me, Cass. I know what I'm talking about.'

'I know. It's in the rules, you told me,' muttered Cass absently. She ran quickly through possible options for arrival times. On her own trip, she had arrived in 1943 on 23 May at 2.30pm. Allowing a full hour, to avoid any possibility of causing temporal damage, she decided Mia shouldn't arrive until 3.30. Cass was about to tell Mia the date and time when another thought occurred to her.

'You can't go from here else you'll appear in some poor person's living room in 1943,' she said.

Mia grimaced. 'Good point. How about the back garden or out at the roadside?'

Cass scratched her head. 'Probably not. The back garden might well have a fence around it in 1943, as it does now, and you'd have to climb several before you reached the road. Also, if you appear on the pavement out front, goodness knows who you might frighten to death. There's an alleyway in George Street we can use.'

'I'm not an alleyway kind of girl,' protested Mia. 'It's not exactly salubrious, is it? Wherever we start from, it's possible someone will see me arrive. But I agree that neither here in the house nor the back garden is a great idea. How about a churchyard or somewhere like that? It ought to be quiet enough there, don't you think? Is there anywhere like that nearby?'

'Yes. All Saints.'

'OK. Where's that?'

'Erm, in All Saints Street,' said Cass.

'Oh. Logical. Lead the way, then,' replied Mia enthusiastically.

'But we haven't talked about what you need to tell Dad, to convince him he should go with you.'

'I'll have The Infinity Glass. Plus I know your name, where you live and a bit about your mother. He'll believe me.'

'How will you bring him home?'

'How were you going to do it?'

'I dunno. Hold hands at the right moment or something, I suppose.'

'I can do that. Ask the sprite if it will work.'

Drusilla chipped in without being asked. 'That should work. Contact between the custodian and the person caught in the wrong time ought to bring him back along with her. Perhaps he should place a hand on the artefact too, though, to be doubly sure.'

'You mean you don't know?' asked Cass, aghast.

'It's unprecedented.'

'Drusilla isn't certain,' reported Cass. 'Holding hands and having Dad touch The Infinity Glass at the moment of departure is her – its – best guess.'

'Ah. I see. Well, there's nobody else we can ask, so there's no point stressing about it. We'll only get one try, unless you can persuade someone else to give it a go if I fail.'

'You won't fail,' said Cass, cracking her knuckles like her father often did.

Mia frowned. 'You're right. We mustn't be negative. I'm sure it will work perfectly. Come on. The sooner we do this, the sooner you'll be happy again. I can't bear seeing you miserable.'

* * *

'Graveyards are such depressing places.' Mia was surveying the array of crooked and mostly illegible weathered and lichen-blotched stones. 'All these people and nobody left who even remembers who they were.'

'You asked for a churchyard,' Cass pointed out.

'Yeah, I know. It's still sad, though. Tell me the date and time I need to go to.'

'Can I say it? When I'm still custodian?'

'Well, the object won't take you there because it's against the rules for you to go twice.'

'Still, I think I'll wait. To be sure we don't mess anything up.'

Mia shrugged and Cass gave a heavy sigh.

'Stop worrying. In an hour, you'll have him back,' said Mia, softly.

Cass nodded, but couldn't meet her gaze.

'Are you ready to detach as custodian?' asked Mia.

Chewing on her lip, Cass nodded again. 'Yeah. Ready. Here goes.' Remembering she was supposed to really mean her words, she lifted her chin and took a long, deep breath. 'I no longer wish to be custodian of The Infinity Glass.'

She didn't know what she expected – a fanfare; a plume of sparks; being lifted into the air amidst a fantastic rainbow light show – but nothing happened at all. It was distinctly underwhelming.

'Is that it?' she asked, deflating.

'Give me the artefact and tell me the date and time I need to go to and we'll find out,' said Mia.

Cass fumbled at the strap of the satchel and handed it to Mia, who opened the flap and reached inside to touch the device.

'You need to go to 23 May 1943 at 3.30pm,' Cass told her. 'Dad ought to be at the caves – you know, Smuggler's Adventure? It was used as an air-raid shelter.'

'Yes, I knew that. OK, here goes. Take me to 23 May 1943 at 3.30pm,' said Mia.

There was a sound like a thousand people simultaneously snapping their fingers.

Patches through Time

PART 5: THE BARGAIN HUNTER's DAUGHTER & THE GLASSMAKER's DAUGHTER

Chapter 34

Double Trouble

Cass shuddered. She stared at Mia, who was rubbing her right arm vigorously and grimacing.

'It didn't work,' Cass moaned. 'You're still here and I'm still custodian. But I meant it. I *really* meant it.'

Mia shook her head. 'No. Look at the inscription on this gravestone. I swear it wasn't that clear before. And see there – the tree?'

'What tree?' asked Cass.

'That's my point. There was a tree over there before I said the destination date and time,' explained Mia, inclining her head to the left. 'Now it's gone. And besides, I can't let go of this blasted Infinity Glass. Drusilla – or Haven or whatever – when are we? And can you detach me from this thing, please?'

Cass was still trying to work out what was going on when Drusilla spoke.

'We are all in 1943, Mia, on the twenty-third of March. The time here is 3.30pm. Well, plus another twenty-one seconds now, to be exact. I have removed the physical bond.'

Mia winced and switched the artefact into her other hand. 'Yeah. Man, that's sore,' she grumbled.

'Why are we both here, Drusilla?' asked Cass. 'I shouldn't have travelled at all. I relinquished custodianship and I wasn't touching The Infinity Glass.'

'I'm not at all sure,' admitted the sprite, after a long pause.

'OK,' said Cass. 'Which of us is the custodian now?'

'Ermmm.'

'See previous answer,' commented Mia with a wry chuckle. 'It doesn't know.'

'I *do*,' insisted the sprite. 'Logic says that, because you can obviously both hear me, you are now both custodians.'

'Two custodians?' asked the pair, in unison.

'That's ridiculous,' added Mia.

'And yet here we all are,' Drusilla replied matter-of-factly.

Mia raked her fingers through her hair. 'Wait. You said we're in 1943, but Cass can't revisit a year she's already been to. It's in the rules.'

This time, Cass had a suggestion. 'But you haven't been here before, Mia. Perhaps you're Primary Custodian now. I don't know. This is all ridiculously unreal.'

Mia giggled softly. 'Time travelling with three coloured blobs inside a glass knot is absolutely bloody mad. Surely this new development is just a bit of icing on the proverbial cake. At least there aren't two of you here simultaneously. Ha-ha.'

Cass raised a single eyebrow and Mia stopped laughing.

'Sorry,' said Mia. 'Well, now we're here and the clock is ticking, so let's go and find your dad.'

Cass gave a single nod. 'What's the time now, Drusilla?' she asked.

'It's 3.31 and a few seconds,' said the sprite. 'I can, of course, give timings to the second, but your father found it irritating.'

'I imagine he did,' said Cass, smiling at the thought of her dad and looking forward to seeing him again. 'Timings are fine rounded down to the nearest minute, unless we have less than five left. I think there's no point us wasting time overthinking why we're both here now that we are. The important thing is to find Dad quickly and get us all safely home. After that, we can discuss the hell out of the situation and try to work it out.'

Mia screwed up her face. 'Assuming we can all return together. I hope there won't be a problem with three people to transport using a single Infinity Glass.'

Cass started along the path towards the road. 'Two of us came, so one more going back doesn't feel like too much of a stretch. Like I said, we have to stop overthinking and get on with it. We're wasting precious minutes. Damn it, I should have thought this all through and suggested we travel from somewhere closer to the entrance to the caves. For goodness' sake!'

'Wait up,' called Mia, sharply. 'What about your clothes? You aren't dressed for the era.'

Cass stopped dead and considered her outfit. She was wearing mid-wash blue turned-up boyfriend jeans, a cable knit crew-neck navy-blue jumper and flat black canvas shoes.

'Damn. The jeans will be seriously out of place here. I don't think even land girls wore them. It would have been way more of a problem if I'd chosen to wear skinnies or jeans with ripped knees, though, wouldn't it? The jumper will do OK. Thank goodness I'm not wearing one of my wackier tops with colourfully worded slogans.' She realised she had subconsciously chosen her clothing to give a positive impression of herself to the glassmaker's daughter. 'This will have to do,' she said. 'I'm not stealing clothes from a washing line. We don't have time and I'm not a thief.'

'Can you roll the legs of your jeans down? That might help a bit,' suggested Mia.

Cass bent down to do as Mia suggested. 'They won't go to my ankles, though.' Her suspicion proved right; they stopped a few centimetres short of full length.

'Never mind. It's not as if anyone's going to recognise you're a time traveller or have you arrested for fashion offences – although they might give you a funny look or whisper behind their hands. We're still in England, Cass. British reserve and all that. I'll bet that stiff formality was even more of a thing back in the 1940s.'

'True. Let's get a shift on, shall we?'

Mia nodded and the pair set off through the churchyard towards the road.

The young women fell into a stunned silence at the sight of the Luftwaffe-induced devastation they encountered on their way to the cave air-raid shelter. Cass had seen the damaged buildings and rubble-strewn roads on her previous trip, of course, but the impact on her was just as intense the second time around. Mia's eyes were like saucers, but she said nothing as she strode resolutely along at Cass's side.

People were out in the streets of the Old Town, some using brooms and shovels to clean up the tinkling shards of glass strewn liberally across both pavements and roads, but most leaving the larger debris to those better equipped to move it. Amidst the tidying-up operation, some people were going about their daily business as if nothing untoward had happened at all and others were holding quiet neighbourly conversations while tucked into house and shop doorways.

'Go to the shelter next time, you silly sod,' said a thick-set middle-aged woman, speaking to a pale bald-headed man who peered back at her through a pair of round wire-framed spectacles. Cass thought the woman's tone was more pitying than reproachful.

'I will do, Maureen,' he responded, nodding solemnly. 'Machine gun fire took out the front windows upstairs. I was lucky I was in the kitchen making myself a cuppa. You've never seen me duck under a table so fast. I thank my lucky stars I wasn't in The Swan.'

The woman called Maureen wiped away a tear. 'Yes. Such tragic losses there,' she said, shaking her head gloomily. 'Several of them were friends, too.'

Mia whispered in Cass's ear, 'How did they live through this? Imagine being here when all this damage happened.'

'My dad *was* here, remember?' replied Cass.

'Shit, of course. Sorry for being dim. Hey, don't worry. You've already been told he's OK; we just have to find him.'

'We don't know he's OK. All we know is that he *was* OK-*ish*. The man I spoke to – a warden, I think – said he'd hurt his arm or his shoulder. Perhaps it was worse than the man thought. Dad could have internal injuries or broken bones or shrapnel lodged in a vital organ or—'

Mia grabbed Cass's arm at the elbow and pulled her to a halt, spinning her around to face her.

'We'll find him and take him home. We can call him an ambulance and get him proper twenty-first-century medical treatment if we need to and he'll be absolutely fine. I promise.'

Cass's shoulders slumped. Mia's promise was optimistic, but optimism couldn't hurt, whereas her own pessimism could. She straightened her spine and found she felt more positive already.

'Yeah,' she said with a sigh. 'Hey, thanks. For shutting down my negativity – which I seriously needed you to do, by the way – and for offering to do this. You thought you'd be coming by yourself to rescue someone you've never even met. It means a lot and I'm glad you're here, despite having a terrible way of showing it.'

Mia nodded. 'Come on, you. Let's do this.'

As they approached the way into the caves, Cass asked, 'How much time have we used, Drusilla?'

'Eighteen minutes,' replied the sprite.

'Is that all?' asked Mia. 'Brilliant. We have plenty of time left. Oodles, as Mum would say. We'll manage, won't we?'

Cass nodded and smiled warmly. 'Yes,' she said. 'I think we will.'

Chapter 35

Ghosts

At the West Hill entrance to the caves, Cass and Mia encountered an unexpected problem. A notice pinned outside told them "Entry for Staff and Military Personnel ONLY. Please use the entrance in Croft Road".

'What if you were in a hurry?' asked Mia. 'Imagine – bombs and stuff happening and you can't get into the shelter.'

'I expect all the locals are aware which entrance to use,' said Cass. 'Besides, if you think about it, crossing open hillside up here during an air raid would make you a sitting duck – any enemy planes flying by would pick you off easily. We need to find the Croft Road entrance, but I'm not good with road names and I don't know exactly where it is.'

A woman of around forty approached the pair. She wore a calf-length plain brown coat, practical flat shoes and had a paisley-pattern scarf tied around her head. The woman's eyes briefly scanned Cass and Mia up and down, then she pursed her lips and quickened her stride.

'Excuse me,' said Mia in her best clipped BBC accent. 'Would you mind awfully telling us how to get to Croft Road? We're visiting relatives and don't know the area.'

Cass failed to hold back a smirk at Mia's attempt to fit in with the way she obviously thought everyone spoke in the 1940s.

The woman raised an arm and pointed back along the footpath they were already on. 'Turn sharp right then keep heading downwards. You'll come out behind The Swan – or what's left of it. Turn left and you'll be in Croft Road.'

'Thank you for your help, madam,' said Mia, with a brief smile.

The woman gave a curt nod and went on her way, walking faster than before.

'What was her problem?' asked Cass. 'She looked like she thought we were muggers or spies.'

Mia shrugged. 'She wouldn't have given us directions if she'd thought we were spies. Thank goodness we found someone to ask. It's weird talking to ghosts, though. Haven, how long have we had?'

'Twenty-three minutes. Almost twenty-four.'

'Still over half an hour left. We'll be fine,' Mia reassured Cass.

'I hope so,' Cass replied. 'What did you mean about talking to ghosts?'

'That woman. She's dead where we come from.'

'Yeah, but you have to remember – we're the ones out of our time here. We're like ghosts from the future.'

'Or shadows maybe. But we have the advantage of knowing how this war will pan out.'

Cass laughed. 'That's true, but it doesn't help us do what we're here to do, does it?'

Following the directions they'd been given, Cass and Mia made their way back into the Old Town. They passed close by the ruins of The Swan, where desperate workers were continuing the backbreaking task of attempting to dig out any survivors. Sticking resolutely to their mission despite the events unfolding at the stricken hotel, the pair continued on their way and took the left turn into Croft Road. There, they soon came upon a sign saying "Air Raid Shelter" with an arrow. The entrance tunnel was approached via steep steps and along a path with high concrete walls either side.

'This is it,' said Cass, stating the obvious.

Once inside, they came to a cavern occupied only by two grey-haired men playing cards at a rickety wooden table.

'He's not here,' Cass groaned.

'Fifteen two, fifteen four and a pair's six,' said one of the men, moving a wooden peg made out of a used matchstick along a narrow playing board. The board had four rows of holes drilled along its length and an additional single hole between the rows at either end.

Cass approached the men. 'Excuse me, sirs, I'm looking for my father.'

'Haven't seen anyone,' barked the second of the men, laying his cards on the table and not glancing up. 'Two pairs for four,' he said to his companion, while hopping his peg along the line of holes, 'four runs for twelve and one for his nob makes seventeen.' He jammed his peg into the end hole nearest to him. 'Hah! I win again,' he exclaimed.

'Only bloke I've seen was the ARP warden,' said the other man, shoving his chair backwards while his opponent laughed heartily and gathered up the cards.

Cass's hope drained completely away, leaving her empty and oddly detached. Her feet were as heavy as lead when she turned to face a crestfallen Mia.

'Wait,' said the man. 'There was another chap. He was hurt. They took him out. You remember, don't you, Tom? It was during our second game.'

The victorious man rubbed a grey-stubbled chin. 'I don't rightly recall. I was too busy winning your money. You owe me three shillings, Burt.'

'Yeah, yeah, you'll get your money tomorrow, Tom. But there was another chap,' said Burt. 'They either took him to the medical room or to the hospital. I dunno which way they went. Took him off on a stretcher. He didn't look good.'

'They took him to the medical room?' asked Mia. 'Where's that, then?'

'That way.' The man called Burt pointed beyond the girls. 'Follow the signs. Just before you reach the schoolroom.'

Cass peered into the gloom in the direction Burt pointed, but the lighting wasn't powerful enough for her to see clearly very far.

'Thanks,' she said.

'You're welcome, Miss. Take care, now.'

Cass gave a weak smile and Mia took hold of her arm.

'Come on. Let's head to the medical centre.'

Cass shook her head. 'What if they took him to the hospital, though? Maybe my timing was a little bit off in my previous trip. I need to get over there, just in case. There won't be time to go to both, one after the other.'

'You won't be able to come back here in time for us to leave, though,' said Mia, logically.

Cass's mind raced, thinking back through all that had happened today.

'I don't think I need to,' she said. ' I hope I'm right, but the fact that I'm here at all means things aren't straightforward. Not that any of this qualifies under the normal meaning of straightforwardness. Besides, I have to go. I can't miss Dad twice. There may not be another chance if I fail a second time. Go. See if he's here. I'm heading across to the hospital again.'

Before Mia could protest further, Cass ran back along the entrance tunnel towards Croft Road.

'Drusilla?' she called, hoping the sprite would still be with her, even though Mia had possession of The Infinity Glass. No reply was forthcoming. With no timekeeper and no watch, Cass would have to rely on clocks or passers-by to tell her how much time was left before… before what? Before she returned home? Before Mia returned without her, with or without her father?

Time would tell. At least if Cass found her father and neither of them returned home, they would be stuck here together instead of alone. She crossed her fingers for the best possible outcome without realising she was doing it.

Cass cursed quietly, turning away from the seafront towards the Memorial in the town centre. 'Matron. What if I get caught? She saw me last time I was here – and clearly thinks me some kind of troublemaker, which I suppose I am from her point of view. With any luck, she'll be off duty by now, or on a tea break. Let's hope, eh?'

Chapter 36

A Tale of Two Nurses

Back in the caves, Mia found the medical centre. There appeared to be a lone member of staff, who was bent over one of the metal-framed beds, changing the sheets.

Two of the dozen or so beds were occupied, the first by an elderly man with a bald head, who was propped up reading a newspaper; the second by an unidentifiable shape curled beneath the heavy blankets with only a few sprigs of hair showing. Mia couldn't even tell whether it was a man. She decided to creep closer and take a peek without either waking the patient or bothering the member of staff.

She sidled to the bedside and craned her neck. The patient didn't stir, remaining instead in a foetal curl. She considered pulling the sheets back, but when she glanced up to check what the nurse was doing, she found a pair of brown eyes staring inquisitively into her own from a couple of metres away.

'Are you a relative?' asked the nurse, her eyebrows arched so high that her forehead was lined and ridged.

'No; I mean, I might be. I'm trying to find my father. Someone told me he'd been brought here. He's got longish brown hair and he had a problem with his arm. I wondered if this might be him, perhaps?' Mia gestured towards the bed.

'No, that's Mr Winstanley. Your father was taken to the hospital. He had a badly dislocated shoulder and he passed out from the pain. Usually we have more staff here, but right now I'm by myself and I'm not strong enough to put a shoulder back. You'll find him at the RESH.'

'Oh, good. I sent my sister to go and look for him there. At least she'll find him. Thank you for your… hey, are you Rose Preston, by any chance?' The question escaped her lips before Mia had time to decide whether it was a good idea to ask it. Rose Preston was her great grandmother, who'd died in 2012; one of the great grandparents she'd discussed wartime experiences with. A photograph of her with her daughter – Mia's grandmother Margherita – took pride of place on the chest of drawers in Lucia's bedroom.

'I am Rose,' said the nurse. 'Do I know you?'

'Erm, no. I think you treated my uncle. I remember him telling me about a pretty nurse who was kind to him, and for some reason your name stuck with me. He told us you were amazing.'

Mia thought through the options. If Jake Patch was in the RESH, Cass would find him. There was no point going after her to help. This opportunity was too good to miss, as long as Cass didn't need her.

'You don't have time to sit and have a chat, I suppose?' she asked her great grandmother. 'Or I could help you change the sheets on the beds if you like.'

Rose beamed, her smile reminding Mia of her mother's. 'Your help would be appreciated, thank you. As I said, we are short-staffed today.'

* * *

265

Cass breathed heavily, climbing a steep flight of steps she hadn't spotted on her last visit. It was the quickest, most direct route from Cambridge Road up to the hospital. She wondered fleetingly whether the steps were still there in her own time, but overgrown, or if they had been completely blocked off or demolished. At the top, she turned left, towards the entrance to the Emergency Department, still with no plan at all about how to deal with Matron, should she encounter her.

The only clock she had noticed on her way through town was that on the Memorial tower. She didn't want to consider how little time she must have left or whether or not The Infinity Glass would return her to the churchyard in the Old Town. Yet time and her father were all she could think about. It must be at least forty-five minutes since they'd arrived. Maybe fifty. Perhaps more.

Running along the front of the building, Cass recognised the window through which she'd had her close encounter with Matron. There was no sign of the head nurse on the other side of the window now, thankfully. Perhaps her father was in there. If so, he must be both conscious and mobile, in which case she could attract his attention and get him to meet her outside. She pictured their reunion – his arms would wrap around her, holding her tight while he wept with joy.

She crossed the grass to the window and peered inside. No patients lay in the corridor now.

'You there,' called a female voice from behind her.

Cass turned, fearing it would be Matron, but it was the young red-haired nurse she'd spoken to earlier.

'I thought it was you,' said the nurse. 'Matron told us to keep our eyes peeled for a female intruder in the grounds dressed in work overalls, but you've changed now. Wherever did you get *those* clothes from?'

'Long story,' said Cass. 'You aren't going to report me, are you?'

'No, of course not,' promised the nurse, checking nervously left and right. 'Did you not find your father?'

'No. I have to find him – and fast. The people at the caves said he'd been sent up here with a dislocated shoulder.'

'Ohhh.' The nurse nodded eagerly. 'I've seen him, then. They were transferring him to a medical ward when I came outside for my break. If you're his next of kin, you ought to be allowed to visit. Don't worry – Matron's domain is the Emergency Department, not the general medical ward.'

'Can you show me the way? Please? Like I said, I need to find him in a hurry. You know your way around this hospital and I don't.'

'I have to be back at work shortly,' the nurse explained hesitantly.

'Please. Time is running out.'

'Don't worry about your father. Honestly, he'll be as right as rain in a few weeks,' the nurse assured her, misunderstanding Cass's words.

'You don't understand. It's sooo urgent that I find him. Pleeease. I'd pay you a thousand pounds if I had it. A million even.'

The nurse smiled. 'Would you, now? Oh, alright, if it truly is as urgent as you say.'

Cass nodded vehemently.

'This way, then,' said the nurse. 'My name is Helen, by the way. Helen Cook.'

'Cass,' said Cass. Trying not to think of Helen as one of Mia's ghosts, she followed her inside.

* * *

He was sitting in a chair when she saw him. His right arm hung in a sling and his eyes were dull and empty, as if he had lost himself.

'Dad!' cried Cass, leaving Helen behind near the doors and haring towards her father.

He turned and saw her. His initial expression of disbelief changed instantly to joy.

'Cass! I thought for a second that my eyes were playing tricks on me.'

She ran to him and he stood to meet her. She wanted to fly into his arms but, realising she couldn't do that for risk of hurting his injured shoulder, she stopped short and grinned at him broadly.

He pulled her awkwardly to his side using his good arm. 'Cass. How are you here?' he asked.

'The Infinity Glass. It came home without you. It was broken. I had it fixed. It's such a long story. What's the time?'

'According to the clock above the door, it's 4.35,' he said.

'What?' Cass couldn't believe it. She should have left at 4.27, and surely a hospital clock wouldn't be out by eight minutes? If it was accurate, she should have disappeared back to her own time before even finding her father. Were they both stuck here now, after all she had done to get them home? At least she had found him. That was what mattered now; it was all that could matter.

She'd have to tell him, of course.

'I think... I think we're stuck here,' she said, despondently.

'What? Where's the device?' he asked.

'Mia has it.'

'Mia? Mia who?'

'She's the daughter of the glassmaker who mended the broken Infinity Glass; the glassmaker who was custodian before you were, Dad. It doesn't matter because Mia will have left by now. She'll be back home, and she'll realise we've been left behind.'

'Wait, two of you travelled?'

'I can tell you all about it later. Are you OK?'

'Yeah, I think so. Some huge bloke with muscles like The Rock popped my shoulder back in. I can't tell you how much it hurt. It's not great now, but at least I'm not likely to pass out and I can feel my fingers again.'

'Sounds like you've been through the wars.'

Patch laughed and Cass realised the irony of her choice of words.

'I need to go,' said Helen, approaching tentatively from behind.

'Yes, of course. I don't want you to get into trouble,' replied Cass.

'I'm five minutes late already. Hopefully Matron will be otherwise occupied and won't realise I'm missing.'

'Good luck,' said Cass.

'Thank you. I'm glad you found him.'

Cass pulled away from her father and hugged Helen. 'Go quickly,' she told her.

The nurse turned on her heels and marched off, tucking a stray strand of red hair back into a hairgrip.

Chapter 37

Staying Put

'Where will we go?' asked Cass, taking the chair beside her father's bed while he sat on the mattress.

'I don't know,' replied Patch. 'We can't go home. I was lucky not to bump into the wartime owners of our house when I arrived. I wanted so badly to take a sneak around and see how different the place looked – or looks – in 1943, but I didn't want to chance getting caught. I legged it onto the road as fast as I could and foolishly decided to walk into the Old Town. I got caught up in an air raid. It was bad.'

'The Swan. Yeah, I read about it,' said Cass.

Patch raised his eyebrows. 'Any survivors?' he asked.

Cass checked quickly that nobody was within earshot. The bed next to Patch's was empty and a man in the bed opposite appeared to be sleeping, but still she spoke quietly. She didn't want to chance being overheard talking about events which had not yet happened.

'A man and a dog are pulled out alive at some point overnight.'

'But not a woman with a kid?'

Cass shook her head.

'Damn. I watched them go inside just before the bombs dropped. It was horrible, Cass.'

'I saw what was left of the hotel. It was horrific. I'm so glad you're OK.'

Silence fell between them as both thought of the people lost during that air raid – people who, until Cass and her father had been here and seen the reality of it, had been unnamed commemorations on a plaque they'd passed numerous times without stopping to read it.

'I was chatting to a porter before,' said Patch, finally breaking the reverent silence. 'He told me that a few people whose homes have been destroyed are living in the caves. Before you arrived, I'd decided to head back there once they're done with treating me here. I thought I'd ask if I could camp there until I could find myself a job. But now you're here with me, things are different. What about your life, your dreams, Cass? You can't stay here.'

Cass shrugged, holding back tears. 'I don't have any choice. Neither of us does. Mia won't be able to come back for us until next year at the earliest, because a custodian can't visit the same year twice. I did, but that was different.'

'What do you mean, you did?' asked Patch.

Cass explained. 'I came to rescue you, but didn't find you. When I went back, Mia said she'd come and bring you home for me, but when she popped out of our time and came here, I travelled with her. I've no idea how or why. I'd hoped we'd get dragged back with her when she returned home, but it didn't happen. So now it's just you and me, stuck in 1943.'

'I see,' said Patch.

Tears spilled down Cass's cheeks and Patch reached for her hand. 'Hey, hon, come on. We'll manage. Can you imagine how cheap it would be to buy a house in the 1940s? Ha-ha.' His laughter was dry and ironic.

'What if they want you to go and fight? What if there's another bombing and we die?'

'I'm not going to leave you, Cass. Now we're together, we're gonna stay that way, and it's not like they're going to send me call-up papers because I don't exist here, as far as the government knows. If you're worried about getting bombed, we can go and live in the countryside. Find a place in the arse end of nowhere and sit out the last couple of years of the war. Your mother used to say she fancied living somewhere rural.'

'But we're literally penniless, Dad. Where will we start?'

He shrugged. 'There has to be a way for a couple of people as resourceful as us to make a new life for themselves. I'll apply for a job – driving buses, perhaps; I don't know. That will have to wait a while, though. This shoulder of mine,' he said, touching it gingerly, 'it will be months before I can use it for anything more strenuous than lifting a cup of coffee.'

'Perhaps I can get work,' suggested Cass. 'Since uni isn't going to happen now.'

He shook his head. 'There must be a way for you to go. After the war is done and dusted, at least.'

'Be realistic, Dad, think about when we are. The Queen isn't even the Queen yet – she's probably younger than I am. Women's rights suck, despite all they did – are doing – for the war effort.'

Patch stared gloomily at his shoes, which were sitting side by side on the floor near Cass's feet. Taking a deep breath, he exhaled slowly, closing his eyes.

'I'm sorry I made this mess happen,' he said, sadly. 'If I hadn't been so bloody greedy—'

'Greedy? What do you mean?'

'The Infinity Glass. I'd never have picked it up if I hadn't been on one of my bargain hunting trips, trying to make money.'

'For me,' said Cass. 'You were doing it for me. It doesn't count as greedy if you're doing it for someone else.'

'It still caused the mess we're in.'

'But your motivation was good. You weren't hurting anyone, either. All you did was try to be a good human being, Dad.'

'For all the good it did,' he muttered.

'You weren't to know.'

'Should have guessed.'

'What, that a bomb would damage the time travel device and send it home without you? That I'd ask the previous custodian to repair it, and then get myself stuck in wartime Hastings with you? How would you guess that, hmmm? Like you said, we're resourceful people. We'll get by here.'

Patch gave a weak smile. 'We're a right pair, aren't we? Swapping roles between being all doom and gloom and thinking we'll be alright.'

'Then let's be on the same side – the positive side. Agreed?'

'Agreed. I'd shake on it, but...' He pointed glumly at his right arm.

'I could cheer you up if you like,' she said, mysteriously.

'Oh, how's that?'

She'd been about to tell him she'd met her mother, but now she hesitated, unsure it was a good idea. She had, after all, prioritised that trip over coming here to try to save him.

'Erm, the Memorial. Did you see the Memorial? There's a clock tower with a spire and everything, right in the middle of town.'

'I knew there used to be one. I bet the town is really different here.'

Cass thought about it. 'Kinda loads and also not as much as you'd think. You'll be pleased to hear that Woolworths is back where it used to be, where the sports shop is in our time. I don't really remember it, but you're always moaning about when they shut Woolworths.'

'True,' he said. 'If there's a plus side to this, it will be having Woolies back.'

The pair fell momentarily silent, then Patch said, 'Hey, I need to get out of here. There's no point hanging about now you've arrived. They left me these awful pyjamas and I'm supposed to change, but I can't change clothes without help anyway, and besides, I'd rather boil my head than stay here a minute longer than I have to.'

'What about your arm?'

'I'll be fine after I've rested and taken pain relief.'

'Where will you get that? There's no NHS here, is there?'

'No. True. That didn't start until a way after the war. I'll have to manage pain relief some other way. They gave me morphine when I first arrived. I thought it would have me as high as a kite, but it didn't – although it helped with the pain when that bloke manipulated the joint back into place. It isn't anywhere near as uncomfortable now, and hopefully it will stay OK as long as I baby it like they told me to.'

'You trust 1940s healthcare?' asked Cass, dubiously.

'It's got to be better than self-diagnosing on the internet,' he replied. 'Hey, how will you manage without the internet and mobile phones, Cass?'

'Easy. I won't even miss them,' she said, casually.

'Liar,' he retorted, grinning.

Cass grinned back. 'Yup.'

'Come on, let's go. You know the way out, I hope?' he asked.

'No problem.'

'Let's make our escape, then, shall we? Before the nurses try to stop me leaving.'

'Sure, this way,' said Cass, crouching to help him put on his shoes.

'You do know hardly anyone even owned a telly in '43, don't you?' said Patch.

'Hey, you want to take care of that dodgy arm. I might have to thump it for you if you carry on like that,' quipped Cass.

Chapter 38

Running Late

Mia loved chatting with her great grandmother. She wished she could spend days talking to Rose about her life as a nurse and her opinions on women's rights, but they had barely scraped the surface of the discussion Mia wanted to have before they reached the last hospital corner on the final bed.

'Hey, what's the time?' asked Mia, realising she could pop out of existence here in 1943 at any moment and give her great granny one heck of a shock, if she wasn't careful.

'Quarter to five,' said Rose, having consulted the fob watch pinned to her uniform.

'What?' squealed Mia. She needed to speak with Haven right away; something was badly wrong. 'I'm so sorry, Rose, I'm going to have to go. I'm late.'

'It would be lovely to meet you again sometime,' said Rose. 'And you can help with the beds whenever you like. Perhaps you should consider training to be a nurse yourself.'

Mia smiled, knowing she'd make a dreadful nurse.

'I've enjoyed meeting you, too,' she told Rose. On an impulse, she wrapped her arms around her great grandmother and squeezed enthusiastically.

'Goodness!' exclaimed Rose, giggling.

'Erm, take that as a thank you from my uncle,' said Mia, stepping back. 'You're doing a great job here. You're an inspiration.'

'Well... thank you,' replied the nurse, blushing.

'Anyway, time for me to go.' Tears threatened to fall at having to leave her great grandmother without telling her they were related. Mia turned and hurried away. Her shoes clip-clopped on the concrete floor, sending eerie echoes reverberating through the sandstone cavern and making Mia think once more of ghosts.

Back in Croft Road, Mia called, 'Hey, sprite, what's going on? Why am I still here? And do you know where Cass and her father are?'

'I am as surprised as you that we have not yet travelled back through time, Mia. The Infinity Glass must be intact – I would know if it were otherwise – yet we have clearly passed the moment when we ought to have disappeared. As for Cass and her father, they are too far away for me to track them. Perhaps they're at the hospital?'

'I need to know one thing – am I stuck here?'

'I don't think so, but I cannot be certain.'

'Well, that's bloody unhelpful,' cried Mia, walking round in circles, clenching and unclenching her fists.

'I am sorry, this situation is without precedent. I have no information for you.'

'Way too much is unprecedented,' muttered Mia. 'Hey, Glass, take me... Oh, forget it. There's no point.' She'd been about to request her return travel, but the rules wouldn't allow it so it didn't make sense to try. She deduced that Cass and her father must still be here in 1943, too. If they put their heads together, perhaps they could devise a strategy for getting all of them home.

Mia set off towards the seafront, planning to make her way to the hospital to track down the missing travellers.

'Where are we going, Mia?' asked the sprite. 'To the hospital?'

'Of course,' said Mia. 'I'm going to find Cass – and hopefully her dad, too. There has to be some way we can all go home.' Then, more quietly, she repeated, 'There *has* to be a way. We can't be stuck here forever.'

Chapter 39

Big Gun

'Excuse me, sir, could you tell me the way to the closest hospital, please?' Mia asked. The man was elderly and frail. His trousers hung around his legs as if they had been made for a considerably chunkier man and he leaned heavily on a stick, forcing Mia to ask her question to the top of his bald head.

With his free hand, the man pointed shakily to the west. 'That would be the RESH. That's in Cambridge Road, dear,' he said.

'Oh, OK, cool, thanks,' she replied, forgetting the formal language she'd been trying to use. At least she was familiar with Cambridge Road. If the hospital was where her racing mind told her it must be, then by 2019, it had been demolished and replaced with housing.

She decided the quickest route would be along the seafront and dashed in that direction.

Mia stared, open-mouthed, at the anti-aircraft gun pointing skyward across the churning grey sea, then at the intimidating rolls of barbed wire that prevented access to – and, more poignantly, from – the shingle beach and the English Channel. Somehow, the damaged buildings and the air-raid shelter where her grandmother worked tirelessly helping the sick and wounded had been things Mia was able to take in her stride and accept as part of life in 1943. But this sentinel of a weapon, although used for defence, brought home to her that people were literally fighting for their freedom and their country. Words spoken in history lessons and copied unquestioningly into exercise books became, in the blink of an eye, a disturbing and almost absurd reality. This town on the East Sussex coast that she took for granted, this Hastings, was part of what had been called the Home Front – a term she now properly understood thanks to a single gun pointing out towards an unseen enemy like an accusatory finger.

Usually cheerful and outgoing, Mia felt simultaneously frightened and deflated. Then, from the depths of her soul, a sense of utter determination germinated and grew like a giant beanstalk twisting upward into the clouds. The people whose lives were here must feel this way too, and luckily history was on their side, although peace would not come for two more challenging years.

Goosebumps rushed along the length of her spine and her arms. She glanced automatically skyward, imagining the drone of aircraft engines, the wail of sirens and the terror that must accompany them. She didn't want to stay here for a moment longer than necessary. Assuming she could get home.

Tearing her eyes away from the huge gun, she sped on towards Cambridge Road and the hospital, knowing she would never again be exactly the same person she had been moments before. She had to find Cass and her dad. Mia's lovely great grandmother would survive the war – that was part of recorded family history – but Cass and her father's safety, along with Mia's own, was questionable and subject to multiple unpredictable factors.

Find Cass, get home. Find Cass, get home, she told herself.

* * *

Cass and her father trotted down the stone steps leading back to the road.

'Do you think they'll arrange a search party when they realise I'm missing?' asked Patch.

Cass shrugged.

'Aargh!' cried Patch, grabbing his right arm with his left.

'What? What happened?' asked Cass, stopping mid-flight.

'I'm OK. Just scraped my arm against the wall and jarred my effing shoulder. Keep going.'

'Are you sure? We can go back if you need treatment.'

'I said I'm fine,' snarled Patch, through gritted teeth.

Cass bit her bottom lip.

Patch heaved a sigh. 'I'm sorry. I don't want to stay in hospital, love. I'd rather we went and made a start on building ourselves a life here. All my shoulder needs is rest and for me to have enough common sense not to go banging it against stone walls. Come on. Before they realise they've lost a patient.'

Reaching the base of the steps, the pair turned left, towards the town centre. Out of the corner of her eye, Cass caught sight of a figure wearing beige dungarees striding up the sloped entrance road to the hospital.

'Mia? Mia!' she cried.

Mia turned, her brow deeply furrowed. Cass grinned, realising her new friend couldn't have been expecting to hear her name called out more than half a century before she would be born. As her eyes rested on Cass, Mia's mouth dropped open, then her lips spread into a wide toothy grin. She ran to meet them and flung herself at Cass, making her stumble.

'I'm glad you're happy to see me,' said Cass, laughing as she steadied herself. 'But why the hell are you still here?'

Mia shook her head. 'No clue. I was chatting to Great Granny when I realised I should have left already. I thought I'd come here and find you. Where did you come from?'

'Down the steps,' replied Cass, ignoring, for now, the reference to Mia's great granny. 'If we'd been thirty seconds later, we'd have missed you.'

'It's brilliant to see you. You found your dad, too.'

'Yes.'

Patch raised his left hand in greeting and gave a tight smile. 'Hi.'

Mia smiled back. 'Hi. Erm, what now, though? How do we get home?'

'I dunno,' said Cass, raking her fingers through her hair. 'Have you asked Drusilla to explain what's going on?'

Drusilla joined the conversation. 'She did. I don't know much, I'm afraid. This should all be impossible. There's always been a single custodian, never two.'

'Hey, wait. What about that weird thing that happened?' asked Cass, frowning.

'To which thing are you referring?' asked the sprite.

'What thing?' asked Patch at the same time. He was the only one of the trio who could not hear Drusilla.

'Bees,' said Cass. 'Bees and lightning. Remember?'

'What?' asked Patch, looking utterly confused.

'Not you – Drusilla,' explained Cass with an apologetic smile.

'Yes, I do remember,' said Drusilla, slowly. 'Perhaps you are right. Perhaps it is relevant to the current situation. It certainly seemed to be related to your custodianship of The Infinity Glass, did it not?'

Cass nodded excitedly. 'Yes, I'm sure it was.'

'What are you talking about?' asked Patch and Mia simultaneously.

'After I became custodian and had the artefact repaired, I was sitting on my bed looking at it. I got this weird buzzy sensation and a feeling like I was tied to time itself by a writhing strand, like the northern lights.'

Mia scratched her head. 'Is that normal?'

'I asked that. Drusilla said no other custodian had mentioned anything similar happening to them, so I put it down to stress and forgot about it. But it must mean something, mustn't it? Especially now this has happened.'

A middle-aged woman wearing a long light-brown coat approached and veered around the group, who filled most of the width of the pavement. The woman eyed Cass suspiciously, then bustled on by, glancing at Patch's arm.

'Let's get away from here. We can't stand next to the access road for the hospital. Where shall we go?' asked Cass.

'How about Summerfields Woods?' suggested Patch. 'It should be quiet there.'

'Where's that?' asked Mia.

'Not far. Come on, I'll show you.'

* * *

'Well, I never knew this was here.' Mia's eyes swept around the pocket of woodland not far from the rear of the hospital.

'No,' said Patch, scanning the immediate area nervously. 'It's bigger than I remember. I haven't been here for years, though – or won't be here for years, depending how you look at it,' he added, stopping to lean against an oak tree heavy with verdant new growth. 'Cass, what was all that about bees and lightning, and how do you think it's relevant to everything that's happened?'

'Like I said, I was holding The Infinity Glass soon after becoming the new custodian, and I felt something weird. It was like a buzzing sensation in my whole body. Then I suddenly had this sense of calmness and peace. It was as if I was connected to the whole of time. I can't properly explain it, but it must be why I'm still a custodian, even though Mia is too. Does that make sense?'

'Not a great deal. Doesn't Drusilla know what happened?' asked Patch.

'No. Drusilla said no.'

'Then it doesn't help us, does it?' Mia chipped in. 'We're still here when we should have gone home. Time was up ages ago. How do we get home? Can we get home at all?'

'Perhaps I wasn't close enough to the device when we should have travelled. Perhaps I made us miss our slot,' suggested Cass.

Mia shook her head. 'It's not your fault. If that did happen, you weren't to know. You had to find your dad.'

'Give me The Infinity Glass,' said Cass, reaching for the bag still slung on Mia's shoulders. 'Perhaps I can wish us back.'

Mia shot her a dubious sideways glance. 'You know it doesn't work like that,' but she reached into the satchel and passed Cass the artefact anyway.

Cass took The Infinity Glass. 'Take us back home,' she instructed it.

Nothing happened. Cass shoved the object back towards Mia, who tucked it away inside the satchel.

Patch emitted a colourful string of swear words, then apologised when Cass's bottom lip started trembling.

Mia pulled Cass into a hug. 'It's not your fault. You mustn't think it is.'

'I wonder,' said Drusilla.

'You wonder what?' asked Mia, adding, for Patch's benefit, 'I'm talking to the sprite.'

'Two custodians. Perhaps twice the normal number of custodians means twice the—'

There was a sound like a thousand people clicking their fingers.

Chapter 40

Two Custodians

'—time,' finished Drusilla as the three humans re-appeared in the churchyard of All Saints and shivered. 'There, I was right,' added the sprite, smugly.

'Oh, thank goodness; we're home,' gabbled Cass, excitedly. 'And we're *all* here. All three of us.'

'Four,' said Drusilla, dryly.

'Of course, but you come with The Infinity Glass. I'm glad you're here, too, though,' said Cass.

Jake Patch shivered as he wrapped his good arm around his daughter's shoulders. 'Th-thanks for bringing me back. It feels a bit unreal right now, but I'm g-grateful to both of you. And you, too, Drusilla; despite everything.'

'Well, I'm not sure what he means by that. Despite everything? Despite what? I was incredibly helpful throughout this whole affair!'

Cass laughed.

'She's moaning about me saying "despite everything", isn't she?' said Patch.

Cass nodded and shrugged.

'Twice the time?' said Mia, looking thoughtful. 'Haven said... Oh, I see: twice the *time*. It still doesn't answer how there can be two custodians, but I'm really g-g-glad to be home.'

Patch shuddered sharply, and then swore – under his breath, this time – and clutched at his shoulder. 'Shivering is not good for a recently dislocated shoulder.' He grimaced. 'Now we're back in the twenty-first century, can we g-get back to the house quickly?'

Hearing a buzzing sound, Cass flinched, nervous that something else was about to happen.

'Don't worry, it's just my phone,' said Mia, taking the device out of her pocket and checking the screen. 'I've had a message from Mum.'

'You took your phone?' asked Cass. 'What for? You couldn't use it in 1943.'

Mia shrugged. 'Never go anywhere without it. Didn't you bring yours?'

Cass shook her head.

'I've got mine, too,' said her father. 'Although, in my defence, I didn't realise I'd be time travelling, let alone getting stuck in nineteen… shit!'

'What's wrong? Are you OK?' asked Cass.

'I don't have it. It must have dropped out of my pocket.'

Cass stared at him.

'Well, never mind; it wasn't expensive, thankfully. The people in 1943 won't have a clue what it is anyway. They'll probably bin it. Either that or they'll think the aliens have landed.'

'Mum's freaking out.' Mia was frowning at her phone. 'She realised where I went. She's sent a dozen messages, look.' She turned the phone so that Cass could see the screen.

'And there's another,' said Cass, pointing at Mia's phone, which buzzed again. 'Perhaps you should let her know you're OK.'

'I think I should go. You need to get home anyway. I'll go back and reassure her.'

'Will you tell her the truth about what happened?' asked Cass.

'Not sure.'

'How about The Infinity Glass?' asked Patch. 'Who's keeping that?'

'And what about your clothes, Mia?' asked Cass. 'Those are at our house, remember?'

'Damn, I forgot all about my clothes. You two go ahead without me – your dad's half frozen, Cass. I'll message Mum and make up a random excuse about why I went out without telling her, then I'll catch you up. Here, you can take this thing, too.' She lifted the strap over her head and passed the satchel containing the artefact to Cass.

Cass opened her mouth to protest.

'Cass, love, please can we go home? I need pain relief and a hot shower and I'm not at all sure which is more urgent,' said Patch.

Mia flapped a hand. 'Go, go! I won't be far behind. I'll catch up with you on the hill. Go *on*,' she insisted when Cass hesitated, reluctant to leave.

Cass nodded and slung the bag over her own shoulder, then she and her father set off briskly towards home.

* * *

Mia hadn't caught up with Cass and Patch by the time they arrived at their front door. Cass checked back in the direction they had come, but there was no sign of the glassmaker's daughter. But, with her dad muttering swear words and gripping his right forearm with his left hand,

Cass wanted to get him indoors quickly, so he could swallow some pain relief tablets and warm back up as soon as possible. She let them inside and told him to sit down while she went to the bathroom cabinet for paracetamol and to the kitchen for a glass of water.

She found him in the armchair with his knees hugged to his chest, his shoulder and arm supported by the padded arm of the chair. She passed him the glass and he held it in his right hand while popping the tablets into his mouth with his good left hand. He downed them in a single glug and passed the glass back to her.

'I'm freezing to death here, but I don't think I can shower until the painkillers kick in,' he said. 'If I went now, I'd have to shower fully clothed because I'd never manage to undress myself.'

Cass trotted back upstairs and returned with the duvet from her bed, which she wrapped around him while his teeth chattered. She herself had warmed up during their swift uphill walk, but his skin was grey and she worried all was not well.

'Shall I call you an ambulance?' she asked.

He shook his head. 'Had enough of hospitals. Give it half an hour and the pain will disappear. If not, I'll ring 111.'

'Sure?'

'Sure. You go and find your friend,' he said.

Someone knocked on the front door.

'Or not. I expect that's her now,' said Patch. 'Better go and let her in.'

Cass opened the door to find not Mia, but Lucia standing outside, her fists on her hips and her lips pursed.

'Where's my daughter?' she demanded.

'Hey,' said Mia's voice. Her face appeared in the doorway beside her mother. 'You talking about me?'

Lucia spun around to face Mia. 'You damned idiot. You time travelled. Why would you do that after everything that happened to me?'

Mia wrapped her arms around her mother, who remained stiff and stern only for a moment before deflating.

Mia unwrapped herself and smiled at Lucia. 'I'm fine. We all got back safely. We saved Cass's father, though I'm not entirely sure how.'

Lucia shook her head rapidly. 'We *all* got back safely?' she asked.

'Long story involving bees and stuff. To cut it short, there are two custodians now and it doubles the amount of time you spend in whatever time you visit. Not that we knew, until we were already back. Even the sprite didn't know what was happening.'

'It took a while, but I did figure it out,' insisted Drusilla, defensively.

'Did you say bees?' asked Lucia.

Mia grinned. 'I'll explain later.'

'And where is The Infinity Glass now?'

'It's safe and undamaged,' said Patch, appearing in the living room doorway. 'Why don't you come in? Cass can make everyone a cup of tea and we can tell you what happened.'

'Mr Patch, I presume?' asked Lucia, unnecessarily.

'Call me Jake,' offered Patch. 'But please don't try to shake my hand.'

'Huh. *She* gets to call you Jake,' grumbled Drusilla, sardonically. Cass ignored it.

'Let's all go and sit down in the living room, shall we?' she suggested.

* * *

'You went to 1066?' Lucia asked Patch. 'I never thought to go back that far.' The two were talking while their daughters made drinks for everyone.

'It was the first date I thought of,' explained Patch. 'Living in Hastings, we all learn the date of the last full-scale invasion of England. I didn't know it was going to take me there – I hadn't learned how the artefact worked at that point.'

'I see, yes. I can relate to that completely. The damned sprite ought to be up front about the rules instead of revealing them one or two at a time. You could get yourself in all sorts of trouble.'

'You're telling me,' replied Patch, eyeing his right arm supported in the sling.

Lucia frowned. 'Is that painful?'

'Not quite so much now. The paracetamol must be starting to kick in. I don't think I'll be working for a while, though. I'm told you made a replacement Infinity Glass when I managed to damage the original.'

'That's right. Quite a task, but I got there, albeit not with the precision of the one I replaced.'

'Amazing job. Well done, you.'

Lucia smiled and looked down at her interlocked fingers resting in her lap.

* * *

In the kitchen, Mia stood next to the quietly whining kettle while Cass dropped tea bags into a pair of mugs and spooned powdered chocolate into two others.

'Imagine if we'd missed each other at the hospital,' said Cass. 'Do you think you'd have come back home without me?'

'I'm not totally sure, but I guess I would have, yes,' replied Mia.

Cass hugged her arms around her waist. 'That's a sobering thought. I mean, Dad and I were both ninety-nine-point-five per cent sure we were stuck in 1943 for good, but we didn't have time to dwell on it. What if we really had been stuck? Hopefully we'd have been OK, Herr Hitler permitting, and we had each other, thanks to you. But we'd be long dead by now. Nothing but ghosts.'

The heavy silence that followed lasted for a few seconds and Cass thought about her mother. She too was merely a ghost, and yet there was a living memory for Cass to cling onto now.

Mia broke the silence. 'Well, I for one am thrilled you're back,' she said, unpeeling Cass's hands from around her waist and holding them gently in hers.

'Oh,' murmured Cass.

Mia tipped her head to the side, then leaned forward and softly kissed Cass's cheek. 'Life's too short to not act on your feelings,' she said.

'*Ohhh*,' Cass's lips curled into a smile.

* * *

'And all you brought back by way of a souvenir was a stone?' Lucia was asking when the girls returned from the kitchen carrying a mug in each hand, along with a packet of chocolate digestives tucked under Cass's arm.

'Yeah. That one up there.' Patch pointed at the top corner of the bookshelf where he'd placed the black and yellow rock as a reminder of his visit to 1066.

'Wow!' said Mia. 'That's astonishing.'

'Sad, I'd call it,' grumbled Patch with a sigh. 'It's just a puny stone.'

Mia put the drinks on a table and went to look. 'No, this honestly isn't just a puny stone at all,' she said. 'If I'm right, this is a pallasite.'

'A what?' asked Cass.

'It's a kind of meteorite.'

'What? How would you know that?' asked Patch.

'Some people like glass, others like antiques. I like rocks,' Mia explained. 'Can I touch it?'

'Why not?' said Patch.

Mia carefully lifted the ancient rock, cradling it in both hands. 'Hmm, yes. Heavier than your average stone, for sure. The greenish-yellow patches are olivine. If you cut it in half, you'd find your rock is full of yellowy bubbles or marbles. This black coating on the outside must be a fusion crust; it forms while the rock is hurtling through the atmosphere. I'd bet money on this being a pallasite. This is so exciting. Is it magnetic?'

'I haven't tested it.'

'Do you have a fridge magnet?'

'I'll get one for you,' offered Cass.

Sure enough, the fridge magnet Cass supplied was attracted to Patch's 1066 rock.

'Is that good?' he asked Mia.

'It shows there's iron in it, which would fit my assessment.'

'How sure are you?' asked Cass.

'Oh, ninety-five per cent plus,' said Mia, grinning from ear to ear.

'Is it worth anything, or is it a museum piece?' enquired Patch, cautiously.

'If I'm right, maybe both. I've never seen more than a small fragment before. This is huge by comparison.'

'Huge? This?' Jake snorted. It was smaller than his fist.

'Everything is relative. Compared to a piece a centimetre or two across, this is enormous. Why would you want to sell such a great collector's piece? It's magnificent. I'd buy it for myself if I could afford it.'

Patch shrugged. 'To me, it's just a rock. If someone else is willing to pay good money for it, I'll take it. I've been putting money away for Cass's uni fund for a couple of years. Can you help me find out how much I should sell it for?'

'Um, you'd have to have it properly assessed first, by a scientist who can identify it a hundred per cent officially. I know someone who could do that. I can give you her email address, if it's any help?'

'I thought you were certain it's a who-je-flip.'

'Pallasite. Well, yes, I'm convinced that's what it is, but I wouldn't want you to rely exclusively on my word. Even I can make a mistake – although I don't think I've done that here. Be sure you know exactly what you're selling, so you can ask the right price.'

Patch nodded appreciatively. 'Thanks for the advice, and yes, please do send me that email address.'

'Well,' said Lucia, reaching for her drink. 'What a lot of excitement for one day.'

Mia gave Cass a meaningful look.

'It's been eventful, for sure,' said Cass, her cheeks reddening as she remembered the peck on her cheek and the lingering kiss on the lips which followed it.

'Perhaps it's time we discussed what to do with The Infinity Glass?' suggested Lucia, matter-of-factly.

'Do with it?' asked Cass. 'What does that mean?'

'Well, we have to get rid of it, obviously.'

'Erm, no,' replied Cass, at the same moment that Drusilla cried an anguished, 'Don't let her!'

'Why get rid of it now?' asked Mia, quietly.

Lucia glared at her. 'You were all for getting rid of it when I was custodian. It's dangerous. You know what it can do, Mia. All three of you nearly got stuck in World War 2.'

'Well, that's not going to happen again, is it?' said Cass.

'Plus there's the whole addiction issue to consider,' Lucia continued. 'Mistakes won't happen if we don't have the damned thing anymore. I vote we either break it or bury it.'

'You vote? *You vote?* You're not either of the custodians,' Cass replied, angrily. 'We are: me and Mia.'

'No, you're right: I'm not a custodian, only the bloody Maker,' Lucia hissed back, her hands on her hips and her eyebrows drawn together.

'But you gave it to me. It's mine now, not yours. Maker does not equal keeper.'

'And you gave it to my daughter,' said Lucia.

'Don't put this on me,' Mia raised her hands defensively. 'I already said I don't want it destroyed.'

'You tell her,' Drusilla cut in, but the joint custodians ignored the sprite.

'Of course you don't! It's got you, hasn't it?' snapped Lucia.

'No!' cried both girls.

'I'm not putting up with this. You clearly don't properly understand what it can do to you. I'm taking it.' Lucia stood and grabbed at the satchel containing The Infinity Glass, but Cass was quicker. She snatched it away before Lucia could close her fingers around it and ducked past the glassmaker into the hallway and out of the front door, which she slammed shut behind her.

Cass ignored her father calling her name as the letterbox rattled. She couldn't stop now. The time travel device was the only way she'd ever meet her mother again and she wasn't ready to let go of that chance. What happened to her father was a one-in-a-million accident, unless she travelled into the middle of a war, which she had no intention of ever doing again.

About thirty metres away from the house, Cass hesitated, unsure where she was going, let alone what she would do when she got there. Behind her, Mia's voice called out.

'Cass! Wait for me.'

Breathing heavily, more from anger than exertion, Cass checked Mia was alone, then waited for her to catch up.

'Mum was over-reacting. Can we go back and talk?' Mia asked.

Cass shook her head. 'She sounded like she meant it to me.'

'I agree,' said Drusilla. 'I told you she couldn't be trusted.'

'That's offensive,' said Mia. 'She can be trusted one hundred per cent. She thinks it's dangerous and maybe she's right, but I know why you won't give it up, Cass. It's because of your mother, isn't it?'

Cass nodded. 'I can't give her up. Not now I've met her.'

Mia wrapped her arms around Cass. 'I get it,' she said. 'Really, I do. Back in 1943, I met my own great grandmother, Rose. She died when I was a kid.'

Down the hill, the front door of the house flew open and Lucia appeared. She checked first towards the seafront, then the other way. Catching sight of the two girls, she marched determinedly towards them.

Cass looked imploringly into Mia's eyes. 'I need time to think,' she explained. 'Time I won't get if we stay here and your mum does what she thinks is best. Will you come with me?'

Mia nodded.

Cass thrust the satchel into Mia's arms. 'Then tell The Infinity Glass a date and let's get out of here.'

THE END (But keep reading for additional content...)

Ten Questions (plus a supplementary one)

I was going to put 'Questions and answers,' here, but I don't want to answer the questions! I like that I've left these (and possibly more) things to the reader's imagination – points for you to ponder. I have my own answers, of course, but I'd still love to hear your suggestions. You can email me at **contact@sianturnerauthor.co.uk** with your ideas. If you do, I'll happily send you a free eBook copy of my short story anthology *A World of Impossibilities* as a Thank You.

Q1: What were the exact circumstances of Jen Patch's death?

Q2: Why is Drusilla attached to/affiliated with The Infinity Glass?

Q3: What was Lucia doing in the past that made her so addicted to time travel?

Q4: Who was 'The Maker'? How did they learn everything they needed to know to create The Infinity Glass?

Q5: Why did Cass experience 'bees and lightning?'

Q6: What about that paradox? How could that happen?

Q7: Does Patch eventually make money from selling a souvenir? How much?

Q8: Where do Cass and Mia go at the end of the story?

Q9: Will Cass see her mother again? What will happen?

Q10: Are there more undisclosed time travel rules for Cass and Mia to get caught out by?

Supplementary question: Are the details of life in 1850, 1943 and 1066 accurate?

I'll answer this one: I tried. I really did. But there were some things I simply couldn't find information about. I've made details of the bombing of The Swan as accurate as I could, using eye-witness accounts and newspaper articles etc, etc, and got help with some other historical details about Hastings in that era (see also 'Thanks, Excuses and Dedications' at the front of the book). But when it comes to it, my novel is a work of fiction – if you can, for a moment, imagine yourself there in 1943, seeing what Patch saw, hearing what he heard and feeling what he felt, then I'm happy with that.

The lady in 1850 is based on my Irish great grandmother, Annie, who actually lived in Folkestone, not Hastings.

As to 1066 Hastings, there was almost no information I could find online or elsewhere. Little snippets about clothing and language from that era was about all I found. But he had to go to 1066, didn't he? He lives in Hastings: when else would you want a time travel device to take you on the spur of the moment?

If you enjoyed reading, please leave a review on the retailer's website. Thank you.

To subscribe to my monthly newsletter and receive a
FREE copy of one of my eBooks, visit
https://sianturnerauthor.wordpress.com/contact-sian/

Find me on Facebook at
https://www.facebook.com/SianTurnerAuthor
See me on Twitter at
https://twitter.com/SianTurner1066

Thank you from the author!

Dear reader,

I hope you enjoyed reading *Patches through Time*. I really loved developing and writing about my main characters, Jake and Cass Patch and the sprite Drusilla/Haven.

In addition to the main characters, I enjoyed discovering Lucia (who honestly deserves a prequel of her own) and Mia (maybe a sequel would be appropriate for her and Cass, should I ever go down that route).

My favourite minor character was Helen Cook, the nurse who helped Cass find her father at the hospital. She was based on stories I've read about wartime nursing, mixed with a dash of my mother (who was actually a nursery nurse in the 1950s) and bits of a few other people who seemed insistent on becoming part of Helen's personality. If you'd like to find out more about me and my novels, or you'd like to join my mailing list or my beta reader team, please visit my website:

https://sianturnerauthor.wordpress.com/contact-sian/

Finally, I'd like to ask ***a small personal favour***. Reviews can be tough to get and can genuinely make or break a book. Your opinions are important to me personally too. So please spend five minutes posting a short review on any relevant retailer's website.

Meanwhile, thank you for reading *Patches through Time* and for spending time with me, Jake, Cass, Drusilla, Lucia, Mia and the others.

Sian Turner

Other Works by this Author

Sweet Erin

Erin Fitzwilliam-Beaumont is struggling. There are problems at school, and at home her work-obsessed parents rarely seem to notice her at all. Then an extraordinary app introduces Erin to a girl named Carys and the pair begin an inexplicable – in fact utterly impossible – friendship. While both girls are struggling to face their own demons, Carys makes an astonishing announcement. Will Carys help Erin find the fresh start she desperately needs, and can Erin help Carys restore her crumbling relationship with her father?

Finding the Falling Man

Faye Dawson's twin brother Drew is literally a man with a vision. When he tells his level-headed sister a stranger is going to die because of him, Faye decides to turn amateur sleuth. But how can they hope to find a specific stranger in densely-populated London and convince him his life is in danger? And what if 'The Falling Man' isn't the only one in peril?

A Shadow's Voice

Jessica Porter, a young woman struggling to come to terms with the death of her gran, is aided unobtrusively by a shadowy entity named Seventh. Unaware of Seventh's presence, Jessica finds hope in an unexpected bequest and the kindness of a stranger. But danger lurks for Jessica, and Seventh is forced to take an unprecedented course of action with extreme consequences. Will Seventh steer Jessica successfully through her time of need, or will Jessica choose to follow a more sinister path?

Vibes
Emma Logan has a secret ability that she calls 'vibes', which means she can physically feel other people's emotions. A new job gives Emma a chance to use her 'gift' for the good of others – and to stop being 'Weird Emma' at last. But danger lurks for an innocent. Will Emma's efforts help or hinder?

Splitting Infinities
A stone is just a stone, right? Except the one Dawn Foster finds has a hidden super-power that makes her think she's going crazy. Then, just when Dawn thinks the whole universe is going to pot, that pesky stone does something that turns her world inside out.

To subscribe to Sian Turner's monthly newsletter and receive a FREE copy of one of her eBooks, visit
https://sianturnerauthor.wordpress.com/contact-sian/

Find Sian on Facebook at
https://www.facebook.com/SianTurnerAuthor
See Sian on Twitter at
https://twitter.com/SianTurner1066

Printed in Great Britain
by Amazon